D0545844

Faith, Hope & Love

f

Cardiff Libraries
www.cardiff.gov.uk/libraries

Llyfrgelloedd Caerdydd
www.caerdydd.gov.uk/llyfrgelloedd

PE

ACC. No: 02743820

Faith, Hope & Love

Llwyd
Owen

ALCEMI

This book is completely fictional.
Although it includes references to actual people
and establishments, they appear in fictional situations
and any resemblance to actual establishments and events
are entirely coincidental.

First impression: 2010

© Llwyd Owen, 2010

This book is subject to copyright
and may not be reproduced by any means
except for review purposes
without the prior written consent of the publishers

Published with the financial support of the Welsh Books Council

Editor: Gwen Davies
Cover and interior design: Jamie Hamley

ISBN: 978-0-9555272-7-2

Printed on acid-free and partly-recycled paper.
Published by Alcemi and printed and bound in Wales by
Y Lolfa Cyf., Talybont, Ceredigion SY24 5HE
e-mail ylolfa@ylolfa.com
website www.alcemi.eu
tel 01970 832 304
fax 832 782

Acknowledgements

Thanks to Spencer, Kitty, Jack and Mary, who all inspired parts of this novel. My family and friends, for their forgiveness. Lisa, for her eternal patience and support. Elian, for giving me a reason to get up every morning; Lloyd Jones for his kind words and similar nature; and Mr Oates, for confirming what I already suspected (ha!). Jamie, for another great cover design. Lefi and Alun at Y Lolfa, and my editor Gwen, for turning what was already a good book (allegedly) into a better one.

ABOUT THE AUTHOR

Llwyd Owen is the author of four highly-acclaimed Welsh-language novels, including *Ffydd Gobaith Cariad* (which won the Welsh Book of the Year Award in 2007), all published by Y Lolfa. He lives in Cardiff with his wife and daughter.

For further information, visit www.llwydowen.co.uk.

For Lisa

"I love this God fellow; he's so evil!"
Stewie Griffin

"Doubt is part of all religion.
All religious thinkers were doubters."
Isaac Bashevis Singer

"Prison wasn't the reforming punishment I thought it would be.
It didn't make me feel guilty, it made me angry.
I realised that prison did nothing to prevent crime.
Prison just postpones crime."
Paul Carter-Bowman

"There's nothing more dangerous than an angry Christian.
With that lethal combination of ignorance
combined with self-righteousness."
Bill Hicks

"Grandpa! Killing yourself is a sin.
God wants us to die of old age...
after years of pain and reduced mobility."
Marge Simpson

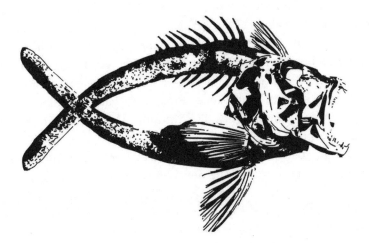

Prologue: THE BEGINNING OF THE END

Blue. Blue lights. Bright. Flashing. Blue lights. Fire engine? Ambulance? Cops and robbers. Saw slicing steel. Sparks. Faceless voices. "This one's still breathing." "He's the only one." "Bag the rest but get this one out." "Make it quick, he's touch and go." Who? Moi? Nah, I'm fine. Tip top. Ticky-dee-boo. A-Ok. Ace. Well, not *totally* fine, granted, but better than Floyd. His sleeping bag looks cosy as it covers his face. Eternal sleep. A crimson shadow where his body lay. Anonymous in death, just like he wanted. Broken glass. Shimmering rain. Shattered lives all around. On the ground. Goodbye my friend. I'll see you soon. Can't feel. Feel nothing. No legs. No hands. No arms. No feet. No feeling. No movement. Numb, numb, dumb. As dumb as Gee as he's dragged from the wreck. As silent in death as he was in life. His body limp like a six foot serpent. A dead serpent, that is. A colossal cadaver. Heavy. A snail's trail flows from his ear. A bloody trail. I'm one with the dash but I'm still fighting.

Dee Dee next. No nurse, just a hearse. The paras peel him from the back of my seat. I feel nothing. Nothing. Cough. Metallic. Blood. The final act. In His name. He and I. The father, the Son and the holy shit. Friends. Respect. Sawing steel. Sparks fly in my face. "Careful now, I want him alive." Dead. Alive. Six of one and aaaaaalf a dozen of the other. I'm neither nor and somewhere in between. I'm nothing without feeling. Bereft of any sensation. Neutral. Damaged. Faulty. Reborn. All of the above and none at all. Movement. From car to stretcher to back of ambulance. Pipes. Oxygen. Just like Paddy's. Maybe smaller. Bright lights. TCP. Numb. Dumb. Cough. Needle. Plunge. Darkness.

Blue light. Bad crash. Doors open. Voices. Eyes open. Distant voices. From this world or maybe the next? Show yourself! Where are you? Deliver me from harm. Your servant. Your son. Your soldier. Wil?! "Al! Hang in there bro! Don't give up. Keep battling. Keep fighting. I'm here. We're here. We're with you. Be strong!" Try to move. Fail. Try to reach. Fail. Can't move. Can't... Fight what exactly? Blonde hair. Haystack. Will. Don't go! Through doors, corridors, confusion, dead end. Will by my side. Pipes in my nose. Oxygen on tap. Alien faces. Alien voices. Alien surroundings. Sign. Theatre. Break a leg. Break your neck. Break every bone in your body. "Stay with us..." "Al. His name's Al." "Thanks, Mr Brady. Stay with us, Al. Look at me look at me, that's it. Stay with us!" I'm not going anywhere, mate! I'm right here! What's the fuss? Oh yeah. The 'accident'. The dead bodies. Rushing now towards the stage. It's curtains up. Good luck luvvie daaarling! "Don't give up, Al, hang in there!" OK Will, I'll do my best. Whatever you say. But Will can't watch today's performance. I'm on my own now... well, almost. He's by my side. As always. At least I think He is. Masked men. Another needle. Another plunge. And then... darkness once again.

Chapter 1: MIXED EMOTIONS

"NEEEEEEEEEEEEEEEEEEEEEEEEEEEEEEEEEEE!!!!!!!!!!!!!!!"

The alarm cracks the whip and I'm up from deep sleep like a slave. My eyes, though, are closing again slowly as the sun seeps past the bars and warms my pale face. I come to slowly; no point rushing, not in here. These last three years, my life has shifted from the slow lane to the hard shoulder. Like iron filings to a magnet, the snores of Knocker, my cell-mate, jerk me closer to the waking state.

There's nothing worse than an alarm at the start of yet another day in captivity. It seems so spiteful: to wake you up for what? To remind us bad boys we're not the ones in charge any more. Control is what you lose once you commit a crime, or at any rate once you're caught and sentenced.

Like most mornings, the stink of urine is suspended in the air along with our sweat. I open my eyes: the clouds disperse. Against the opposite wall, near the poster of Jenna Jameson – that's doing nothing to wilt my Morning Glory – leans Paddy, my friend in spirit, smoking a non-filtered Woodbine. God knows where he buys his cigarettes.

But chances are it's all up for grabs if you live in that limbo between the living and the dead.

"Alright, Pad?" He nods and blows smoke rings up to the rough grey ceiling. Dying's done the old man the world of good, seeing as he couldn't walk or breathe too good back on the other side. His presence messes up my head: on the one hand he sends me on a guilt trip back to all that stuff; on the other, his calm cuts through all that crap. Alive, he was a friend, and now – well, he's good company, quiet and comforting. Everything and everyone I ever had has gone up in smoke, but at least I've got someone with me in this strange world, even if I can wave my hand through him as easily as clearing fag air. He doesn't cramp my style like some second shadow; in fact there he goes now, disappearing into the ether like an odourless fart.

I drag myself out of bed, shivering as my toes touch the cold floor. The weak sun's heat rarely reaches in here. I stumble over to the toilet in the cell corner; yawning widely, letting it all out. I've evolved during my time inside, to better suit my habitat. I've gone down a gear; well, what's the point in racing when there's no finishing line?

But as the mind-mist lifts, a smile confirms the memory of hope. The promise of something quite special for all prisoners. Something new; not brand new like a metallic grey VW Beetle, but something you've tasted before that has retreated to your dreams – like Mam's gravy and Wham Bars. Freedom.

I'm standing at the bucket, dreaming of my future. My dreams are simple now, any childish fantasy wiped out by prison's horrors. I'm not talking about Hollywood-style Death Row horror, but reality: the reason we're all in here in the first place. Violence and unhappiness echo off the walls of each corridor, corner and cell. I want a job, somewhere I can call home. Nothing swanky, just something simple. I want to walk in the woods and look down on the countryside from a mountain: nothing like Snowdon either; Garth Mountain will do just fine. I want to sniff the rising dough of Memory Lane's loaves, feel the sand between my toes; come and go as I please. I want to watch a classic film instead of the box-office rubbish we get fed in here. I want to see Mam and Dad. I want to turn back…

14

"Mornen, butt," Knocker's greeting brings me back into the present.

"Alright, Knock," I answer as a night's worth of urine flows from my bladder.

"I fucken luvs listenen' to you piss, butt. There's somethen very very therapeutic about it."

His voice is pitched low and dark, as rich as a box of All Gold.

"I'm glad you think so, Knock. Too bad if it got on your nerves," I say, noticing the rusty colour of the water, my stomach turning from the smell of Sugar Puffs.

"Aye, it fucken would be, butt," he adds, yawning as wide as Olga Korbut's legs swinging over the pommel horse. He reaches over for his Cutters Choice.

I've shared this fifteen-by-nine-foot cell with Knocker since day one. When I first saw him I was as timid as a mouse in a tomcats' nightclub. Knocker's as tall as the ex-rugby international, Derwyn Jones, but minus the comedy value. But, you know, I was a different person three years back: prison hardens you. I hadn't ever left home when I came in here. You wouldn't believe the culture-shock. One day a cosy nest with Mam and Dad; the next a cold cell with this giant-sized criminal. But fair play to Knocker, he's the happiest, gentlest murderer I've ever met, and you get to meet a fair few in Cardiff Prison.

Knocker's been banged up for over ten years now, since he was nineteen. Life sentence, no parole. Guilt pangs when I think again of walking out a free man in a few hours.

I turn on the hot tap even though it prefers running cold, and Knocker does what he does at the start of every day: rolls a fag. This place turns the biggest drifter into a creature of habit. Wash the face, scrub my pits and shave off two days' of stubble without quite knowing why – I've no one to visit; definitely no one to impress. Then I get dressed in my prison togs for the very last time.

"So today's the day, butt," Knocker announces through a cloud of smoke, as I sit on my bed opposite his.

"It certainly is, Knock."

"Excited?"

"A bit," I admit after a pause.

"A bit! I'd be twitchen like a crack 'ed if I was 'ew!"

I laugh quietly and lie back onto my lumpy green pillow – something else I can't wait to say ta-ta to.

"Well, it's more like nerves mixed with absolute terror if you really wanna know, Knocker."

"Eh?"

"Well, since being sent down I've lost everything, haven't I? Respect, hope, faith and worse than all of those put together, my family." Knocker makes the obligatory mumble we all make when someone's died. "To be honest, leaving prison scares me more than coming in here did."

Knocker chokes off his rollie between the glass ashtray and his huge thumb, and gets up, disturbing the smoke that lays thick in the morning sun. I look away so as not to look at my mate's Full Monty in such a confined space; well, you wouldn't want to see that anywhere, to be honest. I know today will be as hard for him as it is for me. I'm the sixth man to share his cell while he's been in here. We're friends, and soon that'll be over. I've said I'll come and see him but we both know that won't happen. Once out, no one ever wants to come back here.

Having completed his morning ritual – smoke, piss and a quick wash – Knocker gets dressed before the second alarm gongs for porridge time. The doors bang open together and we join the rush to the cafeteria.

After breakfast, a meal that'll ensure my next will taste like one of Delia's finest, it's time for work. As a new boy I had a choice of tasks: data entry, cleaning duty or on the box production line. I chose cleaning for one reason only: it would be a new experience.

My parents are... were... very traditional. Mam looked after the house; Dad earned the money to pay for it. With that cosy setup all my life, I never had to raise a finger. Don't get me wrong, I did keep my room tidy, but the rest of the house was Mam's territory. Not that Dad was a chauvinist pig or anything; just that was the way things were at home.

So it was cleaning prison floors for me. A baptism of fire, if ever there was one. First day some old boy called Harry Monroe showed me the ropes: how to mix the liquids and how to tread the line between working up a sweat and leaving the dirt for people to notice. By now I find it quite therapeutic. The monotony sends me into a kind of trance, unless it's just the chemicals talking. It's almost like some mysterious Martial Art, like Mr Miyagi and his wax on, wax off.

Another bonus is that it means I get to move about, shake my booty. Maybe it sounds crazy, but two of our prime preoccupations in here are sleeping and sitting around… apart from the dudes of Muscle Beach… or Steroid Corner just beneath the barbed wire next to the canteen's waste disposal overflow, to use the full address.

I have to brush and mop the floors of Wings A to D, with each wing taking about an hour. Usually I tackle them in alphabetical order. Having finished floors A, B and C, I approach D Wing, the butterflies somersaulting in my stomach. Here is the Zoo, the home of the worst criminals in here. I always feel the chill, the terror when I approach. I know the animals are locked up but it still creeps me out to be only metres away from their warped minds.

Outside the entrance I bump into Mr Carver, the prison's governor, with his *Western Mail* under his arm. He's a decent bloke, and close to retiring.

"Morning, Alan, how does it feel then?" Fair play, he never forgets anything. I've got to think before answering.

"Don't know really, Mr Carver. I mean it's good to be leaving but things aren't so good on the outside, you know…"

I trail off, and Mr Carver nods his understanding, wishes me well, and walks away down C Wing's crumbling corridor.

On D Wing I start at the far end and work my way back towards the door so that I don't leave dry footprints on the wet floor. When I reach Carl Sweeney's door – he's one of the nut-jobs – I take a look in through the hatch. Never, in almost three years of mopping, have I done anything like this. The heart of his cell is as bare as a newborn baby's bum – that should suit the paedo just fine.

Looking at him staring at the ceiling, knowing that he'll be doing the same thing exactly when his hair's turned white and his skin is slack, is enough to keep me away from this place once I'm out. Cold fingers scale my spine as I turn away and finish off the floor.

17

Back in my cell the three of us, counting Paddy, sit in uncomfortable silence and wait for the call. My stomach is twirling like an out of control carousel, and my mind is full of false hopes. This confusion is totally new. After leading such a sheltered life, the future reels on like a perpetual horror film.

The hatch opens and Watkins looks in on us.

"Say your goodbyes, Brady. Time to go."

The hatch closes; I look at Knocker, shaking my head.

"I can't do it, Knock. I wanna stay."

"Course ew don't, butt."

"I'm serious. I don't know what I'm going to do out there. I've never been alone in my life..."

"What about Paddy?"

"You can see Paddy?"

"No, but I can feel 'im. And I ear ew talken to 'im sometimes."

"But Paddy's not real, Knock." Paddy raises an eyebrow. "What *is* real though is this, me leaving. I feel lost, Knocker. I don't know where I'll go... I should never have turned down Accommodation Assistance." Tears fill my eyes then break their banks.

"I don't want to leave, Knocker!" I wail.

Knocker stands up, and reaching for my shoulders, pulls me tight to him. Binding me in his strong embrace, he sets things straight.

"Don't be so fucken daft, mun. Think of me for a second, would ew? I'm nevva gonna leave this place, like; I'm gonna die in ere an old man. What you've got is a second chance, Al. To start again, like. Sayin ew wonna stay is bloody well insulten, to tell ew the truth. Whateva you're scared of, whateva really happens, being out there 'as gotta be betta than stayen in ere to rot."

His words make me feel so selfish. But they don't make me change my mind. I've lost everything and now, for the first time in my life, I'm on my own. Still, by being so negative about my own future, I've forgotten that Knocker hasn't even got one.

I'm still sniffling like a girl when Knocker pushes me gently away. He takes no notice of the pool I've spurted across his pecs. I stand in the middle of the cell, head spinning, and my friend fetches the silver cross that has hung by my bed for months.

"You don't wonna forget this, butt."

"Thanks, Knocker," I tell him through the mist, "but it just doesn't mean the same to me anymore. How can I believe in anything after what I've seen... what I've been through... outside and in here..."

"Well it meant a lot to you once, butt, so maybe it'll mean something again some day..."

"Doubt it."

As delicately as a harpist plucking strings, Knocker' flicks closed the clasp around my neck. Then he gets out a piece of paper from his pocket and gives it to me. I look at it and see a name and number.

"What's this?" I ask, even though I already know the answer.

"Mate o' mine, like. Name's Quim. Give im a buzz and he'll help you get back on your feet, butt."

"Thanks, Knocker," I say, knowing I'll never make the call. No way am I breaking the law again. Not ever.

"C'mon, Brady. Time to go." Watkins' voice through the hatch again.

Knocker offers me his hand and we shake warmly.

"I couldn't have made it without you."

"Course ew would ave, butt. You're tuffa than ew think."

With the tears streaming, I turn towards the door, to wherever freedom might take me. I swallow back all today's mixed feelings and open the door. I don't intend looking back.

But I hear Knocker shout, "Al! Al! Ew forgot your books, like," and I turn and take them – all my worldly goods – that is, a first edition of my favourite novel, and my own book of poems. I'd forgotten the poems existed, to be honest, since I haven't written a word since doing what I did. There was a time I used to write regularly – total rubbish, truth be told, but inspiration comes easy when you've got a handy Muse. The silky material of the book's cover is soft against my sweaty palm, and I watch as Knocker disappears behind the steel door.

I arrive at the administration block and exchange my prison uniform for a black suit, a white shirt and some very shiny shoes. These drag me further into my downer, reminding me as they do of the last time I wore them: at Mam and Dad's funeral. The officer gives me my parole licence and reminds me to phone Parole first thing tomorrow. I nod, words choked back in fear. I look to my right at the glass door with no bars. I'm so close...

I sign my name and get my own money: my last pay packet, and also my release grant of £43, a week's worth of Jobseeker's Allowance. Ta very much! The whole process is so systematic, it's like checking out of a hotel, or being a piece of lost property returned to its owner...

"Are you ready then, Brady?" the officer asks, jangling his keys like some teasing Jim'll Fix It.

"Yes," I lie. I've never in my life been so unprepared.

The officer takes me over to the door leading to the unfamiliar universe beyond, and I'm half-expecting a lost continent on the other side. But my body won't listen to sense: my heart is galloping, clip-clop-echoes ringing between my ears; sweat is creeping down my face, and my jelly-legs will not move.

The door opens and the room is flooded with spring light. The officer turns and waits for me to walk towards my freedom. He'll have to wait a while...

"I have to close the door now, son," he announces.

"OK," I say.

And after another spell of silence he adds, "You have to leave first, son."

The officer prods me forward and I step out. I'm free. I hear the door clicking shut again. I'm on my own. I'm on my own! I'm... panic!! The world starts to breathe: the pavement, the cars, the buildings, the plants. In-out-in-out-in-out: retching violently like a dolphin on dry land. Welcome back, Alun Brady. Breathing along with the Earth's cruel rhythm, I know I've got to focus on something... anything. I can see workers in uniform, visitors in civvies – lovers, parents and children coming and going. Everybody's smoking. Nobody's smiling. The flagpoles above are shaking in the wind and I'm in danger of banging my head unless I move. All the unfamiliar sounds are deafening and I'm sure that all this ebullience hides an undertow of ridicule. I want to go back, knock on the door and beg for help. Though my body is refusing to respond, still my mind is awake. I must be strong. But it's hard to be brave...

I force my legs to move, and slowly, slowly, like a solar-powered car on a cloudy day, I make my way through the crowded car park to Fitzalan Road. I wait and let a lamppost take my weight, trying to ignore all the unnecessary details and concentrate on the building in front of me. It's one of Cardiff's sad excuses for a skyscraper. I've been looking at it every day through the bars for nearly three years without knowing what it was. But on this side of the wall I can see that it houses the Wales Tourist Board, Arriva Trains and Railtrack. I've dreamt of this moment: being on this side of the wall, and now that I'm facing the glassy grey building, the only thing I can think about is how small it looks...

I'm choking; I cough and spit on the ground, the green globules glossing my shoe leather. The world around me seems unreal. Surreal. I stare at the cars, the buildings, the people walking past – they obviously know where they're going with their lives – and it nearly makes me cry again.

I can't cope with the exotic warmth of the sun, so I cross the road into the shade. I take a breather against the wall by the phone box in front of the office block. The swamp of stubs suggests this is where the Brunel House smokers huddle, and here they come, right on cue: a crowd approaching, lighters alight, aloft like the audience of a Scorpions' concert. I've got to move, but I've no idea where to go. I look around for some clue but I'm lost at every level. After years of order, of captivity, freedom feels like a cruel joke.

I escape hesitantly: over the road, reach the unwelcoming bars of the NCP and flop against them. I'm steaming out sweat, and run my fingers through my short brown hair as I look around again helplessly. The smokers' voices carry on the wind: they sound happy, and that shadows my world a seventh shade of black.

The last speck of hope is about to fade away when I see Paddy leaning on a lamppost a few yards away, puffing coolly on a Woodbine. He thumbs for me to follow him. And even though my unfamiliar leather shoes are already pinching, I follow, like one of Hamelin's young citizens, blindly towards Newport Road.

Chapter 2: MUMMY'S BOY

The early autumn colours rush past the window, creating a glorious collage in front of my eyes. On a day like this, with the sun shining in the bluest of skies above the city, God's presence is easy to behold, in the leaves' soft whispers and in nature's complex weave. The engine's soft purr and the classical music – *Gloria in Excelsis*, if I'm not mistaken – encourage my eyes to close. The journey home from chapel is made in silence every Sunday morning. I don't know if my parents are thinking about the sermon we've just heard, but the holy words, which are still fresh in my mind, affect me in the same way every week. Serenity. Tranquility. Contentment.

Right now, I'm pondering what this morning's sermon meant to me. The Prodigal Son. A story I've heard a thousand times, if not more, which is as relevant to me today as it's ever been. It would be relevant to you too, if you had a brother like mine. You see, we're a pretty traditional middle class family, and like every *true* Welsh family, we've got our very own Black Sheep...

Dad drives his Viking-blue Volvo V70 like a saint. He keeps to the speed limit at all times. He coughs lightly into his closed fist as we turn our backs on Roath Park Lake and climb Celyn Avenue towards the welcoming pastures of our snug middle class suburbia, also known as Cyncoed.

After stopping to buy the papers – the *Sunday Times* and the *Wales on Sunday* – in Lakeside, Dad soon eases the car onto our driveway's fine chippings. He silences the engine, which allows the birdsong to reclaim its rightful place on the soundtrack to my life.

I step from the car and come face to face with the weeping leaves of our ancient willow. I rush around to the other side of the car to open the door for Mam. She reaches for my hand and I gently assist her onto her feet. She thanks me with a smile and heads for the back door. Only strangers use the front door of our home.

With my hymnbook tucked under my arm, I follow her towards the house. I hear a *miaaaaaw* somewhere behind me and turn to welcome Dwdi, the most important member of this family, as he rolls towards me with his nose and tail held high. When Dwdi first arrived, he was a fit and playful cat, but after eight years of wheedling food out of my parents, he's more Sumo wrestler than Siamese cat.

I stop to pet him, but as I bend down, he bolts for the door and the promise of a tasty snack. It reminds me of a cartoon joke about the training procedure for cats: "It isn't difficult: mine had me trained in two days." I smile and step towards the house with Dad by my side.

At the back door an invisible wall of aroma hits us, created by the huge chicken that's been roasting for the past couple of hours in our absence. The smell makes my mouth water, and as we both *mmmmmmmm* and *ahhhhhh* appreciatively, we exchange our leather shoes for our slippers and go in.

Dad disappears as usual into his study to put his feet up and read his paper, and I join Mam in the kitchen.

"Can I help?" I ask, but as always, she doesn't accept my offer.

"No thanks, bach," she says, opening the Aga and planting a fork in the chicken's golden-brown flesh. "You can set the table if you want, though."

Mam would do everything for us if we let her, and as it happens, Dad *does* let her do everything! But I can't. I'm a modern man... well... I like to think that I am...

23

I hang my jacket behind the door, loosen my tie and leave Mam to tend to the food. Apart from my bedroom, the dining room is my favourite room. The warmth, the dark oak floor; the open fire and Kyffin Williams's 'Shepherd' that hangs above the mantlepiece; the solid table and the fertile garden beyond the patio doors. This place holds a lot of memories for me, good and bad. This is where I used to skate across the polished floors in my socks. Also where I burnt my hand in the fire's flames: on my brother's orders.

Against the wall opposite the 'Shepherd' stands an antique Welsh dresser displaying commemorative plates and antique crockery, a constant dusting duty for my Mam. I open the door and reach for six table mats made from the finest Llanberis slate. I place the mats carefully on the table in perfect symmetry – three facing the dresser and three facing the fire – before adding forks, knives, spoons and wineglasses.

By now, the smell of Dad's cigar is vying with Mam's feast for my attention. I don't like him smoking but all he does is claim he might 'get run over by a bus tomorrow'. Fair point... I suppose.

The gentle notes of a Tchaikovsky piano concerto reach every room through Dad's elaborately networked central speaker system. One of his legendary 'little projects' which took him three months to plan, two weeks of aimless struggle before accepting that he didn't have the necessary skills or patience to do the job, and two leisurely days for Mr Jones, the sparky, to finish the task. The joke is I've heard Dad boast to guests and visitors about his 'handiwork' on more than one occasion!

I love standing with my back to the garden, as the sun kneads my shoulders through the double-glazing. The light creates a whirlpool on the glass covering the wall tapestry of 'The Last Supper', but I'm dragged from my daydreams by a crooked knife on the table. I rectify the defect as the front doorbell rings, announcing Will's arrival. For once, he's on time.

As Will, Mia and Sophie enter, the peace of the morning disappears. The fussing is already well under way by the time I reach the door.

"*Wel, helo 'na Sophie, sut wyt ti heddiw – wyt ti 'di bod i'r parc,* blah, blah, blah, blah, blah..." She asks breathlessly, but Sophie just stares back vacantly. All women love to fuss, an instinct amplified after her children have flown the nest, and much aggravated if among them is a son or two.

"You know she doesn't understand Welsh, Mam. It confuses her, coming here. She leaves your house and expects to see some uniformed guard holding a massive leek, standing knee-deep in a puddle of phlegm, asking to see her passport..." Will says, a cloud of Cuban cigar smoke blurring his blond mop. I want to say to him that Sophie *needs* to learn the lingo. She needs to *hear* the language. That children are like sponges and it's a disgrace that he doesn't speak to her in his mother tongue. We were raised in a bilingual home, me and Will, and spoke Welsh to Mam and English to Dad during our childhood. But, as Will grew older, he decided to turn his back on the language. I embraced it like a true patriot. I'm proud of my language, my heritage, my birthright and use it every day as part of my job. When you think about it, it's about the only thing that sets us apart from our neighbours on the other side of Offa's Dyke. Anything that makes us stand apart from our dear oppressors has got to be a good thing. I mean, otherwise aren't we just an irrelevant principality clinging to our bastard brother's underbelly? Without our own language, we're no more of a country than Kent.

Dad comes downstairs and gives Mia a long, tight, squeeze. He holds his own cigar in his right hand and hugs Mia with his left, while simultaneously trying to shake hands with Will behind her back. It's so awkward. So fake. A sad state of affairs, but it's really not our fault. It's Will's! He just doesn't make the effort. Never has. We don't see much of my brother and his harem: he's too busy, otherwise engaged. He's a disgrace, that's the truth. They only live a couple of miles away! I'd love to see more of Sophie and Mia, but I'd never say so. You see, unfortunately for me, Will's bagged all the confidence of this family, so I keep my mouth shut and melt further into the background.

After Dad releases Mia, Mam takes over as Dad turns to Sophie. As Mam pokes her nose into Mia's business, Dad makes those noises that you only hear adults direct at children under three years old... or an animal.

No one seems to see me. I'm a fly on the wall. A voyeur without

25

a subject. As anonymous as a lampost during daylight hours. Will sucks on his cigar before sending a plume of smoke spiralling towards the ceiling.

"Do you *have* to smoke that, Will?" asks Mam.

"Doctor's orders," is Will's answer to everything. He *is* a doctor, well, a surgeon to be technically correct.

Mam huffs her reply and leads Mia and Sophie towards the kitchen, promising her grandchild a tasty morsel to tide her over until lunch. I'm about to step out of the shadows to say hello, but before I can do or say anything, Dad leads Will towards the front door so they can savour the rest of their smoke in the fresh air.

I'm about to ascend the stairs and retire to read in my bedroom, when I feel a tug on my trousers. I turn around and look down to see Sophie staring back.

"Al!" She spits, through a gap-filled smile.

"Hello, Soph, what you doing?" I ask.

But before I can say another word, she scampers towards the lounge, her blonde curls bouncing on her head. I turn and start on my way to my bedroom, but stop myself after two steps as I realise there's no one around to watch her. Where are her parents? Otherwise engaged. So I follow her to the lounge where I find her messing about with Dad's records... and... oh no, she's started licking them too! I rush towards her in order to avert disaster.

"Sophie! No!" I exclaim, and amazingly she stops straight away. What discipline! One thing's for certain, she can't take after her father if she's that obedient. I step towards her, take the vinyl and put them back in the appropriate sleeves. Dad loves his records as a normal person loves their family. If the house went up in flames, the vinyl's the first thing he'd save (that's why he chose to house them on shelves with wheels!), followed by Mam carrying the hi-fi...

By the time I've put the records back in alphabetical order, Sophie's disappeared again. I find her in the hallway licking the rubber plant. She looks at me brazenly: she's mocking me! Maybe she is more like Will after all.

"Sophie, don't do that! It's ucky..." I whisper with as much authority as the word 'ucky' allows me, but she carries on licking the leaf as if it's a lollipop. Her eyes sparkle and then I notice her pink T-shirt and the lie that's written on it in garish silver glitter: 'Angel'.

"No, Sophie!" I raise my voice and this time she listens. I smile and say, "Well done", but her eyes well up and her smile disappears.

Her screams fill the whole house. I just stand there staring at her. What on earth? But when I step towards her the reason for the change in her mood becomes apparent. The air in the hallway is thick with Sophie's 'natural' odour, as well as her crying.

I run to the kitchen and open the door. Mam's busy mashing something, while Mia sits at the table sipping a glass of Chardonnay.

"Mia, you're needed in here…"

"Alright Al, where did you come from?" I have to fight the desire to tell her bluntly where I've been – looking after her responsibility – but whisper "I was here all along" while staring at the floor.

Mia puts her glass on the table and gets up. I try, but fail, to stop myself staring at her long legs, which are on show today thanks to her short black suede skirt (belt). Mia's a bit of a tart. A trophy wife, there's no doubt about that. But… well… she's soooooooo sexy… I guess she's about the same age as Will – early thirties, about three years older than me – but it's hard to tell as she has the body of a teenager and wears far too much make-up. She reminds me a bit of those make-up monsters who work in Debenhams. Wait a minute, does her nose look smaller than the last time I saw her…

She pushes past me on her way out of the door, and as her breasts brush against me she looks into my eyes and smiles. My knees begin to buckle so I breathe deeply. Her aroma fills my nostrils. I turn and follow her, eyes drawn again to her long legs. Behind me I can hear Mam struggling to lift the chicken from the oven. For once, I don't turn to help her. Otherwise engaged.

Mia steps towards Sophie, who's still sobbing by the rubber plant. The sunlight coming through the stained-glass window on the landing lends her a halo. Mia looks like some kind of angelic figure for the end of the millennium. A cloud passes overhead, returning my sister-in-law to her true form.

As she bends down to comfort Sophie, her short skirt creeps further up her thighs. I'm transfixed. I stare at her like a famished dog at a butcher's window. I don't hear the kitchen door open behind me. Without warning, a hand grabs my testicles and my… my… the hand holds my manhood hostage. Rumbled.

"Not bad, ey Al? You can fuck her up the bum for a hundred quid…"

Will's words make me sick. What's wrong with him? Suddenly, he turns me around and gives me a big hug. I almost suffocate in the soft leather of his Neo-like longcoat. Then he grabs at the hairs of my armpit until my eyes fill with tears. I can't let him see my pain. He lets go when Mam calls us all to the table.

I can still feel my brother's dirty paw on my privates. Unfortunately, I can't do anything about it because I'm carrying a jug of Mam's jellified gravy in one hand and a bowl of new potatoes in the other. After delivering my load to the table, I head back towards the kitchen and try to claim back my nether regions using my liberated hands.

At last, the table's ready. Dad's carved the meat and glasses are charged.

Without permission, Will starts loading his plate. This almost makes my Dad choke, although Will doesn't notice.

"Will, wait a minute! We have to say grace," Mam exclaims, tapping his knuckles softly with a spoon.

Will sheepishly turns to Mia. "I forgot we have to pray first…" he mumbles, which shows how often he visits us. Dad's bald head and three-chins become a worrying shade of crimson. He sips his water to cool down, before gesturing for me to lead the prayer.

I keep it short and simple. After all, I don't want to bore anyone, especially Him. My hands are closed in front of me and I hang my head at an angle so no one can see that my eyes are still open. I scan the table. My parents' eyes are closed in contemplation, as are Mia's. Sophie stares without a clue as to what's going on. Amazingly, she's sitting still – which is more than can be said for her father.

His disrespect towards me and my parents, *especially* my parents, makes my blood boil. What sort of example is he showing Sophie? I almost lose my temper when he stealthily steals a slice of meat and stuffs it his mouth. I can feel the tension mount. I choose to ignore his immaturity, and as I recite the last line of grace, I steal a glance at

Mia. With her hands in front of her in the classic pose, she reminds me of a praying mantis.

"Amen."

We all tuck in while Will's voice clamours for attention, the authority of his delivery belying the vacancy of his thoughts. On and on he prattles.

"And I got us one of those flat screen plasma TVs, a grand it cost me, didn't I, Mi," he says. Mia doesn't work. Not since Sophie's arrival anyway. She doesn't need to as Will makes more than enough to fund their lifestyles. And even though it was Will's idea for her not to return after Sophie was born, he likes to remind her on a daily basis of her lack of contribution.

"And I've booked for us to go to the Maldives for a fortnight in February, you know, before global warming and the rising sea levels reclaim them..." He's read that nonsense in some quasi-liberal rag like the *Guardian* or *New Statesman*. He doesn't actually posses any personal convictions: he recycles other people's ideas. That's his style. Even though he's a surgeon, my brother comes across as an unintelligent man.

I look around the table as Will continues his eternal monologue. Me, me, me. Blah, blah, blah. Cash, cash, cash. Want, want, want. Mam tries to join in, but even she's outgunned. There's no hope. Buy, buy, buy. Spend, spend, spend.

Mam turns to Sophie and tries to make her eat some vegetables. No chance. Will sees this and can't help himself.

"Don't bother, Mam. She only eats sweet things these days, you know, difficult stage an' all that," before turning his attention to his daughter. "You don't have to eat that, babes. We'll get you a Happy Meal on the way home..."

Sophie yelps her appreciation, as Mia stares at her husband through blazing eyes. Will's reaction? He stares sarcastically right back. Mia turns back to her food.

The most awkward of silences descends, which prompts Mam to turn to Mia.

"So how are your parents? We haven't seen them for ages."

Mia fills her in on her parents' wellbeing – nothing deep, just superficial chit-chat between strangers – before Dad asks, "And how's Sophie doing in nursery school, Mia?" And, maybe for the first time ever, Mia actually has something to tell my parents. Suddenly, there's a spark in her eyes.

"She's doing very well actually," she says, smiling. She's so beautiful when she's happy. But I'm afraid that's a foreign feeling for my sister-in-law. "She's made lots of friends, and she's a bit of an artist by all accounts…"

Her accent is upper-class-Kaadiff: all *aaaaa*s and no *rrrr*s; it lacks the usual sharp edges which makes many Kaadiffians sound like the bastard offspring of Frank Hennessy and Charlotte Church.

She's happy to have the opportunity to talk proudly about her greatest creation, instead of being drowned out by her husband… again.

My parents *mmmmmm* and *wwwwww* as she speaks, but before Mia can elaborate, dear William wrestles the attention away from her.

"They tell us she's artistic but it's hard to believe really, innit Mi, cos, well, I'm totally scientifically minded and don't have an artistic bone in my body. And neither has Mia. You've got no talent at all, have you love." Once again, that was not a question. Fact. Black and white.

Silence. The stereo replaces one CD with another (although my father is huge believer in the sound quality of vinyl, he chooses to listen to CDs when eating, so as not to have to get up every twenty minutes or so to flip the record over). Will is the only one who hasn't noticed any awkwardness. He reloads his plate and tucks into his second helping.

I look over at Mia and realise she's staring right back at me. Her blue-grey eyes hold me and for once I don't look away. I see sadness in her sclera, regret in her retinas and loneliness draped over her lenses. A strange sound fills the room: some sort of bell, a ringing phone… Everyone looks at Will. Who else? He places his cutlery on his plate, leans back on the chair's hind legs and takes a tiny phone from his pocket. Without excusing himself from the table, he crows into his latest gadget.

"All right, Floyd. Wotsappennnnnin' bra?" My parents stare at him. They can't quite believe his arrogance. His rudeness. How did they conspire to create such a creature? Will's voice is turned up to eleven. He's always struggled with the concept of talking properly on the phone. Some people instinctively shout, as if the person on the other end is deaf... or very far away. Which they are in some cases, but you know what I mean... "Yeah, no worries. No. Just a half, mate. No, he's lying. Yeah. Yeah. You're right, he can be a proper twat sometimes."

That word – the pregnant goldfish – affects every adult sat at the table. Except for Will of course. Mam almost gags on her Sancerre; Mia stares at her husband accusingly before turning her attention to Sophie; and Dad just shakes his head before refilling his glass with his favourite Rioja.

"OK, Floyd. Yeah. Yeah. *HAHAHAHAHAHAHAHAHAHA HAHA!* True. True. What? No. Look, I gotta go... I'm... Wossat? Nah... nothing *that* exciting!"

I don't know what everyone else is thinking at this precise moment, but the only word that comes to mine is 'poseur'. I've read a lot about these mobile phones, but they'll never catch on. It's just a craze. A short term fad. Call it what you will, but they won't be around for long. They fry your brain, that's what they say. Amazing that they're legal if you ask me.

"Safe as... Later, Floyd. Easy now..." I'm embarrassed for him. He's in his thirties, a hot-shot surgeon but chooses to talk like a fifteen -year-old schoolboy!

He puts the phone on the table and resumes eating. Sophie reaches over but before she can get to the mobile, Will whips it away from her and mocks his daughter by baring the contents of his mouth. She laughs.

"It's amazing isn't it, Brian," Mam announces, which makes Dad jump. He has long since discovered his internal off-switch, and has perfected the art of melting into his surroundings. Or, to put it another way, he doesn't listen very often and therefore has no idea what Mam just said.

"The phone, Brian," she explains. "Will's phone! It's so small!" Dad mumbles and reaches for the wine.

"You'll be able to take photos and send them with these things in a few years, I'm tellin' you. And use them to check emails and surf the web an' all tha'.'"

I almost laugh but manage to keep my thoughts to myself by filling my mouth like a greedy hamster. Mam's attention returns to her grand-daughter, as Will fiddles with his phone, unable to keep chatting at the same time. I'm lured into my own head by the soothing music. I've been able to do this my entire life, thanks to Dad's musical obsession, and in no time my mind's free from the inane conversations around me.

After Will's finished on the phone – probably sending a message to Coach, Piltch, Moose, Rex, Rang, Billy Reii, Baboon, Big Jim, Monkfish or any other ridiculously-monikered member of his middle-class massive – he sits back, picks up his wineglass and says, "So, Al, have you found yourself a bird yet then? Or a bloke, come to that?"

Dad coughs violently and reacquaints his masticated beef with his plate. Mam's jaw hangs open. Mia backhands Will on his shoulder. I just stare across the serving bowls at my brother. I can't say anything. I don't *know* what to say, although I'll have plenty of clever retorts in a few hours after he's left...

The silence returns. What Will just suggested will torture my parents far more than me... and I'm about to visit a whole world of pain. Will's smile widens as he looks around the table.

"What? What's the matter? Surely this isn't a revelation? It must've crossed your minds..." Silence. "Seriously? Jesus..." He couldn't have chosen a more effective curse, but instead of apologising, he laughs and tells me, "Until I saw you appreciating my wife's fine body earlier on today, I really did think you were a gay boy, Al. And so did Mia come to that, didn't you, luv?" Mia's cheeks flush and she avoids eye contact. "I mean, it's an easy mistake to make, Al, especially when you consider the evidence..."

"Evidence?" Dad, simmering.

Will looks me up and down, considering my sexual make-up. "Well, he's always been a proper little mummy's boy and you know how things go..."

"No, how?" Mam snaps, worrying that she's somehow at fault for... what exactly? Everything.

"Just look at Jimmy Savile, Mam, or Dale Winton..."

"Who?" Mam and Dad together.

"Dale Winton, the handbag who does *Supermarket Sweep* on telly. Pushing forty, probably lives with his mam, gay as fu..."

My parents stare at him without a clue who he's talking about. "Never mind, look, Al's nearly thirty, he's never left home, he's never had a girlfriend... He never goes out. He watches classic films, and that's 'classic' in inverted commas too. Some bloody arty-farty camp bollocks from I don't know... Luxemberg, Latvia, Lesbos. I mean, if he's not a gay he must be a girl. Are you a girl, Al?"

"That's enough, William!" Mam roars, like a bear defending her cub. Once again, Will looks around the table. His smile remains. I fold the napkin on my lap while thinking of some way of defending myself. Blank. I've got nothing. I'm not gay, I'm sure of that. But it's true I've never had a girlfriend. "And anyway Will, Alun *has* got a girlfriend, haven't you, cariad? What's her name now, Alun – that girl you're seeing from work?"

I mumble 'her' name – Rhian – and as I do so my eyes meet Mia's across the table. This time, it's my turn to look away in shame. Shame because of the lie. Shame because of my hopelessness. Shame because of my shame.

"That's right, yes, Rhian. You've been seeing her for a while now haven't you, Al..."

"Have you met her then, Mam?"

"Not yet, no. All in good time..."

"Can I meet her then? We could go on a double date – me and Mia, you and *Rhian*." Silence is my only weapon, while my brother owns the biggest arsenal known to man. I simply cannot lie properly. My eyes betray the truth without having to move my lips. And that's what I'd have to do right now – lie – as the truth is 'Rhian' doesn't exist. Well, there is a girl called Rhian who works in my office but she's married. I only said I was sort of seeing someone because Mam was trying to set me up on a blind date with the niece of someone she knows from chapel.

33

The tears start flowing and I run from the room. Before reaching the stairs, I hear Will ask, "What did I say?"

"You're such a prick sometimes, Will!" Mia replies. *Sometimes* she said?

I take the stairs three steps at a time to my attic room, where I throw myself onto my single bed. I curl into a foetus. Through the haze I see the face of my favourite actor, Jack Nicholson, staring insanely at me from the framed poster on my wall: "Here's Johnny!"

This is how it's always been. Will got all the ability, all the confidence. I don't even respect him, so how can his opinions affect me? But as with a paper cut, the smallest slice causes the worst pain.

I sniff and snort in a tangled web on my mattress, under the watchful gaze of the Black Rock Cross, which reminds me of my Irish roots on my father's side. I have to stop myself from reaching for my notebook and adding to it a doom-laden verse. I don't even know why I write. Maybe it's because my speaking voice is so weak that I have to release some emotions, some feeling.

As the blue sky slowly becomes a collage of reds and yellows outside the Velux window above my bed, I hear Mam calling me. They must be leaving. There's no way I'm going down. I release myself from the womb and tiptoe to the dormer window looking onto the front of the house. I spy through a tiny gap between curtain and wall, and watch as Mia helps Sophie into her child seat in the back of my brother's Mercedes. Will's already behind the wheel. Waiting impatiently. He's wearing driving gloves. After Sophie's secured, Mia kisses my parents and steps around the car to the passenger door.

Before entering the vehicle, she looks up towards me. She looks straight at me. Through me. I freeze, although I'm pretty sure she can't see me. She stares for a good few seconds, before smiling and taking her place next to Will.

I remain standing, staring out of the window and allow the peace to return to my home. I turn away from the window and come face to face with my own damp-cheeked reflection in the mirror above the small sink opposite. I see staring back what I've always seen – a little boy. Mummy's boy.

Chapter 3: LOST

I'm following Paddy, walking a good twenty yards ahead of me past the Mayor's mansion on Richmond Road. I'm still admiring the new buildings that have popped up in my absence when I hear a voice addressing no one in particular.

A man is walking towards me wearing a slick grey suit and carrying a black briefcase. His dark hair sticks to his head with serious assistance from his styling gel; he has swimmer's shoulders and a confident strut. He is also undoubtedly insane. He's not shouting, but his words are clear.

"Tell Russell I'm on my way, would you, Sally," he commands as he walks past me. "I'll be there in three minutes," he adds after dramatically consulting his watch. I stare until he rounds the corner and melds into the city's comforting greyness, before shaking my head and continuing on my way.

The outside world leaves a prisoner behind when under lock and key. That's stating the obvious, I know, but it's also undeniably true. The city has developed – evolved even – so much since I, like Lister and Cat, have been in a state of stasis for the past three years. The luxury flats on my left as I walk along Crwys Road, with their 'stunning views' of the crumbling mosque on one side and the railway track on the other, as well as the flimsy-looking purpose-built student accommodation on Richmond Road that I passed not long ago, are proof of this unrelenting civic development. But, the main thing I can't believe is that everyone, and I mean *everyone*, is talking into tiny little mobile phones, confirming my brother's laughable prophecy of a few years ago. Everywhere I look they're hanging from the population's ears, like a feather from Mr T's lobe, with the power to turn the volume on everyone's voices right up. There doesn't appear to be such a thing as a 'private' conversation any more. But I suppose anything's better than talking to yourself like that bloke I passed a minute ago.

So what else have I missed while I've been in limbo? The start of a new century for starters. There was a bit of a party in prison, but it was all a bit subdued. After all, what's the point celebrating when you know you'll be waking up behind bars come morning? If I remember correctly, I played chess with Knocker until just after midnight, and retired without much ceremony. Party on, Wayne! Nine eleven too. I mean, it's not as if we weren't aware of what happened, it just didn't affect the majority of us. Tension mounted between eastern and western factions for a few days, but nothing serious. Not even a stabbing. Prison's so insulated. You live life from minute to minute, hour to hour. You dream of the outside, of freedom. But they're nice dreams mostly, positive dreams, not the hideous reality that lurks beyond those bars.

Another recent development I've noticed is the litter – it's everywhere; like a plague of plastic bags. Or maybe it's just that I don't remember the mess. Maybe I've created a perfect and nostalgic image of the city in my head: a rose tinted utopia that now reveals itself to be nothing but a lie as I'm faced with reality. Who knows? I know who's to blame around here though: the students. This, after all, is their turf. They're everywhere, all different shapes and shades. Punks, Goths, squares and skaters; rugger buggers, stoners and moshers. Everyone co-habiting happily, rushing around Cathays going nowhere for at least three years... The amazing variety of people is comparable in a way to the prison population I've recently left behind. People from all walks of life – different religions, backgrounds and so on – are thrown into the same cauldron to simmer together. Although, of course, there are some major differences too: life moves at a snail's pace on the inside compared to out here, and getting your hands on a kebab is almost impossible. I'm on a different planet from the people that rush past me, as I crawl after Paddy, savouring every step, every breath, everything.

I'm saddened to see another new Spar shining brightly on the corner of Woodville Road, but my nostrils are soon filled with sweet memories as a long forgotten aroma whips me back to my childhood – chips! But not any old chips either, but chips from the XL Fishbar – my family's traditional 'local' chippy. After three years of tasteless tucker, the smell floods my palate with saliva; I must give in to temptation.

After completing the transaction – something else I'm not used to doing – and receiving my order from the greased-up chipmeister, I leave the chippy and sit down on the wall outside the Co-op to enjoy my meal. Paddy stares at me impatiently before disappearing, like a chameleon, into the ether. I open my greasy package carefully, like a cautious child on Christmas morning, before digging in to my Clarks Pie and chips. The chips are better than I can ever remember, but after one thousand and eighty-three days and three thousand two hundred and forty-nine prison meals, that's no great surprise.

After an initial burst of scoffing, I slow down a little and let the grease settle. I take off my coat and bask in the sunshine, watching the world go by. After three years of a neutral existence, watching the people rush around brings me to the conclusion that everyone's a prisoner in some respect: to time, a career or family… It also makes me feel tired from just watching!

As I melt back into my surroundings, the combination of warm weather, a full stomach and foreign, yet familiar, sounds exorcises the fear I felt on leaving prison. Hearing the Kaadiff accent reminds me of travelling on the bus to work, shopping in Asda with Mam and watching the Blue & Blacks with Dad. Sadness suddenly grips

37

me as I think of my parents, although I know exactly where Paddy's leading me now.

After sharing the rest of my feast with a couple of greedy pigeons I place my litter in an already overflowing bin, and go and look for my companion. I find him beyond the empty fruit boxes, which are parked illegally on double yellow lines outside the Veg Rack, standing outside and staring at Glenn Abraham, the estate agent's window. I join him and do the same, almost choking on what I see. A hundred grand for a flat! A quarter of a million for a terraced house! Have the workers' wages increased at the same rate, I wonder, or just their debts?

I turn to share my thoughts with Paddy, but he's already on his way. Before taking a second step, the agency's door opens and Paddy literally walks through the body of the young man leaving the office. In his blue-black silk suit, which really brings his rich brown Pharaoh-like complexion to the fore, the estate agent beams a chubby smile in my direction. He hops into his light blue Mondeo and drives off to his next appointment without being aware in any way of his recent brush with the nether world.

I follow my guide towards Whitchurch Road – a street that's always confused me slightly as it doesn't take you to Whitchurch and neither is it near that particular suburb – passing a patchwork of people representing a variety of cultures, while doing my best to side-step all the black bags, which colonise the pavement like the seals on Skomer's beaches. Before reaching Cathays' Gothamesque library, Paddy takes a right down Fairoak Road and crosses the street towards journey's end. Not far now. Paddy walks through the gates of Cathays Cemetery and I follow him, although I have to open the gate first, for obvious reasons...

As I walk along the cemetery's paths, past gravestones that stand like sentinels guarding their masters' ashes and bones, my own memories of my last visit to this place come flooding back, bringing dark thoughts with them. Paddy's still ahead of me, but I don't need his help anymore. Although I've only ever been here once before, and although the cemetery's so vast, I know exactly where my parents rest.

The last time I neared their graves, the circumstances were very different, although my shoes were causing me the same grief then as they are now. The rain fell from the darkest of skies, which reflected the mood of the many mourners who surrounded their graves. As I approached, the congregation turned as one to face me; their eyes like poisoned arrows. They emitted a mixture of emotions – hate, anger, shame and disbelief amongst them. The fact that I was handcuffed and flanked by a pair of mean-looking prison guards didn't help. Like a hooker between two props, I walked towards them, but didn't join them. Even away from prison, a convict will always be an outsider. The only smile I saw all day was from Sophie. She was stood between her parents under a bright pink brolly, and she looked over towards me on more than one occasion, which is more than can be said for Will or Mia. At the time I regretted going, but I'm glad I did by now, even though I knew my extended family would find it difficult being that close to me. I'm the living embodiment of the Bradys' worst nightmare – a dark period filled with sad memories – but I've given the whole episode so much thought during my sentence that my conscience is clear and I don't regret what I did. What I do regret though, was not having the chance to explain my actions to my parents. This fact will haunt me until my dying day.

I turn left by the derelict chapel and pass a concrete angel deep in prayer under a covering of moss. The gusting wind of central Cardiff has given way here to a light breeze dancing in the trees.

I spot Paddy standing by their grave, but when I approach he disappears. I never got this close to them on the day of their funeral, mainly because my family defended the grave like a bunch of Orcs at the gates of Mordor. At least I was 'released' that day, though, a privilege I wasn't granted for my grandad's funeral at the beginning of my sentence.

I felt so alone at my parents' funeral. But right now I feel like their son once again. I stand there, staring at the ground, struggling to picture their faces. Emotions bottled up over the years explode to the surface. On my knees, I cry uncontrollably. Regaining some composure, I sit cross-legged, ironing the grass with my open palm. Through the fog, I read their simple gravestones.

BRIAN BRADY
1946–2001

AND HIS DEAR WIFE

GWEN
1947–2001

GOD IS LOVE

The fresh daffodils, lilies and tulips – Mam's favourite flowers – that decorate their plot, show that my brother visits them more often in death than he did when they were alive.

The tears continue to flow. I hadn't realised how much I miss them. After a lifetime of companionship – and even prisoners have permanent, although admittedly enforced, companionship – the loneliness hits me. I've never craved for friendship during my life, as I had the best friends possible living at home with me. But now, sitting here alone, it dawns on me that it's not a matter of *wanting* friends, but rather a *need* for friends. After a lifetime of familial friendship, I'm totally lost and truly terrified.

As the tears continue, I mourn for the first time since the accident that ended my parents' lives: a coach crash on the way home from watching Oberammergau's world famous Passion Play. When I heard the news I was heartbroken of course, but I hadn't seen them for over a year and, to tell the truth, I was already accustomed to their absence. I understand why they were so disappointed in me – after all, what I did went against everything they believed in – but the worst thing is that I never got the opportunity to explain that it was an act of love. Although I didn't want to apologise to them either. After all, parents aren't right about everything.

I also know that they'd both believe that they've gone to a 'better place'. But as I sit here in the unique silence that hangs above every cemetery I've ever visited, I find it hard to agree. All I see is cold earth and I know they'd be much happier at home, relaxing to the sounds of some classical master or getting their hands dirty in the garden.

The sun disappears from view behind the nearby buildings and the sky above is painted red. I'm torn between the darkness of mourning and the relief of being free. That I can watch the evening close around me in the open air in itself leavens the sadness that I'll never properly be able to bid my parents farewell.

I kneel, remembering a trip to France when I was about five. T-shirts from St. Jean du Monts. Blue for me, red for Will and green for Dad. Sunburn and frites; crepes dripping with syrup – the true taste of misbehaving; Asterix, Obelix and Getafix, the Smurfs and being bored in the Bayeux Tapestry. I remember the frustration I felt as I struggled to build my Airfix models and Zoids, and the way Dad made it all look so easy. I remember Mam reading me bedtime stories. Gerald Cordle on the wing for Cardiff and Dad's scathing opinion of his lack of handing skills; Thorburn's kick from half a mile and Elvis Evans side-stepping his way to the most amazing of touchdowns against the Jocks. Swallowing an apple core and the disappointment that no tree grew in my stomach, like Dad promised. Singing in the school choir at St. David's Hall and my parents' faces smiling proudly at me from the front row of the audience. I remember the love they projected towards me, and once again the tears flow.

"'Scuse me mate," says a voice from behind me. I turn to face it, and he doesn't bat an eyelid. He seems familiar, a mixture of all the inmates I've just left behind: arms covered in tattoos, numerous scars, crew cut and roll your owns. But, there is one thing that sets him apart from the tenants of Cardiff Prison: a suntan.

"Sorry 'bou' this, mate, but I gots to lock up in abou' ten minutes like. OK?" I nod and he leaves me to it, wheeling his barrow towards the chapel.

I get to my feet and wipe my face with my sleeve before looking around for Paddy. I don't know what to do now, but I hope he'll have some idea. I can't see him anywhere at first, but as my eyes adapt to the descending dusk I spot the burning tip of his Woodbine off towards the exit, leading the way.

I follow Paddy out of the cemetery and walk down Allensbank Road, leaving the terraced houses behind as we approach suburbia. My mind's like a portrait by Pollock as Paddy takes a right by the

Mackintosh, which spews the stink of its microwaved meals into the dark, adding to Wedal Road's already overpowering personal hygiene problem. As I walk towards the Juboraj I'm surprised to see the grand red-bricked houses which have sprouted uncomfortably up between the rubbish dump and railway. If you *could* afford to live here, I'm pretty sure you wouldn't *choose* to live here...

We turn left onto Lake Road West and I can smell the Juboraj's Eastern aromas. I realise my legs are aching. I haven't walked this far for a long time. Although you can easily keep fit in jail, that sort of exercise doesn't appeal to me. I'd much rather climb a mountain or get lost in a forest in order to stretch my legs, as opposed to treading the mill or cycling on the spot in a gym. In jail, I was already caged like a hamster, without feeling the need to act like one too.

We reach Roath Park Lake. Scott's spot-lit lighthouse reflects perfectly on the still water and I sit for a while on a bench, drinking in the view. The last time I walked this way was on that terrible day over three years ago. My life's point of no return. The colours merge and separate on the water's slow-moving, almost stagnant, surface and I think of Knocker, that he'll never see anything like this again. Paddy's gestures grab my attention, so I get to my feet and follow him once again, limping along because of the blisters that have appeared on my left heel and under the big toe of my right foot, towards the tree-covered islands at the opposite end of the lake.

Before reaching my destination – Will's home which overlooks the lake – I sneak past the flock of geese, so as not to disturb them, and watch an angler land a tiddler. He seems disappointed with his catch, but what do you expect to catch in Roath Park Lake – barracuda?

I join Paddy and we sit on a bench by a picnic table, our backs to the barely-rippling water. When I look at him he nods his head towards the house across the street. What I witness in the window makes my heart pound. Mia. I've only visited their home a couple of times, and seeing her in the backlit window is both a shock and a pleasure at once. Her hair is shorter, without being short – I believe the technical term for the style is a 'bob' – and there's a hint of red in there somewhere too. However, her features are unmistakable – her button nose, deep dimples and Manga eyes haven't changed at all. I stare at her from afar, the same old story, and shiver a little as I give a warm welcome to another emotion, one I didn't think I'd have to deal with today...

When Sophie joins her at the window, holding a fat ginger cat that must be Dwdi, guilt rises within me and I cry again. That's the thing about guilt and time – the images cloud over but the feelings live on. I thought I'd be able to just walk up to their door; that's why I refused the prison's offer of temporary accommodation. But now, as I sit and stare at them through the window, I know that I can't do it. That would be totally unfair on everyone. I don't want to open the old scars... not yet, anyway.

Paddy lights another Woodbine as I watch Will walk into view, wearing a bright Pringle sweater and holding his mobile to his ear. He strokes Sophie's hair gently, before snapping his phone shut and placing it in his pocket. He mouths something to Mia. She laughs. Things seem to be much better between the pair these days.

Seeing my brother fills me with dread. We've never been close, although our relationship did get better during the months leading to my conviction. After a lifetime of bickering and bullying, the scars run deep. But much worse than anything he ever did to me was the way he treated our parents.

The term 'black sheep' was coined for people like Will – he went against everything my parents believed in, just out of malice. Our parents gave us everything – support and love – but that wasn't enough for my brother. He wanted to see them suffer, as if he was trying to prove something by making them unhappy.

But in my current frame of mind and state of isolation, I love him more today than I've ever done before. Having a brother is hard to explain, but there's an undeniable connection between us. He is all I have left...

After the funeral Mr Arch, our family solicitor, visited me in jail. After sharing the limpest handshake, he delivered the news in monotone. Despite my brother's lack of respect towards Mam and Dad, despite years of abuse, ridicule, lies and self-centredness, it was Will that received all my parents' inheritance. According to Mr Arch, Dad changed the will just before my trial reached court. I was already aware that they were ashamed of what I had done. But wasn't I the good son, regardless of what had happened recently? I was the faithful one. I listened to them, indulged them, respected them, and loved them. I… I… I'm starting to sound like Will now…

The monetary situation hasn't affected me until today, as finding the rent wasn't a problem while the taxpayers were paying. But as I sit here watching my brother basking in the bosom of his family, I long for home – my parents' house that is. Unfortunately, according to Mr Arch, Will sold my home for a pure profit of around half a million. I'm enraged. I'm disgusted at my loss and his unexpected and undeserved profit.

Question: What do you give the man who has everything?
Answer: More.

I know this probably sounds like sour grapes on my behalf, but believe you me, what I did was not even in the same league as my brother's attitude and behaviour towards our parents throughout his life.

Paddy continues to smoke beside me as the leaves above whisper sweet nothings to the night. Mia gets up and leaves the room. Sophie starts skipping as Will speaks into his phone once again. Mia soon returns carrying a small child in shocking pink pyjamas, which confirms that the happy couple had a second daughter while Uncle Al was 'working away'.

Mia passes the toddler to Will. He holds the phone between ear and shoulder in order to multi-task and help his wife. As Mia steps to the window once again to draw the curtains, she stares directly at me. Even though I'm certain she can't see me, my heart beats louder in the full beam of her gaze. She smiles and then pulls the curtains closed. I stare at their home for a little while longer, before realising that I'm holding the silver cross that hangs around my neck. As I run my fingers and thumb over the cold metal, I notice the smile on Paddy's face: he's happy to see the comfort his gift is giving me.

I get up and leave Paddy where he is, and limp back in the same

44

direction we came earlier. I don't need a guide now. I know exactly where I'm going to sleep tonight… although I would appreciate a piggy-back.

I reach the main entrance and scale the rusty railing before creeping quietly past the dark house and derelict chapel. I find a sturdy sack along the way before reaching my parents' grave once again. Clouds have gathered in the sky above, creating a heavenly blanket for the city's homeless to lie beneath.

I release my throbbing feet and massage my aching toes. As I lie down on the soft grass above their graves, I realise that there's one thing I regret more than anything. I never had the opportunity to thank them before they died. I never had the chance to tell them how much I loved them. But more: I regret not having the chance to say goodbye to them…

Chapter 4: FRUSTRATION

"You'll nevva gess wor I urd off tha' Leeeee-anne Rolff girl?"

"No, wozzat Debs?"

"Ye', wo?"

"I urd tha' tha' Jow-anne Delaney girl from da Malfa, you nowz 'er, short 'air, blonde, looks like wossername off Eestenduz…"

"Pat?"

"No, nor Pat, the fa' one wo' my dad fancies."

"Sharun."

"Yeah, Sharun. Righ', well, I urd she got urpies from suckin' Nathan wossisface…"

"Buttla?"

"…Yeah, suckin' Nathan Buttla off behind vu Spa'."

"Who, Sharun?"

"No' Sash, no' Sharun. Jow-anne innit. From da Malfa."

"Oh…"

"She ain't a full shillin', vat girl…"

"I knowz Kez. She's well rank."

"Urpies? Wossa'r'en Debs?"

"Wo', you don't knowz wo' urpies is like?"

"Well, yeah, but no, but ye… You knowz I knowz, I jus' can't remember innit. Worrizit Debs?"

"It's a SDP innit, like da clap an' rabies but you gets it from suckin' cocks an' fingering an' all tha', innit Kez?"

"Ye'. My mum gor it last yur like. Caught it off sum Doctor down da Philly. My Dad was well fucked off wiv 'er."

Welcome to my nightmare. It's early Monday evening and I'm on my way home from work. Right now, I'm trapped in a bus stop, with Debz, Kez and Sash in front of me and about twenty other contortionists squeezed into the shelter outside the Toucan Club. The rain's bucketing down, hence the overcrowding, soaking the city and her citizens to the skin. It was pleasant this morning you see, with blue skies and a gentle breeze, so I, like many others, came to work sporting nothing more than a light jacket over shirt and tie. Now, that would be considered a mistake in springtime, while it's complete madness in the autumn.

Regardless of the dampness and tightness of the situation, it seems to me that everybody's smoking, as the fumes dance above the scrum like steam rising from a herd of cattle. The girls who stand in front of me – loaded with bags from Primark and Peacocks, their stained Regal fingers heavily burdened with Sovereign rings from Argos – discuss… well, you already know what they're discussing. And I don't mean characters from popular soap operas either. Sucking… penises… as if it's the most normal thing in the world. *Their* world maybe, but not mine. Everyone can hear them but that doesn't stop them. They have no shame. Obviously. I regret not bringing my Walkman to work today.

A man of Asian descent joins the ruck and squeezes in right next to me. An Indian, or maybe a Pakistani, his skin the colour of an old naturist from Nevada. As he settles into the human cushion, our eyes meet but he doesn't seem to see me. He just looks right through me as if I'm not there. I slip my hands into my trouser pockets and am relieved to feel my keys and wallet safe and sound. Not that I mistrust him on the grounds of his ethnicity, you understand, but 'they' do warn you about pickpockets when travelling abroad, while no one seems to consider the possibility that people make a similar living at home too. This situation is perfect for a pickpocket – everyone pressed against each other with wallets poised to pay their fares. Western governments have succeeded in making us all paranoid about anyone who's 'different' from 'us', and through this fear, some kind of control is achieved. These criminals – thieves, murderers, rapists – walk amongst us, looking 'normal' but lacking in values, morals and more.

Shortly, typically, and with a seemingly-huge collective sigh of relief, two buses arrive at once. I let everyone else go ahead of me. I can think of only three things: a steaming whirlpool bath, a good novel and an early night. The perfect Monday evening. I can't wait to get out of my sopping clothes which cling to me like lycra. I show the driver my return ticket and push my way towards the back, apologising and excusing myself. No one makes any kind of effort to get out of the way. I grab a pole and look around. Everyone looks so depressed – so sad, so bored – like caged animals in a badly-run zoo. I spot a couple of elephants sitting in the disabled seats, their flesh bulging over the sides of the narrow pews. An open-legged orang-utan sits in the middle of the back row, picking fleas from his ginger thatch, while a silver-backed gorilla nods his head to the beat of his personal stereo. A vulture and hyena reach at once to retrieve a stray five pence from under their feet. I see a baboon, a gazelle, and three chimps squeezed into the same seat, and through the herd of hairy buffaloes I spot one of nature's most stunning beasts sitting a few feet away from me. A panther.

My world falls silent as I stare in her direction. I watch her as she watches the world pass by the steamy window through an opening she's made with her paw. Her dark hair glistens under a damp covering of dew. My eyes wander from her auburn eyes, beyond her Merlot lips and down towards her breasts, which are completely covered by a denim jacket, leaving everything to my imagination, before reaching her silky legs, which stretch towards the dirty floor beneath her high-heeled toes.

I'm paralysed. Unfamiliar feelings are stirring, the desire is almost overpowering. I begin to tremble as a rush of blood causes a commotion in my... I look away to try and stem the sensation but as the 'ping' of the bell denotes a nearing bus stop, I anchor myself to the pole and await the rush of bodies as they hurtle towards me.

As the bus slows down, I look again towards the panther and see her get to her feet. She straightens her legs and her short skirt lifts a little to reveal the pale skin of her upper thighs above her stockings. I'm rooted to the spot and just stare as she readjusts herself and brushes past me. I turn away to avoid stabbing her with my sword, and gaze longingly after her as she moves her dancer's body towards the exit. It's only after she's gone that I notice that the tepee in my trousers is pointing straight at the face of an old lady who's sat down beside me. Fortunately for both of us, she seems completely unaware of this intrusion, thanks mainly to the polka dotted plastic hood that covers her head.

I ring the bell in blind panic, even though the bus isn't close to my home, and try to tame my manhood using my right hand, which is buried deep in my trouser pocket. I manage to snare the snake between my belly and the elastic of my underpants, while pushing my way to the front.

The walk home is a wet nightmare, filled with guilt and frustration. I feel guilty for viewing that girl as nothing more than an object. Something to look at, something to have. Like a model in a magazine or much worse. I'm frustrated because... well... you know... and she wasn't even *that* amazing either, just fool's gold in a sea of silver. Beggars can't be choosers, so 'they' say, and after twenty-nine years of waiting, I, without a shadow of a doubt, fall into the first category.

I walk the full length of Cyncoed Road – from Penylan, past the water tower, the college and the suburban mansions – which slithers towards Llanishen like a gigantic asphalt anaconda. The rain has stopped by the time I turn on to my street, Hollybush Road, but this just makes things worse as my clothes start rubbing against my skin. I walk the last quarter of a mile in serious pain as my feet start to blister. At times like this, I regret not completing my driving lessons when I had the chance at seventeen.

I limp towards home, dreaming of the bath, some hot soup and my warm bed. Monday night is my night in our house. With Mam at her am-dram practice and Dad down the golf club, finishing a day on the links with a few drams at the nineteenth hole, I've got the place to myself. Just me, Dwdi and a good book.

But I know there's something wrong immediately, as both my parent's cars are parked on the drive. I'm relieved to see through the kitchen window both my parents sitting at the table, deep in discussion.

I take a deep breath before opening the door. At least they're ok... alive. I always expect the worst: I can remember standing on a chair, straining to see out of the upstairs window when I was a child, worrying about my parents when they were only a few minutes late coming home.

Their heads turn to face me as I come in, smiling uncertainly.

"What's wrong, what's happened?" Mam gets up to fetch a mug from the cupboard; Dad sits there staring into space. Mam looks at me.

"Alun!" She clucks. "You're soaking!"

I nod and take off my shoes, placing them on the floor by the Aga.

After filling my mug with coffee, Mam gestures for me to join them at the table. I stay where I am in an attempt to dry off a little. With my back to the Aga, I smell the coffee and appreciate the rich aroma before taking a greedy gulp.

"Come on then," I demand. "What's going on?"

Once again, no one answers. They look at each other. Mam's eyes are bloodshot; Dad's are glazed and tired.

"Gwe..." Dad says at last, passing the baton to Mam.

"Brian, he's your father!"

"I know that, but come on, you're much better at explaining these things..."

"Alun," she says, looking at me with a half smile. "Patrick... your grandfather... Brian's dad... is ill..."

"What's wrong with him?" I blurt out.

"Patience, Al!"

"Sorry, Dad. Mam. I just... you know."

Dad nods his head and slurps his coffee. Mam absent-mindedly fiddles with the spoon in the sugar bowl. I look at the wrinkles around her eyes which are more noticeable tonight.

"Well, he's very old, you know that. How old is he now, Brian?"

"Eighty-seven."

"Eighty-seven, that's it. Well he's... I don't know how to say this... he's lost... he's lost his legs..."

"What?"

"Gwen!"

"Sorry, sorry, no, no, no! He hasn't lost his legs at all, but he has lost the *use* of his legs..."

"How?"

"We're not really sure, are we Brian, not one hundred percent anyway... old age..."

"Wear and tear..."

"Thanks bach, yes, wear and tear. He needs two new knees, you know, fake ones..."

"Artificial."

"That's it, he needs artificial ones, but because of his age and his history of heart problems the doctors won't treat him..."

His heart problems. That's one way of putting it. About twenty-five years ago, my grandad smoked sixty non-filtered Woodbines a day, though allowing for exaggeration over the years, I'll call it forty. So: he had a heart attack. Not life threatening, but enough of a warning for most. While recovering in the hospital, he was warned daily by the doctors to stop smoking or the next heart attack would be fatal. But the first thing he did when he came out was go down the shop and buy a fresh twenty.

A month later, he had a second heart attack that would have killed most people, and back he went to the hospital. This time, he listened to the doctors' warnings and his wife's pleading and when he left the hospital he found another habit to fill the void vacated by smoking. Sweets. When I was a child, going for a spin in his car was like visiting Willy Wonka's mobile factory – there were dental dangers everywhere! In the glovebox, under the radio, in the doors, the tape holder and always in Grandad's mouth. The only thing missing was the Oompa

Loompas, although now I think about it, I never looked in the boot. His health recovered over the years, but he lost his teeth in no time. I can still hear him complaining – "Well, the toffees gave me lungs a rest but they rotted me bloody gnashers!"

Although I spent many Christmases, birthdays and Easters with him, the only story I have about him is of dubious authenticity. We've never been close and now it looks as though I'll never have the chance to get to know him...

"To tell you the truth, Al, that's what we were just discussing before you walked in... Alun?"

"Al!" Dad plucks me back to the present.

"Huh, sorry Mam, what was that?"

"We're thinking about looking after him ourselves. Here..."

"Who, Grandad?"

"Of course, who else?"

"What about a nursing home, with round the clock care?"

"That is an option," Dad explains. "But we want the rest of his life to be as comfortable as possible..."

"As happy..."

"Yes, as happy as possible. Dad, and Mam before she passed away, have given us so much as a family over the years, we want to repay him a little, that's all..."

"That's what families are supposed to do; care for each other..."

"I just want him to know that we think the world of him and appreciate everything he's ever done for us..."

That's understandable, but...

"You think we're mad, don't you Al! Brian! Look at his face... look!"

"Calm down, Mam!" I plead. "I think it's a great idea. A bit of a shock, but a great idea nonetheless."

"Sorry bach," she says calmly. "I didn't mean anything..."

"I know. It's ok."

She reaches a hand towards me so I step towards her and give her a big wet hug. Despite the obvious emotional burden, I sense a great determination in my parents tonight. My grandad's time is obviously ticking towards its inevitable conclusion.

A guttural *Miaaaaaaaw* breaks the silence and Dad, without any hesitation, gets to his feet to feed Dwdi.

"We're off to Merthyr to see him in a minute," Mam explains. "You should come if you've got nothing better..."

"Gwen, I'm sure Al has..."

"No, Dad, I want to come. Just give me ten minutes to get changed."

I run upstairs to my bedroom, taking three steps at a time. I am strangely desperate to see my grandad. To make up for lost time. I want to talk to him, get to know him. Right now. The way I've ignored him throughout my adult life makes me think of one person in particular. Will. That comparison doesn't sit comfortably on my conscience.

We're in the Volvo, on our way to see Patrick Brady, cruising past Whitchurch Golf Club. We leave the city at exactly seventy miles an hour, and pass under the fantastical shadow of Castell Coch in complete silence.

The rain has stopped but the road is still soaked with surface water. I sit in the passenger seat staring straight ahead at the street lights. The weariness, sadness and guilt rush through me as Dad slows down carefully – from 70mph to 50 at the eternal road works of the A470.

In the cockpit's low light, Dad's profile reminds me of Grandad's, although Dad's middle-age spread is the opposite of Patrick Brady's beanpole frame. Dad inherited his 'big bones' from his mother, but he has the same nose as Grandad's and the same dimples.

Unlike my mam, who's of pure Welsh stock, Dad's a proper mongrel, which makes me one too, I suppose. Grandad emigrated around 1930 to Wales from Blackrock in Dublin when he turned eighteen. The reason for his exile is shrouded in mystery and is talked about in whispers by members of the family. He worked in the port of Fishguard for ten years and during this period he met Gwyneth, my gran. They married and moved east to look for work and chase their dreams, settling in Cascade where grandad found employment in the nearby Penallta Coal Mine.

He still lives in the village, a stone's throw from their matrimonial home, in a tiny, one-bedroom bungalow, where he has his meals delivered. He moved within a couple of months of losing Gran. It's with absolute shame that I admit I can't remember the last time I visited him. I don't have any way of getting there… apart from the train, the bus… ok, so I don't have any excuse for neglecting him… for forgetting him. I just hope it's not too late to make up for my misconduct.

I rejoin the world in time to see Cyfarthfa Castle hiding in the trees beyond the lake to the right.

"Right by here!" says Mam.

"I know," Dad whispers, slipping the car into second as we start our ascent toward the Gurnos.

The atmosphere outside changes as soon as we reach the estate – which is notably darker due to the many streetlamps that have been vandalised. Many windows are boarded up, and the burnt-out car shells, which are dotted around, transport me to another world. A shanty town. A favela on my own doorstep. Society's rubbish dump. Where the weak and the poor, the mute and the helpless congregate. Once you find yourself in a place like this, it's almost impossible to ever escape.

"Watch out by here, Brian!" Mam exclaims from the back seat, referring to a gang of youngsters hanging around a bus stop drinking cider and… it's hard to say… but isn't that enough? Especially on a Monday night! As Dad drives past on the wrong side of the road, avoiding the mass of bodies which spills from the pavement onto the tarmac, I can feel fifteen pairs of eyes staring towards us. The Gurnos is a proper ghetto. A place and a community that politicians would rather forget.

Mam insists that Dad parks the car close to the main entrance under a streetlight. We walk towards Prince Charles Hospital arm in arm with Mam in the middle. The puddles underfoot reflect a sky awash with stars. The grey building, turning black in places, is as sad as the estate that surrounds it and the patients who occupy it.

A cluster of people stand by the main entrance – patients, relatives and various health workers – adding to the NHS's already mounting problems as they puff away next to a concrete trough of dead flowers.

The picture I paint of the outside might be bleak, but it's Edenesque compared to what awaits us within. I follow my parents towards Ward 3, Orthopaedic, as they tread the same path as they did five years earlier during Gran's final days.

We pass a security guard en route. In the hospital's sepia-toned light, his pale skin and bulging beer belly suggest that he might need medical attention himself soon. As we pass him, he takes a long swig from his can of Diet Coke and reaches for a packet of crisps, which he greedily begins to devour.

The stale aroma of hospital food makes me retch. We pass patients suffering from various illnesses and ailments: from jaundiced ghosts to a legless amputee screeching around the corner on two wheels. Two sisters embrace tearfully. We see slings, plaster of Paris, stitched skulls, people with Parkinson's... and sense an atmosphere thick with anxiety, heartbreak and death.

The ward sister points us in Grandad's direction. He lies there in the far corner of a room full of old men mumbling, snoring, farting or whistling tunelessly through damaged lungs. He is utterly still. His closed eyes reveal a small birthmark on the right lid. His arms lie lifelessly by his side. His chest rises and falls under his pyjamas with assistance from a nearby oxygen tank.

We stand at the foot of the bed, staring. He's not at all like I remember him... that's such a stupid thing to say... and my hopes for getting to know him disappear before my very eyes.

After a long silence – on our part as opposed to the other patients – Mam starts to sob quietly. I put my arm around her and pull her close as Dad takes a seat at his father's bedside. He gently strokes the old man's left hand and I can see the rough contours of a lifetime of physical work shifting beneath my father's fingers. As well as working down the mine, Grandad tirelessly worked on his allotment in Fleur de Lis throughout his life until only about a year ago. His manly hands are something else I haven't inherited. Although, now that I think about it, it's not possible to inherit such hands... without doing some physical work of your own, that is.

"Mr Brady?" asks a voice which makes all three of us turn around to face it. "I'm Doctor Thomas and I was wondering if I could have a chat with you... in private." Dad stands up, takes Mam's hand before following the good doctor towards an office near the ward's reception.

I stand for a moment not too sure of what I should do next, but the answer is so obvious. I sit down beside him, in the chair recently vacated by my father. My eyes are drawn to the tubes protruding from his nostrils and I listen to his lungs as they struggle to operate. The flesh of his face hangs loosely from his chin and his white hair is like a thatched roof dusted with snow.

Shamefully, the only thing I feel towards this relative stranger is pity. As I look around the ward, all I see are old men, wise men, who have lost their dignity. I turn my gaze towards Grandad and hold his hand in mine. Amazingly, considering his lifetime of graft, his skin is like gossamer hanging delicately from his fleshless fingers.

I long to explain myself, but don't feel able to speak. So I do something far more practical instead: I close my eyes and pray.

Chapter 5: AN UNLIKELY SAVIOUR

The early morning traffic rumbles beyond the barred windows, welcoming me back to consciousness, and as I open my eyes I see Knocker standing over me with the day's first fag hanging precariously from the corner of his mouth.

"No, Knock, not yet..." I protest. "The alarm hasn't gone off..." I close my eyes again. But my friend doesn't listen: he bends down and shakes me gently back to life.

I open my eyes and through the morning mist I notice that Knocker seems much smaller than usual. His shoulders don't need their usual 'Wide Load' warning. He shakes me once again, but I'm determined not to leave my bed until the alarm goes off.

"C'mon mate, wakey-wakey!"

I sit up faster than an uncoiling cobra when I realise it's not Knocker after all. The figure steps back, holding his hands in front of him.

"Easy now, mate, take it easy," he advises. I look around and see nothing but gravestones stretching towards the horizon and remember where I am.

I'm shivering under a plastic sheet covered in condensation. I get to my feet and stretch, then reach for my shoes, but remember my blisters.

"Are you all right, mate?" he asks.

I recall seeing him in exactly the same spot last night. Like myself, I don't think he's changed his clothes since then either. He still sports the same 'Motörhead – No Sleep 'Til Hammersmith' sleeveless T-shirt, denim shorts which were obviously a pair of jeans in a former life, and heavy Caterpillar work boots. His short spiky blond hair – a flat top to be technically correct – mischievous eyes and gravy-coloured complexion makes him look at least five years younger than he really is.

"Yes, I think so. A bit cold..."

"A bit! I'd be fuckin' freezin' out here if I was you. Haven't you got anywhere better to sleep?" He looks at me, pulls hard on his rollie and blows the smoke towards the sky. I stretch again.

"I actually haven't... and now that I think about it, that's one of the best night's sleep I've had in ages..."

The man chuckles, tilting his head so that the golden hoops hanging from his left ear sparkle in the morning sun.

"Well, I'm glad of that, but you can't stay 'ere again. OK?"

"Of course, it won't happen again."

"Safe. No 'arm done. They your parents a'they?"

I turn to look at the graves.

"They were..." I correct him.

"True. I'm sorry." And I believe him too. He's got such a friendly face and such a crooked smile, that it's hard not to. "Look, my name's Floyd," he adds, thrusting his hand towards me.

I introduce myself, "Alun, but my friends," (cough!) "call me Al," and we shake hands. Floyd invites me to his shed for a cuppa.

I pick up my sack-stroke-duvet and place it in his wheelbarrow along with my shoes. We head towards the far corner of the cemetery, past the chapel and the house by the entrance. Floyd tells me about his job as the cemetery's caretaker and I try my best to conceal the pain of walking barefoot along the rough paths. I stop suddenly and wince as a pin-sharp stone burrows into my flesh.

"Why don't you walk on the grass verges, Al? They're softer than puppies and don't yelp when you step on 'em," says Floyd. I chuckle and do as he suggests.

After about a hundred yards, we veer off the public path, leaving the graves behind us, and cross a parched stream called 'Nanteeweedle', according to Floyd. We walk along a rock hard dirt track into the trees.

"There she is," Floyd announces, nodding towards a cluster of thick foliage in front of us. I stare for a second and still can't see what he's on about.

"What? Where?"

"There... HQ. My office, laboratory, storeroom, garage, workshop, kitchen and lounge." He smiles broadly as the sun penetrates the canopy, lighting up a very well camouflaged work shed. "No one knows she even exists... which is just the way I like it. You're a privileged person, Al. If you tell anyone about her, I'll have to kill you..."

"What?" I ask, slightly startled.

Floyd lets go of his wheelbarrow and turns to face me. My heart pounds.

"Al, you gotsta chill, mate. I was only joking, like, but I can see from the look on you face that you're shitting it. You're very jumpy... but I'm sure there's a good reason for that..."

I almost butt in and explain everything that's happened to me, but he spreads his hands.

"Look, Al. I don't care what happened to you or why you're kippin' like a bepp by your parents' grave. It's just, well, when I see a man in a suit crying his eyes out and then freezing his nuts off, least I can do is offer him a cup o' tea, know what I mean?"

After unlocking the door's three heavy bolts, Floyd steps in and switches on a bare bulb. I stay by the door, leaning my shoulder against the frame, understanding why Floyd wants to keep the place a secret. The shed's pretty much how I'd imagine the headquarters of Trotters Independent Traders to be: chock-full of CDs, Lacoste polo shirts, shoe boxes emblazoned with names like Adidas, Puma and Nike, various electrical goods such as toasters and kettles. And three dubious-looking plants standing to attention in the far corner under the unrelenting glare of some UV lamps. Even though I'm completely inexperienced in that particular field, I know exactly what they are. To the left of where I stand there's a stainless steel sink and a rusty kettle, a mini fridge, a camping stove, a radio and a filthy window sporting a crispy-looking roller blind which is doing a pretty bad job of keeping the contents of the shed a secret. To my right there's a workbench, overflowing drawers and garden furniture hanging from hooks on the wall; and in front of me sits a 28-inch TV on a pine table. It's hard to tell if this piece of kit is contraband or here for entertainment purposes. But, from looking at the dust on it, I'd guess that it doesn't serve much of a purpose at all.

"Scuse the mess, Al, I don't do much entertaining in this place. And don't stand there like a bouncer, mate, come on in. Make yourself comfortable," Floyd fills the kettle. The water boils and he retrieves a couple of sun-loungers from the corner, gesturing for me to join him. But, as I'm about to take my first step, Floyd shouts "Stop! Sorry mate, but you might want to put your shoes on before coming in, in case you step on a nail or some glass or summin'."

"That would probably be more pleasant than putting my shoes on, Floyd…"

"That bad, ey. All right, stay there for a sec…" He heads for the pile of shoeboxes and asks, "What size are you, Al?"

"Size?"

"Feet. Shoes. What size?"

"Nine."

"Bingo!" And he turns to face me, smiling, holding an Adidas box. "You can have these. They're Sambas, Adidas Samba. Y'know, like the dance."

"Are you sure, Floyd?"

I'm embarrassed that this bloke, this stranger who's *already* been too kind to me, is now giving me a brand new pair of daps as well. And even though the contents of his shed suggests I shouldn't, I trust him almost completely already.

'They' say that prison can erase your ability to trust others, but things were different for me, thanks to Knocker. Truth is, it was behind bars that I made my first true friend – apart from my immediate family. Now that I'm on the outside, I'm beginning to realise just how important friendship really is. I wouldn't have lasted a week inside without Knocker and I'm determined to survive now that I'm free.

"Yeah, of course. They've just been lying there for the past few months. Maybe even years. I'm not the best salesman, see – I buy all this stuff off people, know what I mean, then after an initial burst of floggin' down the Arches like, I just don't bother any more... can't be arsed I s'ppose... anyway, they're yours if you want 'em..."

I thank him and put them on by the door, then park my behind on one of the floral-print chairs. While I tie my laces, Floyd pours boiling water over two teabags and shuffles off into the shadows. The next thing I know is I'm hit in the face by a cotton shirt.

"Put that on too, so you don't look like an undertaker..."

Thanking him again, I exchange my formal one for this bright red Lacoste polo shirt. I sit and watch Floyd stir the drinks. I realise just how short he is. 'Five foot and a fart' as Paddy would say. Paddy! I almost forgot about him... but I'm sure he's ok. After all, a cemetery should be the best place for him to find some friends.

"D'you want any sugars, mate?"

"No thanks."

"More for me, then," Floyd grins, dumping three heaped spoonfuls into his mug and adding the milk.

Floyd puts his mug down on the worktop and reaches for his rolling papers. But I don't believe it's tobacco in his stinking pouch.

"What are these, Floyd?" I ask, pointing at a pile of plastic cases. "CDs, are they?" Floyd looks at me, confused, as he eagerly chops some herb in a plastic bowl on his lap with a pair of nail scissors.

"Not quite. They're DVDs..."

"DVDs? I've never heard of them."

"Serious? Fuckin' hell, where 'ave you been 'iding, mate?"

I pause for a second and consider whether I should just tell him everything...

"I've been away for a while..."

"Oh yeah, travellin' is it?"

"Not quite. The complete opposite really..."

"The complete opposite of *travellin'*?" I glug my Glengettie and nod. "What? Sitting still?"

"Pretty much..."

"Fuck, I knows now!" He grins at me, nodding quickly as he fills his king-size paper with tobacco and finely-chopped grass. Without taking his eyes off of me, he licks the paper and rolls the perfect cone, smiling and nodding the whole time. "You've been banged up, haven't you? The suit, the kippin' rough, it all makes sense now."

I don't say a word to begin with, trying to work out my best move. Then I consider his generosity, his honesty and... I admit everything... almost.

"I have. Yes. I got out yesterday after serving three years of a four-year stretch..."

"What was you in for, Al? If you don't mind me asking..."

"Some other time, Floyd, if *you* don't mind?"

"Of course mate, no worries," he says, holding his palms up in front of him once again. "I've done some time myself, like. Two stretches, one for armed robbery when I was well young, twenty years old I was, five years of an eight-year stretch. That taught me something, that did..."

"What?"

"Never get caught!"

We both burst out laughing like a couple of Bond villains.

"What else were you sent down for?"

"Did another year about ten back for dealing draw..."

"I see you've reformed well on that front, Floyd!"

"Of course! What about you?"

"Reformed?"

"Aye."

"That's a difficult one to call, really, as I don't think I did anything wrong in the first place..."

"True, we're all innocent on the inside..."

"I didn't say I was innocent of what I was accused of," I explain, taking another swig of my tea. "I mean, the evidence was stacked against me. I confessed to everything anyway. I just know what I did was the right thing to do at the time..."

My words silence us both, so Floyd places the joint between his lips. Before lighting up, he says, "You've got nowhere to stay, have you – no family or nothin'."

"I *have* got a family, but nowhere to sleep, you're right. Why?"

"Well, I was just thinking. You can stay here if you want, till you get back on your feet, like. I knows it's not much, but it's better than kipping on the floor like a tramp."

I think I've found my guardian angel! I thank my new friend, and even though my new, temporary, home is a garden shed, it's better than a bench, a grave or a cell. "Do you trust me, Floyd? I mean, I haven't even told you what I was in for…"

"I don't know if I trust you yet, Al, but I've got a good feeling about you. And anyway, everyone deserves a second chance in life, don't they?"

"You're right. But what about the house by the main entrance? Does anyone live there?"

"Nah, just the occasional gippo and the resident ghost."

"Ghost?"

"Yeah, that's why the gippos never stay too long!"

Floyd's eyes sparkle and he lights his herbal cigarette, its tip crackling as the smoke rises towards the ceiling. Having emptied his lungs, he gulps down some tea and melts into his chair with a stupid grin.

The tranquility is torn by Floyd's mobile phone ringing. He looks at the handset, mumbles "Unknown number, fuck" before answering.

"City Gardening Solutions, Floyd speaking… Hah! You gotta be pro, Clyde, I'm not psychic… Yeah, I'm all right, sun's shining weather is sweet, what more can you ask for… anyway, what can I do for you… How much? Fuckin' hell, big weekend is it?… Nah, shouldn't be a problem, mate… safe, call by later, we'll sort it out…"

It's hard not to listen.

"So, do the council mind your on-the-job higher state of consciousness then, Floyd?" I regret my joke immediately, but after an 'uncomfortable silence', Floyd erupts with laughter.

"I don't know about a higher state of consciousness, but the council don't say anything about me being caned all the time. In fact, I don't think they've ever met me sober… but it don't matter. See, they employ my company, not me personally, I think they call it... y'know... fuck, I forget, fuck... doesn't matter. So they employ my company, City Gardening Solutions, to look after the place, y'know, keep it clean an' tidy. Nothin' too strenuous. I don't have to do any gravediggin' or anything dark like that, they employ a firm of specialists to do all that shit. All I gotta take care of is maintenance. Just maintenance."

He pulls hard on the joint once again. "It's ideal for me really, stress free, fresh air, well, as fresh as you can get in the city like, but you knows what I mean. It's good physical work, keeps me fit like. I mean, I used to do martial arts like. I mastered Tao Do Chaung, you know, Ninjitsu. Serious stuff like," he unconsciously tenses his biceps. "Now I just do some gardening and a few press-ups every day to keep in shape... but, best of all I get a year-round tan without going to those salons what turn your skin orange... Outsourcing! That's what they call it, outsourcing... Truth is, I hardly ever see a council worker down here. As long as I keep the place lookin' tidy, no one cares if I'm off my box all day. Ideal."

He offers the joint to me. Now, the smokiest things that've passed my lips are salmon, mackerel and some Bavarian cheese, and I didn't really plan to discover a dirty habit today. On the other hand, I don't want to insult my new friend. Instinct kicks in, however, and I shake my head.

"Don't give me that, Al. It won't bite you; it'll give you a whole new perspective on the day ahead..."

"That's from *Easy Rider*." Not one of my favourite films starring Mr Nicholson, but there's no denying the man's charisma, charm and talent, even in that mess of a movie.

"So you knows *Easy Rider* do you? If that's the case you definitely want some of this," and he hands me the spliff, leaving me no choice. I look at the paper, which has turned black under the drug's special effects, and then at Floyd who's grinning like a fool. "And anyway, Al, what have you got to do today? Fuck all, that's what!" And like the coward that I am, I lift the joint to my lips and suck... before coughing as the smoke hits the back of my throat. I need some water. A lake full preferably...

"Don't murder it, Al. Just toke it easy."

But I've already passed it back to him and swiftly step to the sink where I run the tap and slurp at the water. Floyd laughs out loud. Once my throat's stopped feeling like it's on fire, I sit back down and wipe the tears from my eyes.

"Ahhh, virgin lungs," Floyd says, offering me the spliff. "Mine are shrivelled up like a pair of raisins by now. You want some more of this?" And as I want to appear hard in front of my new friend, I take it off him. "Now, don't pull so hard this time, Al. You don't want to choke again." I pull smoothly and softly, sucking the smoke deep into my lungs. I don't cough. And if I'm honest, it's quite a pleasant sensation. After passing the joint back to Floyd, I recline in my chair and let the herb work its magic.

After a minute of complete internal panic as my mind contorts and expands, causing the room to melt all around me, things start to settle as I begin to relax a little. Floyd is lying back, and I glance over at his face: his eyes closed, an etched smile. I do the same thing, and for a minute that feels like an hour my mind's full of chaos and madness as the guilt and greenery take a hold of me. Thankfully, before things get too weird, Floyd comes back to life and drags me with him.

"Well I don't know about you, but I'm fuckin' starvin'," and he's right too, my stomach's been moaning for a while now. "It's breakfast time, mate. I'll take you to the best caff in Cardiff. My shout."

We struggle a little to sort ourselves out but manage to leave the shed and meander leisurely through the trees back towards civilisation.

After rejoining the public path, we glide past the empty house and crumbling chapel. The sun feels strange on my pale skin. My feet take to my new trainers like a hermit crab to an empty shell, and the cemetery appears like a 3-D image. The whole world seems clearer, more defined somehow – the gravestones jump out and the trees and plants seem to be breathing softly in the wind… beautiful, maaaaan.

Without warning, Floyd holds his arm in front of my chest, bringing me to an abrupt stop opposite Morgan Signs on Fairoak Road.

"Check that out," he says, pointing in the general direction of the buildings on the other side of the street.

"What?" I ask, trying my best to concentrate on what's in front of me.

"The graffiti on the van, man."

In the dust, someone has written: "I wish my wife was this dirty."

We both keel over, cackling like hyenas, tears streaming down our cheeks. This moment seals our budding friendship, and suddenly I'm feeling undeniably hopeful.

Once our breathing has returned to normal, Floyd points at the shop next door to Morgan Signs: Mossfords' stonemasons.

"Now that's prime fuckin' real estate and prime location for a stonemason, ey Al. Mr Moss is a fuckin' millionaire and it's all thanks to the positioning…" Right on cue, Mr Moss steps out of his empire's HQ and waves at Floyd. Floyd waves back and shuffles away in case the old man comes over for a chat. "He's always fuckin' smiling, he is, and it's no fuckin' wonder is it, I mean, everyone's gotta die someday. That's the only certainty in life, innit. Death. We're just blank cheques on legs to him. He looks at us and thinks of cash, 'cept he won't get anything from me, no one will…"

"How do you mean, Floyd?"

"Unmarked grave for me, Al. Absolute anonymity in death, just like William H…"

"William Hague?" I ask, completely confused and astounded at Floyd's Conservative leanings.

"He's not dead yet, Al. And anyway, no, not William fuckin' Hague! William H Bonney…"

"Who?"

"Who? Are you serious? Billy the Kid, Al. Billy the fuckin' Kid." We carry on towards Crwys Road, laughing at the absurdity of it all.

I spot Paddy leaning on a gravestone near the electricity generator and feel a bit guilty for abandoning him in favour of Floyd's company. He doesn't seem to have made any 'friends' either but he soothes my emotions with a wide smile and a thumbs-up, before disappearing.

We go into Café Calcio and sit down. I ask Floyd where the menus are and he points at the tablemat with its extensive selection. My mouth starts watering and my belly groans.

"There's no choice really," says Floyd. "I recommend the Big Bastard Breakfast, it's massive and it'll set you up for the rest of the day."

As he lights another rollie, I notice the smoke for the first time. *Everyone* is smoking – the students, the customers, the workers. The air is so heavy that I can practically see the walls yellowing.

"Can I take your order?" Our waiter is in torn jeans and a dirty T-shirt, and is a bored cross between Plug from the Bash Street Kids and the BFG.

"Two Big Bastards please," says Floyd without consulting me, and off goes Plug back to the kitchen.

Floyd smokes and I stare at the world passing by in super slo-mo outside the front window. I decide to count my cash, but as I fish into my pockets I hook out something a little more serious than pounds and pence. Panic envelops me as I hold up my Parole Licence.

"Oh, no!"

"What's up?"

"My parole officer…"

"What about him?"

"I forgot to… I have to call him this morning."

"So why do you look like you've seen your ex-girlfriend carrying a nipper that looks just like you?"

"Well, I'm stoned for starters… and anyway, what do I tell him? I've got nowhere to live…"

"You have, the shed."

"Well, yes, but I can't tell him that, can I, they'd think I was mental. I told them I was staying with my brother, see, and I'm not so I can't give them that address or maybe they'll call round to see me…"

Floyd laughs.

"Al, mate. Chill out. In my experience, they're never gonna call round to see you, it's you that goes to see them… if at all. Look, I've got a plan that'll get the fuckers off your back for good. I'll call him if you want, on your behalf like. I'll tell him you're living at my address

67

so any correspondence can be sent there like, and I'll also tell him you're working for me, City Gardening Solutions, and if he wants to see you he can call by the cemetery. How does that sound?"

Brill!

"I don't know what to say Floyd, thanks. But will it work?"

"Course it'll work… look, I know how hard it is to get work after doing time. I mean, no one wants to employ an ex-con. Why d'you think I set up my own business?"

"Why?"

"Cos I don't ask myself for a reference, do I… I don't care what those equal opportunity fucks tell you, no one wants an ex-con working for 'em. I'm tellin' you; we're more prejudiced against than the fuckin' Taliban. I mean, I wish I could give you a job an' all that, but unfortunately, the council don't pay so well, know what I mean…"

Then, after choking his roll in the ashtray, he grabs the card from my hand and says, "I'll be back in a sec, mate". Before exiting, he turns and shouts, "What's your full name, Al?"

I answer and watch him lean against the café's front window, holding his tiny phone to his ear.

I catch myself staring – unintentionally – at the backside of the girl at the next table. It makes my stomach turn: her bum-crack is peeking at me from above her hipster jeans, reminding me of a slot machine at a seaside amusement arcade. The tops of her cheeks bulge above her belt, and I only stop staring when Plug returns with two heaped plates. The meals comprise half a pig disguised as sausages and bacon, a couple of eggs, a tin of tomatoes, baked beans, mushrooms, a clump of congealed animal blood and two rounds of fried bread. I tuck in immediately, swallowing a Babe's worth of bacon in ten seconds flat. Floyd returns, his eyes open wide. He puts down his mobile and my licence before stuffing his own face.

"How did it go?" I ask eventually.

"Sorted," he says, through a mouth full of meat and grease.

Chapter 6: THE BLOODY BAT PHONE

"They're here!" Mam shouts up the stairs, ending our 'normal' lives once and for all.

It's a stormy Saturday afternoon and I lie on my bed, pen and pad in hand, attempting to write a poetic masterpiece. But, as usual, I'm failing miserably. I've long come to the conclusion that I'll never be a Poe, a Dodge or one of the Dylans, but for some reason I keep on trying.

A fortnight has passed since we visited Grandad at the hospital. I can't wait to get to know him, and since he's pretty drugged up, I hope he's compos mentis enough to communicate with me. All I ask for is a chance to speak with him... to listen.

We stand hopefully at the front door but it is apparent that the old man is oblivious to anything, including our presence. His eyes are closed and his chest still wheezes its deathly symphony.

"Where d'you want him, luv?" asks the lead paramedic as if he's delivering a new washing machine.

Mam looks pale after a long day of spring-cleaning, even though Grandad is likely only to ever see one room. I've already noticed a change in my parents over the past few weeks. The wear of preparing for the coming weeks – months, years – is already showing. The prospect of comfortable retirement has retreated and I've heard them quarrel more over the past few days than I have in the preceding decade.

"Upstairs, second door on the right," Mam directs the paramedics. We watch the patient being pushed, carried and manoeuvred towards the first floor and Patrick Brady is in his bed within a few minutes and the strangers in green are almost ready to leave. As one sets the breathing apparatus by the bed, my father asks, "The doctor said he didn't need that…"

"He doesn't need it all the time, like. But it could come in handy at some point…"

"We hooked him up before leaving the hospital," the other one adds. "Just to make the journey more comfortable for him."

"When's he likely to come around?" Mam asks, as she wipes a bit of dust that she must have missed earlier off the windowsill.

"Couple of hours tops, probably less…"

"More like an hour I'd say."

"Aye, an hour or so. He might be a bit groggy when he does but that won't last long…"

"From what we hear off the nurses on the ward, Paddy here's quite a character…"

"He certainly is," Dad beams, obviously proud of his own father's reputation.

But this is quite a shock, as I remember him as a quiet man. A serious man even. I'd go as far as to say he was almost surly. Kind, but never a 'character'. One of the paramedics hands Mam a bulging carrier bag.

"Here's his medication." He opens the bag. "There's about a month's supply in there. You know where to go to get more, don't you?" My parents nod. "Good. Now, I'm sure the doctor's explained that young Patrick here's not to leave his bed. His legs aren't strong enough, and what with his chest problems on top of that, if he puts any weight on them he'll be back in hospital quicker than you can say haenathrosis patella synovitis." He grins.

70

"Yes, Doctor Thomas explained. Thank you for your help."

"No worries, Mrs Brady, just doing our job."

My parents lead them out of the room leaving me alone. Leaning against the portable television, I stare at my grandfather's wheezing shell. He looks so peaceful in his unnatural state of sedation, under the shadow of Christ on the cross, which hangs above the headboard, protecting his soul. Will this be our relationship: me watching a sleeping body, with no opportunity to get to know him? This is probably all I deserve. With a heavy heart, I return to my room and my notebook, hoping that my dark mood might add a little bite to my weak couplets.

I give up on the poetry and listen to some music and read before joining my parents in the kitchen for tea. French bread, cheese, tuna mayo and a bowl full of crisps; our family's traditional Saturday supper.

As usual, Dad's pretty quiet, but tonight, for once Mam isn't filling the void with inane chatter.

"How was he then?" I ask, as the old man woke about half an hour ago.

"Not brilliant," says Dad through a mouthful of cheese. "He was pretty confused to start with, a bit groggy too, but he'll be fine by now if you want to go and say hello. Just don't expect too much. He's very different to the way you probably remember him..."

"I'll go up after finishing here." Mam hasn't touched her food. "You ok, Mam?"

"What? Y-y-yes. Not much appetite that's all, bach." I reach over and squeeze her hand.

"It's going to be alright, Mam, you'll see," I say, masking my uncertainty with a smile.

I send my parents to the lounge to relax, and I wash the dishes before visiting the patient.

As I climb the stairs there are butterflies doing flick-flacks in my stomach. But the old man is fast asleep. Again. I sit down and wait in the hope that he'll wake up shortly.

The wheezing is almost deafening in the absolute silence of the room. The oxygen cylinder aside, the lamp's low light and the velvet-textured wallpaper gives the room a Victorian quality. I feel like Sherlock Holmes by the bed of the main witness in an important case. I look around at the old man's belongings, searching for hidden clues to Patrick Brady's past history.

On the bedside table lies an ancient looking hardback book – *A Portrait of the Artist as a Young Man*. My favourite book ever! Grandad's favourite book? Maybe. Hopefully. This is a fortunate development and a bonding implement of the finest order. My mind overflows with possibilities, as my eyes roam around the room and settle on his kind face, his open mouth and the drool dripping from it.

On the loose skin of each of his once mighty forearms are two fading tattoos – an anchor on the right, a crab on the left. Then I look at his right hand and even though I've heard the story many times before and remember being amazed by it when I was a child, this is the first time as an adult that I've studied his fingers… or his *lack* of fingers, to be precise. Indirectly, Patrick's missing fingers are responsible for my birth. Some kind of skipped generation insemination, if you like.

When working in Fishguard Harbour back in the 1930s, he lost the index and middle finger of his right hand. A heavy metal door had closed on his hand, cutting the fingers clean away. According to the legend, Patrick went straight to see his manager, who insisted that he went immediately to the hospital for treatment. But, as he had the rest of the day off – a rare occurance in those days – Paddy didn't go anywhere near A&E. Instead, he went straight to the S&A, the Ship & Anchor. With his hand in an ice bucket, and the beer and whiskey numbing the pain, he was back at work the next morning with his hand in a homemade bandage and two fingers less than he was born with.

Some years later, at the beginning of the Second World War, Patrick Brady, along with hundreds of other young men from West Wales, went to an army training camp in Haverforwest to prepare for battle. But, to Patrick's dismay, and the absolute delight of his fellow soldiers, he couldn't fire his weapon properly because of his missing digits. Patrick Brady, or 'Paddy Shoite Shot' as he was known from this moment onwards, became the butt of many jokes. However it turns out that Patrick was the lucky one, since he was posted to an American base on Swansea's outskirts, as a driver to some Colonel or other for the duration of the war. His fellow trainees, meanwhile, were sent to fight on the beaches of Normandy. Not one of them returned. So, if the story is to be believed, if Grandad hadn't lost his fingers in Fishguard, I wouldn't be here now telling you this story...

His missing fingers give me a new perspective on life and confirm that someone else is guiding my fate, my destiny, my existence. If I needed further confirmation of God's existence, Patrick's missing fingers are that proof.

"So you like the Count then, Alan?" I turn to look at the old man's face. His eyes are still closed, but he slowly opens them and looks at me. He cracks a crooked, toothless grin at my incredulous face. "Count Basie, Alan," he repeats, sitting up slowly. He grabs the glass of water off the bedside table and puts his false teeth back in. "I heard you listening to him earlier. That was you, wasn't it? I know your dad only listens to classical..."

"It was me, yes. I do love jazz, but I listen to all sorts. I can't see the point of listening to just one kind of music, I'd feel I was missing out..."

"Same here, Alan, same here," he agrees in a rich blend of soft vowels, hard consonants and the rrrroundest rrrrrrrs I've everrrrr hearrrrrrd. "I am partial to a little jazz though, I have to admit. I caught the bug from the negro soldiers during the war..."

"You can't call them 'negroes' any more!"

"Why? It's not racist if that's what you're thinking."

"Well... it's not politically correct..."

"Politically what? Bloody hell, it's better than nigger, coon or spade, isn't it? And that's what most people called them. Anyway, the whole world thinks it's fine to call us Irish Micks or Paddys, the Scottish Jocks and you lot Taffys... same same. And Alan my boy, when you get to my age, you're too set in your ways to change and too old to care."

He looks so sad for a split-second that I decide to play along with him. "I'll keep the noise down from now on..."

"No, no, no. That's not what I meant at all. I liked it. And anyway,

73

you can hear everything that goes on in this house from this bed – your Ma's constant activity, I mean, does that woman ever stop? Your music and everyone's footsteps… including the cat's."

"Do you want a stereo then, and some jazz CDs so you can listen to them in your own time?"

"Really, Alan, you'd do that?" I nod. "Thanks, son, that would be grand, but only if it's not too much trouble."

"No trouble at all, it's nice to know we've already got something in common." Grandad's proving to be a different person to the one I remember. I don't actually remember ever speaking to him before. Not like this anyway. Gran was the focal point of our visits, the one full of fuss and chatter. He'd just sit in the corner reading quietly and taking it all in.

"So, how are you feeling, Granda… Dadc… I'm sorry, I'm not even sure what to call you anymore… I've been such a poor excuse for a grandson, I've neglected you so mu…" I almost burst into tears but the old man cuts across me and drags me out of the darkness.

"Don't be so soft, Alan!" he spits. "I'm pushing ninety and I certainly never expected you to come and see me every day, week or even month. We've all got our own lives to lead, so stop that now. Your parents have always been good to me and you know, I always had a good feeling from you when we did meet up." He pauses. "How is your brother anyway?"

"I don't know really. We hardly ever see him."

"That's a shame, it really is. Family's very important… Anyway, where were we, Alan? Ah yes, I remember. You can call me Paddy like everyone else." I fight the urge to say 'only if you call me Alun or Al like everyone else'. "This Dadcu business doesn't seem right cos you know I can't speak Welsh. And I feckin hate Grandad, it makes me sound too respectable!" He gives me a sly wink, but the look on my face betrays my unease at his casual cussing. "What's the matter, boy? Oh, I get it, the swearing." He takes a swig of the water that only recently housed his dentures and licks his crusty lips. "I know, I know, it's not right and we're all good Christians. But do you really think that God can't take a little swearing. I mean, murder and rape, of course they're unacceptable, and so they should be, but let's face it, the Almighty must have called Judas a buggering bastard bollock after what he did to his son! If you ask me, there's nothing wrong with swearing, after all, they're just words. And anyway, God must've invented feckin' swearing." His straight talking and skewed logic puts a smile back on my face. "And to answer your earlier question, Alan, I've been better, as I'm sure you can guess. I mean, I was working my allotment a few months ago, growing some prize-winning pumpkins I was, and some of the tastiest potatoes outside of Pembrokeshire." I nod again in sympathy. "And look at this!" he exclaims, pointing at the brand new bright red phone on the bedside table. "Look! Look what your parents got me – the bloody Bat Phone! Well, if they think I'll be using that if I'm in trouble they're well off the mark. If that happens, I won't fight it... I mean, the Bat Phone for God's sake!" His chest wheezes as he laughs at the absurdity. I laugh even though Mam and Dad just want to look after him. "And what's this?" he points at a little device on a second table.

"It's a baby moni..."

"I know what it is, Alan, but it's much more than *just* a baby monitor..."

"It is?"

"Yes, it's the perfect example of life's cycle and old age regression if ever I saw it. You see, I'm practically back to being a baby now. I'm completely dependent on others to care for me; like a new-born child, but without the cute jim-jams." I smile. "The main difference though is the loss of dignity. You see, a grown man lying here being bathed, wiped and fed: he's lost his dignity, whereas a baby doesn't have any in the first place." Maybe his body's rotting from within, but his mind's as sharp as a Shaolin's sword. He reverts to his rattling breathing.

"I see you're reading Joyce, Paddy..."

"Why do you sound so surprised, Alan?" he asks, on the defensive. "It's my body that's buggered, not my brain. And I'm not really reading it either, I know the book so well I could recite it to you with my eyes closed..."

"Me too," I chirp excitedly. Ever since Dad bought me a copy for Christmas when I was about twelve, maybe thirteen, I've re-read the novel on an almost yearly basis. To meet someone who shares my passion for the book is a major moment. Major. And the fact that it's Paddy makes it a hundred times better.

"Well, well." And now it's his turn to be impressed. "Did you know that we've got a lot in common; me, Joyce and Stephen…"

"You're both from Black Rock – you and the author, that is…"

"You're right. And like Stephen in the book, I left Ireland to follow my dreams…"

"And you all appreciate the arts and understand their importance to the human soul…"

"We do, Alan, we certainly do. The pills might help the pain, but it's art that soothes the soul." And we both sit there staring at each other for a moment, full of admiration. Paddy reaches for his copy. "This is an original too. First edition. A gift from me Ma before I left Dublin. A proper family heirloom if ever there was one. This is your inheritance, Alan. It's yours when I'm gone…"

"Wow, thank you. But don't say that…"

"Why not. C'mon, we all know I've not got long left here, there's no point denying it…"

"You never know."

"Well I hope to God it won't be too long, the sooner the better if you ask me. So tell me, Alan, whet else do you like apart from Joyce and jazz?"

"Poetry," I say, without hesitation. "And films, especially Jack Nicholson…"

"Poetry, you say. Anyone in particular?"

"I like Poe a lot, how he imagined those horrors I'll never know… also the two Dylans, Thomas and Bob…"

"Dylan Bob, never heard of him!" He frowns.

"No, Paddy! Bob Dylan." We both laugh. "He's very underrated if you ask me." Embarrassed, I add that I also try to write a little.

"Really, you write poetry too. Well, well, Al, you're an absolute bag of tricks, aren't you."

"They're not very good."

"Don't put yourself down, boy. The fact you're actually *attempting* to create something sets you apart from the majority of us. I'd like to hear some, if you wouldn't mind."

"Well, yes, you could of course, but I've never shown them to anyone. They're not very good."

"So you've already said, but let me be the judge of that. And anyway, doubt is an integral part of every poet's psyche. And not only poets, I'll have you know. Every great creative thinker – be it poet, painter, musician, writer and so on – doubts their own ability. It's what spurs them on to create something original and challenging every time they pick up a pen, instrument or whatever..."

"Really?" I manage to say, although it's not *really* news to me.

"Yes. Really. Take your man Dylan Thomas. Undoubtedly a genius. A legend in his own lifetime, no less. But he was so full of doubt and insecurity that the first poem he submitted for publication in the Westen Mail wasn't even written by him. Not the best start to a career, granted, but look what he went on to achieve. A bit of doubt is quite healthy. I mean, to be certain of your own greatness is to be certain of nothing at all..."

His zeal is too powerful. Why didn't I inherit any of this Brady passion? Oh, yes, I almost forgot: Will got all the good stuff...

"There's an old proverb which says it all, I believe. Doubt is the beginning, not the end of wisdom." He falls silent for full effect, a cheeky grin spreading across his face. His eyes twinkle.

"I'll fetch my book if you want to hear some, it'll be a world premier..."

"To tell the truth, Alan, I'll have to pass tonight. I'm a bit tired after the journey and all the drugs they pumped into me. Next time, ok. Maybe tomorrow." And he smiles once again, this time full of respect. I want to give him a bear hug but I'm afraid I might crush him. "Can I get you anything before you go to sleep, Paddy – some water, a cup of tea..."

"No thanks, Alan... although there is one thing."

"Name it."

"Do you think you could maybe smuggle me a bottle of whiskey tomorrow – something good, nothing cheap? Brian refused point blank when I asked him earlier and I dare not ask your Ma, but it helps me sleep, you see." It's the little things that make life bearable when you're as ill as Paddy. So I agree to his request.

I get up to leave and watch Paddy pass out before I even turn off the lamp. It appears that he doesn't need *that* much help to go to sleep after all.

Chapter 7: EXTRA-CURRICULAR ACTIVITIES

The heat and sweat must be what woke me in the end. The shed is hotter than a sauna and my bum is brushing the floor through the thin material of the camping bed which Floyd bought me from the Army & Navy Store on City Road.

I open my eyes and greet Paddy – who, like Leon, sleeps upright in a chair by the door – with a grunt. I think he's trying to protect me from the cemetery's resident bogeymen, but I'm not scared in the slightest. Is it because of Paddy's presence that I feel so at home here or because my parents are nearby? I am alone, which is what scared me more than anything when I left prison, and yet I don't feel lonely.

I down half a pint of water from the glass by my bed; check my watch. Like yesterday, it's gone half-nine already. The main reason for these lie-ins is that the shed is darker than a cave, even in daylight, thanks to the closed blinds and the covering of trees.

There's no comparison with my previous home in Cyncoed. But it's definitely better than my old cell, where during my first week inside I was kept awake by a cacophony of unfamiliar sounds. It was only after Knocker bought me a pair of earplugs from Chris 'Corner Shop' Barker, who ran the black market on the inside, that I managed to get any kind of sleep.

I get up slowly, fold the bed and put it away for the day. I open the door to let the air and light flood in, roll up the blinds and fill the kettle. As the water boils I blow the grime from my nostrils, which are as full as a pub ashtray at the end of a busy night. I wash my armpits, my face and wet my hair so I can comb it. I need to look my best today. After drowning a tea bag in a mug, I let it stew as I have a quick shave, ridding my chin of the pathetic three-day growth of bumfluff. The water, ice cold, is welcomed by my scorching body.

I think of Floyd and how generous he's been to me. Apart from the shed, the clothes, the shoes and the bed, he doesn't even come over – to his work HQ that is – before ten in the morning so I can rest and get my head together. He's a saint...

Floyd moved his 'shrubbery', as he calls it, yesterday, to place them in the basement 'grow room' that's nearly ready back home in Thornhill. I really enjoy his company. I mean, what's not to like? He's funny, lively and full of unbelievable anecdotes. Having a friend like him – a peer as opposed to an older family member – makes me regret not making much of an effort in the past. We visited Café Calcio each morning, Floyd insisting on paying, and it's because of his generosity that I've refused his invitation to join him down the Three Arches in the evening. It's not that I don't want to go but it's so embarrassing when he pays for everything. He knows I'm skint and that's why I'm going job-hunting today. I know it'll be difficult but I have to try. I must find something to focus on because after a lifetime of order and conformity – especially during the past three years – I'm desperate to return to some normality and rejoin the workforce.

After drying myself with the Cardiff City towel Floyd lent me yesterday, I slip into my black trousers and walk topless out of the shed towards the clearing in the green canopy. The open space is perfect for drying clothes and is far enough out of sight from the graves.

My white shirt dances in the morning breeze, and I look up at the blue sky. My pasty skin laps up the warmth. I put on the shirt and am hit with nostalgia. The warm material on my skin reminds me of the way Mam used to place mine and Will's clothes in the airing cupboard about half an hour before we woke up during the winter. She did spoil us. Just a little. I smile at the sweet memory as I meander back towards the shed.

As I approach my new home, the sun hits something that glitters. I go and investigate. Leaning on the shed next to the shelter which houses Floyd's mowers and strimmers, is a load of old pipes, rusting in the elements. Amongst them, like a pair of a tiny aluminium tusks, I spot the handlebars of an old rusty racer.

The bike is so corroded that it's impossible to guess its original colour. After giving it a quick wipe, I search the shed for a pump, and find it in one of the drawers. After filling the tyres with air, I check the brakes and oil the chain. I take it for a test-ride along the uneven path. Even though the journey is far from a comfortable one – thanks to the blade of a saddle, the extra thin wheels and the rough ground below – the bike seems to be working fine, and just like that, I've got some wheels. It's better than walking, and when you're as poor as I am, even catching the bus seems extravagant.

I wash my hands again, check my clean clothes and devour two slices of toast. The torturous shoes are my only choice, since my daps don't go with my suit. Off I go on my steel stallion towards the nearest exit on Fairoak Road. I hope the road will prove to be a smoother ride, but when I share this with Paddy, who's walking by my side, he ignores me completely. Even after all this time, I'm still not sure if can hear me.

I find Floyd by the old chapel, raising a new sign warning people of the building's dangerous condition.

"Health and safety, innit," Floyd explains. "We've got to cover ourselves in case some stupid kid or alky wanders in there and has a fall on the way home from the pub."

According to Floyd, the cemetery's used in many ways apart from burying the dead, including Satan-worship, gay sex and sniffing glue. I haven't seen nor heard anything too bad during my time here, though. But now that I think about it, the bloke in the shed probably comes top of the weirdo food chain…

"You look smart, Al. Where you off?"

"Job hunting, like I told you yesterday. Is it still OK for me to use your mobile number as a contact?"

"Of course it is," he says, before noticing the bike.

"I found this near the shed, by the way; you don't mind me borrowing it?"

"Not at all. Does it work?"

"Seems to, and anything's better than walking in these shoes…"

"Aye," he agrees, taking a long drag on his smoke before offering it to me.

"No way, Floyd. Thanks all the same, but no way," and just in case he didn't hear me, I repeat: "I'm off job hunting."

"Why? You should enjoy your freedom, take a few weeks off, like."

"No thanks, I'm already going loopy after just a few days. Plus I need the cash…"

"True, true… although you know I'd lend you some if you want."

"I know, cheers Floyd. But I want to get back on my feet ASAP and the first thing I have to do is find a job."

"Anything in particular, I heard there's a vacancy down Bute Street."

"What is it?"

"Rent boy!" And he laughs out loud, before turning his attention back to the job in hand.

"See you Floyd."

"See ya, mate. Oh, and Al, come down the Arches after you're done. I'll be there from twelve…"

"Twelve!"

"Aye, half day on Friday like," he explains, before adding with a wink: "Extra curricular activities."

"It's Friday, is it? All right, Floyd, see you later." I mount the racer and leave my friend to his morning's work and Paddy to his eternal wandering. As I join the other vehicles on Fairoak Road, I hear Floyd shout "Good luck". I thank him under my breath, knowing that I'll need more than luck today…

I bomb down Cathays Terrace towards the centre of town, and join the Taff Trail near the Millennium Stadium. I decided to come this way in order to avoid cycling past the prison. Too soon, I suppose. I'm heading for the Bay, to Mount Stuart Square and the new offices of my old employers.

Before I got banged up, I worked for six years at ENCA Ltd, a company that promotes the Welsh language to Wales and the world. My first job after leaving college. My only job. Ever. I say 'leaving college' but in truth I didn't *go* anywhere, as I studied Welsh at Cardiff Uni and lived at home. I'm a translator... I *was* a translator, and I'm hoping that my old employers will take pity on me today and offer me some work.

Brains Brewery spews its sock-like scent into the air making me wonder why anyone would drink something whose brewing smells so bad. My right trouser-leg gets caught in the chain, getting torn and almost bucking me off the bike. I'm so angry after all my efforts to look smart that I almost turn back. But, knowing how bad that would make me feel later, I tuck my trousers into my socks and carry on.

Passing the high-rise flats and the urban decay, I start feeling even more pissed off. This is home to the city's mainly black and Asian population, and is as deprived as anything London or Birmingham has to offer. Close by, in the Bay proper, the city council has been spending millions building flimsy flats and American-style amusement centres for the city's moneyed masses. It just makes my blood curdle. Even though its not as obvious as in South Africa, Australia or the southern states of America, what I see before me is some kind of apartheid at work. It dawns on me that I'm cycling through an open prison... Cardiff's Gurnos, if you like. The posh restaurants and yacht clubs of Cardiff Bay beyond mask the city's shameful face.

Most people think that prison isolates criminals from the rest of the world, and that's true to a certain extent. But oddly, prison insulated me from the reality of the outside world, and there's a part of me that wants to go back there. At least you could forget about inequality there. Inside, we're all more or less equal, as everyone's in the same situation. Of course, there's a hierarchy at work, but everyone's equal because everyone's locked up. Separation and inequality are actually far more prominent in the outside world.

I reach Mount Stuart Square's regenerated esplanade and leave my bike around the corner from ENCA's entrance, just outside the Coal Exchange. I don't lock it as I don't have one yet, but if anyone wants to steal it, good luck to them – they obviously need it. As I walk towards the entrance, I can't help but compare the new HQ to where I used to work in town. This area is so much more pleasant, with the bay itself only a few hundred yards away, separated by a building site where the Assembly will be housed, along with something called the Wales Millennium Centre.

I'm buzzed in and approach the reception desk, straightening my tie and cursing my torn trousers. I wanted to give a good impression, the best impression, but... it's too late now. The reception area is slick compared to the old one. This one boasts two dark leather sofas, fresh flowers, slate floor and large windows. The company's logo stands six feet tall on the wall behind the desk. Nice.

But the same eyes stare back from behind the computer – Shiranee's. She's a stunning girl from Indian descent: her cocoa-coloured skin, pitch-black hair and wide doll-like eyes are a mesmerising combination. But, unfortunately, she has a thick covering of hair on her upper lip which ruins the image for me, and which has probably contributed to the fact she's known as the company 'bike'. I've even heard some people refer to her as Sir Walter. As in Raleigh. Although her muzzie's a definite turn-off, just being this close to a woman, as well as knowing all about her notoriety, is almost enough to send me over the edge. I beam my best smile at her, hoping that she'll remember me, but she hasn't got a clue who I am.

On her desk, there's a sign that promotes her bilingualism, so I start the conversation in Welsh:

"*Bore da, Shiranee, fi 'di dod i weld Neifion...*"

"'Ave you gots an appointment?" She asks in English, which sort of makes a mockery of ENCA's commendable policy of encouraging people from ethnic minorities to try for menial jobs at the company on the condition that they try to learn Welsh. It makes for an interesting workplace when you can speak Welsh to Dan the Rasta in research or Jamshad, from Bangladesh, in distribution. Unfortunately, Shiranee's efforts seem to have fallen by the wayside, so I don't push my luck.

"No, I don't have an appointment," I concede. "But I used to work here a few years ago and just want a quick chat with Neifion. My name's Alun Brady…"

And she looks at me as if the name rings a bell but the face isn't singing quite the same tune.

"Take a seat please, Mr Brady, I'll see if ee's available now."

But before I have a chance to start reading Buzz Magazine, Luned, the head of the translation department walks past, does a double-take and stops for a chat.

"Al! Is that *you*?" And I get to my feet to shake her hand. When our hands touch, flesh on flesh, my whole body shudders, and I struggle to speak without st-st-stuttering. Not that I fancy her or anything. She's alright, don't get me wrong – nothing special, and not bad for a middle-aged woman either. The reason I'm shaking is that she's the first woman I've touched in over three years and the sensation is so alien, confusing and frustrating that it's all completely involuntary.

"Hi, Luned. How's it going?" I manage to blurt out eventually.

As she shakes my hand I notice two things: her wide, fake, smile; and her eyes, which look everywhere at once as long as its not in my direction. Even though she's uncomfortable, she's pretty friendly, which helps me relax a little. I take a deep breath and say, "I've come to see Neifion. Just for a chat, that's all."

"Looking for work, is it?"

"Yes. It's time to rebuild…"

"Come over and see the team after you're done with Nei…" she suggests, straining to escape.

Maybe I will go and see them later on, but no, seeing the same old faces comfortably drifting towards their pensions will do nothing to help my current state of mind. Seeing them will only make things worse.

Within a couple of minutes, Neifion appears in reception like Robert Kilroy-Silk… with extra cheese. He's a handsome man in his fifties, single and still in the depths of the mid-life-crisis he's been suffering since his twenties. He dresses 'young', if that makes any sense, and flirts openly with every female employee younger than him. According to the company grapevine, he's a homosexual in denial.

85

His silver hair shows his true age, while his cheeky goatee betrays his insecurity.

Neifion manages the company: but is really the boss' puppet or lap-dog. He's a two-faced coward. A mass of confused contradictions. A spineless, racist homophobe whose primary faith is his own importance. He's the kind of man who probably played Herod every year in the nativity play in chapel. As the boss is hardly ever present at the office – due to lobbying, promoting and extensive hob-nobbing duties – Neifion is responsible for the day-to-day running of the company. Because of this power, he struts around the place thinking he's Tony Montana... but mincing more like Richard Fairbrass.

"Alun, Alun, Alun! How's it going *mate*?" He asks as if he's greeting an old friend – something I never was. "Follow me to my office. You want a drink? Tea, coffee, water?"

"No thanks, I'm alright..."

"Sure?"

"Yes. Positive. Thanks."

"Shiranee!" He barks. "Black coffee, now, there's a good girl."

I follow this bully towards his office and sneak a look over my shoulder to offer sympathy or solidarity to Shiranee, who obviously doesn't need it. She's holding up her middle finger defiantly, suggesting there'll be more than just hot water being poured over Neifion's granules.

"Take a seat, Al," he orders, and we have a little chit-chat about nothing much. He puts his feet up on his desk, his hands behind his head, and asks, "So, what can I do for you today, then?"

"I'm looking for a job..."

"There's nothing available in the translation department at present," he butts in.

"I'll do anything. I just need a chance to start again, that's all..."

He nods his head slowly, giving the impression that he's deep in thought. He then starts stroking his goat. As he tickles his tuft, my mind wanders and I'm hypnotised by the sound of the fan whirring on Neifion's side of the desk, keeping him cool while I sweat away on the other side like a sumo wrestler following a game of squash.

"Actually, Al, there's nothing I can offer you at the moment, but if you leave your phone number I'll be sure to buzz you when anything comes up. Ok?"

What I want to say is 'No, that's not OK, help me!', but as usual, my testicles have long abandoned ship, leaving my voice to doggy-paddle towards the coast.

"Great, thanks, keep me in mind. I'm available as of today," I manage, scribbling on a scrap of paper. "This is a friend's number. Leave a message with him and I'll get back to you as soon as I can..."

After shaking hands again, I leave the building without visiting my old department. And even though I know that I'll never hear from ENCA again, that doesn't really bother me. That's what I was expecting: prejudice and fear, because there's nothing scarier to the middle classes than an ex-con. Even one as lame as me.

No one's stolen my bike, so I jump on and cycle back down Bute Street towards town. As it's still quite early, I decide to visit the Job Centre and maybe a couple of temping agencies. I leave the bike outside the Job Centre on the corner of Charles Street. The sweat is collecting between my shoulder blades. My face is also drenched, and as I wipe my forehead with my sleeve, I get a waft of BO which almost makes me choke. I almost head for home as today is slowly developing into a nightmare, but I force myself inside as I *have* to find a job.

As well as the propaganda and lies which welcome me inside the centre, there's also... air conditioning. I bask for a moment. Apart from the security guard there's no staff around. There are plenty of 'job seekers' dotted about the place, though. The workforce is separated from the public by a barrier of desks, which are all unoccupied.

Eventually, someone appears at reception and gives me a form to fill. After completing it, I take a number from the machine – like the ones you see on a cheese counter in supermarkets – and join the motley crew of job seekers to wait my turn. After ten minutes, I decide to check out the noticeboards. I keep one eye on the queue and one eye on the workforce. Or, the *lack* of workforce, to be more exact. There's so little activity on the 'other side' to make me feel like offering my own assistance.

There are plenty of job notices which appeal – clerical work, gardening, and even waiting tables or bar work – but I don't take down the details just in case there'll be some bureaucratic complication. After a long wait, I hear my number being called by some young woman, so I take my form and my fragrance over to her desk. I smile warmly and offer my hand but she doesn't even see me. When she looks up she just stares through me for a while. I sit staring back at the top of her head. Her blonde hair cascades over her bare shoulders, while her summer vest shows her lack of breasts. If only she'd smile, I'm sure she'd look pretty. But that's not going to happen. No chance.

"Address?" She sighs. Having failed to recall Floyd's address, I decide to be honest.

"It's a bit complicated really…"

"Where do you live, Mr…"

"Brady."

"Brady. Yes. Where do you live? We need an address before we can continue, before we can *help* you."

"Well, it's in Cathays…"

"You need to be a little bit more specific than that, Mr Brady!"

"Yes, of course. I live in Cathays Cemetery."

"Cathays Cemetery? Really? In that old house by the entrance, is it?"

"Not quite, no. I live in the caretaker's shed…"

I realise how ridiculous I must sound. The girl looks at me properly for the first time. Her words are both patronising and phoney, "So you're homeless, Mr Brady?"

"No, not at all…" She gets up and walks over to a nearby filing cabinet. I blush a little when she returns, but she just hands me a leaflet.

"Here's a leaflet that might help you. It's a charity that helps the homeless find somewhere to live, an address, so that you can sign on and rejoin the mainstream…"

"But I'm not…"

"Mr Brady!" She says authoritatively. "Until you register with one of the centres for homeless peole, we can't help you. It's that simple, unfortunately. Now please contact this number; they'll be able to assist you further. "

"But I'm not…"

"Goodbye, Mr Brady," she adds, before pressing the button on her desk for the next 'customer'.

I get out of there in a foul mood, but the system's so laughable that it's hard to stay angry for too long. I decide not to go to any temping agencies today and return to my shed, via Lovely Baps – without doubt the best named baguette shop in the galaxy – considering how unfair it is that there are people out there who don't want to work but are forced to find some, while I'm desperate to work but am not allowed.

Taking off my shirt and washing my pits for the second time today, I come to the conclusion that this world is a complicated place. Paddy agrees with me, I think, and after putting on casual clothes and comfy daps, I go in search of Floyd. I wander around the cemetery then remember he's down the Arches for the afternoon. I wheel my bike across the gravel to the exit on Allensbank Road and head towards the pub in the hope that my friend can lift my spirits.

The pub's main entrance leads into the large and empty middle bar. There's no one here except a table of four businessmen enjoying a long, lazy, liquid lunch. Their faces are blotchy from the booze. I can count on one hand the amount of times I've been to a pub, although the last time I went it was actually here, in the company of my brother, a few months before I got sent down. The Three Arches is a strange pub, and according to Will the three rooms within represent the three classes of society. At the weekend, when the place is packed, the middle classes claim this room as their own. It's pretty comfortable, with carpet underfoot and plenty of chairs. To my right, through a heavy brass door, lies 'Bel Air', as Will calls it. This is where the snobs of Cyncoed, Lisvane, Llanishen and Roath sip their large brandies and double Baileys as they discuss their assets and neglect their manners. In the public bar to my left is where I expect to find Floyd. Here the working classes congregate, having twice the fun as the others put together. This is where you'll find the TV, the pool tables, the jukebox, the bandits, the skittle alley and a floor so sticky it makes the short journey to the toilet seem like a moonwalk. There are no frills here – no cushions on the seats or clean ashtrays every half an hour. But this is the pub's true heartbeat. Without the customers of the public bar, the Arches would probably struggle to stay open.

I find Floyd sitting on a stool by the bar between two companions. The three of them are glued to the telly, their bodies subconsciously trotting in unison with the horses on the screen. I lean on the bar and watch them. Floyd, for the first time since I met him, has changed out of his dirty work clothes and into black jeans, a striped polo shirt and the shiniest pair of white Lacoste daps I've ever seen. I think he might be ready for the weekend. The two men who flank him have come straight from work... either that or they haven't returned to work after lunch. Their clothes are a collage of colours and textures. If I had to guess, I'd say they were a pair of painters and decorators.

"*C'mmmmmmmmmmmmmmmmmmmmmmmmon* my son!" Floyd shouts as the horses gallop down the home stretch. As they cross the line, my friend is on his feet punching his fists wildly in the air. He calms down, and only then does he notice me. His smile is broad.

"Al, fuckin' hell, I didn't think you'd make it! Did you see that? Jeezuz H Cribbins, that don't happen very often, does it Jeff?" Jeff, who sits by the bar holding his head in his hands, mumbles something incoherent in response before ripping his betting slip dramatically. "My Son, sixty-to-one for fuck's sake! Hardly worth a punt, you'd think. Well, you'd be wrong!"

Floyd is extremely excited. He turns to the barman who's come to see what all the noise is about.

"Drinks all round, John; I've just won six hundred fuckin' quid!"

"So that's why you're acting like a child is it, Floyd?"

"Fuck off John, don't be so miserable!"

And the whole room, six people that is, make their way to the bar to choose their prizes. After everyone has settled once again, John turns to Floyd.

"Pint of the usual for you, is it Floyd?"

"Aye, and whatever Al by 'ere's 'avin'."

And it feels like everyone turns to stare at me. I'm under some pressure to choose wisely and not make a fool of myself in front of my new friend. Floyd beams at me again as I scan the bottles and pumps.

90

I mutter, "Half a shandy, please", knowing at once that it's the wrong thing to say. There is a chorus of laughter.

"Bitter or lager?" John asks professionally.

"Lager. Stella. Pint. OK Al?" Floyd answers on my behalf. I don't say anything, but my cheeks are red.

I join Floyd, Jeff and Jase. Jeff is in his late fifties, chewing an unlit thick cigar which gives him the most crooked of smiles. He has a bald head and one lazy eye. Jase is his son: they work together. Jase, who's in his thirties, has long, blond, surfer-dude hair, and tattoos on show wherever clothes don't cover his flesh. His smile is as wonky as his father's, and he chain-smokes Benson & Hedges as if his life depended on it.

After taking a swig of the Stella, savouring the coldness on such a hot day, Floyd introduces me to his friends.

"Boys, this is Al…"

"From the shed?"

"Yes, Jase, from the shed."

"It's only temporary," I add, somewhat defensively.

"Of course it is, Al."

After some initial small talk, the four of us are soon laughing and drinking like a college reunion. After my first pint disappears, and just as Floyd's getting another round in with his winnings, he remembers my morning's mission.

"Fuck Al, I almost forgot. How did it go this morning?"

"What happened this morning?" Jase, through a cloud of smoke and as nosy as Mrs Mangle.

"I went job hunting," I explain. "No luck at all though. Where I worked before, they were polite but I know they'll never get in touch…"

"I told you so," says Floyd and I nod in agreement.

"I went to the job centre but all I got was this!" I show them the homeless leaflet. "It's hopeless! All I want is a job so I can get back on my feet but they wouldn't even let me register because of where I live."

I take a swig of my second pint, feeling the first tickle of intoxication in my stomach, as the four of us fall silent. But, out of the darkness comes hope.

"John, d'you need any bar staff?" Floyd asks the manager – a fat man in his forties who's trying to mask his blatant alcoholism with plenty of Brylcreem and a sensible tie.

"As it happens, I do," he retorts, looking in my direction.

I smile back, full of hope.

"Look no further, John, Al by 'ere's the man for the job." Thanks, Floyd.

"Have you got any experience?"

But before I have the chance to answer, Floyd does it again on my behalf.

"Course he fuckin' has, John! And anyway, it's hardly fuckin' difficult now is it!" John stops staring at me and turns his attention to Floyd. The threat is there for all to see… except Floyd that is. "What? What? Don't even think about arguing the point, John, or I'll come round there and show you how to pull a pint… a few fuckin' pints come to that!" Everyone laughs and the tension fades.

"You can start tomorrow, Alan, if you want."

"Yes, definitely. What time?"

"I've got two shifts to fill…"

"I'll do them both," I butt in without thinking.

"You sure? It's hard work." And I nod as Floyd, Jeff and Jase laugh at John's claim.

"I need the money and I won't let you down…"

"As long as you turn up on time, you won't."

And there we have it; I've got a job. I turn to Floyd to share my joy, but my friend's on his way out through the door in the company of a young man. I'm not exactly sure what's going on, but I could have a pretty good guess.

"Where you from then, Alan?" asks Jeff, and I turn to answer him, trying to emphasise my true accent.

"Caaaadiff," I say.

"Fuck off!" says Jase. "There's no way you are. Your accent's more like, I don't know… not proper Caaaadiff anyway."

"Are you really, born and bred like?" asks his dad.

"I am," I confirm. "I spoke some Welsh at home, though. With my mam – it's her first language. Dad's from Irish decent so he can't speak the lingo like… That's why my accent's so hard to pin down, I suppose." I know I'm mimicking them to some degree, but that's understandable, isn't it? I just want to fit in. I just want to be accepted. "I know I don't have much of a Caaaadiff accent, but I've lived here all my life…"

Jeff nods and says, "There's a little bit of Caaaadiff in there, Alan, certain words like, but it's much softer than mine, Floyd or Jason's Crystals Caaadiff twang. It's nicer if you ask me, I mean, you've heard that Frank Hennessy, well, if I sound anything like that cunt, I'd rather be English!" He pauses for a second, considers his statement, then says: "No, not really… not at all…"

"But he does sound like a cunt," Jase agrees.

"Yes, son, he does. So you're Welsh then, Al, *proper* Welsh I mean, fluent native speaker and all that crap…"

"I *can* speak the language, yes. I went to a Welsh school and worked as a translator after leaving Uni, but my Irish roots are just as important to me…"

"Say something then," Jase again. "Say something *rude*."

I hate it when this happens – which is pretty much every time anyone who's never heard the language finds out you're bilingual.

"OK, here goes. *Mae Jase braidd yn dwp.*" Jase's face lights up on hearing his name. It may just have been the alcohol talking, but I instantly regret it… not that Jase has any idea.

"What did you say, Al?"

"I said Jase's got a huge penis…" and he nods his head slowly, proudly. Jeff on the other hand, shakes his in disbelief.

"Whatever the language, you can always tell when someone's talking bollocks."

"Like father like son then innit, Dad!"

"Unfortunately, yes."

And after Jase makes me repeat the sentence over and over again so that he can say it himself, Jeff brings us back to the subject of nationhood.

"I've never met a Welsh speaker before, you know. I mean, I knew they existed because of the road signs and that, but I never *met* one before today. I seen that SC4 on the telly but I've never watched it,

I mean, what's the point when you can't understand a bloody word they're on about?"

"Most programmes have subtitles these day, Jeff…"

"I'm sure they do, Al, but you see, I'm not a brilliant reader, never have been. I mean, I read the *Sun* and the *Sport,* like, but that doesn't really count, and when it comes to watching telly I can't be arsed with it all. I never go to the cinema to watch a foreign film 'cos of the subtitles, so I'm not gonna start watching foreign shit on my own telly…"

Before the conversation veers towards a drunken nationalistic debate, Floyd returns.

By six o'clock, I'm drunk as a skunk for the first time in my life. I've guzzled four pints of Stella and have even joined Floyd and Jase in the car park for a cheeky smoke on two occasions. The first time was a mistake. The second complete and utter madness. I blame the booze, myself.

I've experienced the whole range of emotions: been close to tears thinking of my parents; guilt, shame and longing while thinking of Will and Mia. Regret when Paddy's fate and my part in the whole mess came to mind. Relief at my freedom, and pride for finding a job. I've hugged Floyd more than once, and I'm pretty sure I've also called him 'my besht mate' too… I'm a walking talking emotional contradiction. Also known as 'a bit of a mess'.

By half-seven I've polished off another couple of Stellas and the whole world is turning. The people around me are blurred and the lights are kaleidoscopic, spinning like a carousel. The world is alien to me tonight and nothing makes much sense anymore. I'm excited one minute, then depressed the next. I haven't stood up for the best part of an hour and am scared if I do it now I'll collapse. The pub's full of cloud-like faces, all male, and Floyd's introduced me to many people that I'll never recognise if I see them again. I'm happy. I think.

As well as the six hundred pounds Floyd won on the gee-gees earlier, his 'extra curricular activities' must have doubled his money. He's visited the car park with complete strangers more often than a bulimic goes to the bog, to borrow one of Jase's sayings. I haven't had to pay for one drink.

Without warning, the contents of my stomach – scampi and chips from the 'award winning kitchen' (when did they start giving prizes for microwaved meals?) – make an appearance in my mouth. I sit there with a mouth full of warm soup trying my utmost not to panic. I'm still sat at the bar – John, my new boss, is serving right in front of me and I try my hardest not to spew all over the bar and get the sack before even starting my new job. I swallow the lot and wash my mouth with the dregs of my Stella. I get to my feet without falling, mumble something to Floyd, and make my way to the exit. Stumbling towards the door, Jase announces at the top of his voice in dodgy Welsh that he's 'a bit thick'. I don't feel guilty. Not now. Alcohol's great! I then feel my stomach rumbling and get out of there just in time to empty its contents on the asphalt. That was close. Thanks to the fresh air and empty stomach, I feel instantly refreshed. Rejuvenated. I start walking home.

"You all right, Al?" asks Floyd, who's caught up with me in the car park. "You look fucked!"

"Aye, aye, aye," then I point at my chest, adding: "I am. Drunk! Me!"

"Where's your bike, mate? Did you bring your bike?"

"Yes, no. Yes, I think so… don't know… maybe…"

And he leads me by the arm towards the main entrance through a throng of underage drinkers enjoying the beer garden (beer yard, more like). Floyd props me up by the wall, finds my bike and helps me across the road.

"You all right to get home now, Al?"

"Yes, yes," I try and fail to get on my bike.

"You can't ride home, mate…"

"Zimmer… frame…"

"Good idea, ya pissed bastard! Use it as a zimmer and be careful."

So I hug him again and thank him; then I start spewing again, this time all over the bike's saddle. He laughs and rubs my back as if I'm his wife. Floyd returns to the pub and I zig-zag home a different person.

Chapter 8: CELTIC CROSS

As October becomes November, the night and the temperature fall hand in hand as I come home from work. My home, literally and spiritually, is cloaked in darkness. I open the back door and find Dad reading the *Western Mail* at the kitchen table. I put down my Dixons bag, fondle Dwdi and liberate my feet from their leather torture.

"Alright Dad, good day?" I know the answer before he opens his mouth, since the bags under his eyes are bulging.

"Don't ask!" Although daytime is difficult for them all – my parents and Paddy – I'm certain that it can't be as bad as the nights. I can't tell whether or not Paddy is having nightmares, or if the pain is too strong. His groans and occasional screams make it very hard to get any sleep at all.

Paddy's been here for twelve days now and his condition has already deteriorated. There's nothing wrong with his spirit – apart from the regular references to death – but physically, there have been some 'developments'. As well as his buckled legs and limp lungs, his eyes are sinking deeper into his skull, which, I'm told, is a sure sign of malnutrition. His oesophageal stricture – a little lump which has developed on his oesophagus causing him problems while swallowing – is beginning to affect him too. On top of all this, his back is covered in bedsores, which give him continuous pain. Watching him rot before my eyes is so hard, especially now that I'm getting to know him properly.

As his condition gets worse my parents unravel as they try to look after him. The challenge is too great for them, but since each is as stubborn as the other, they'll never admit it. They'd rather keep on battling quietly until nature takes its course.

"Where's Mam then?"

"In bed."

The situation is affecting Mam more than anyone, even though Paddy is Dad's father. She seems to spend every spare minute asleep. This upsets me too since Mam's normally such a busy-bee.

"Is she ok?"

"Yes, she's just tired. We're going out in an hour or so..."

"Where?"

"The theatre. To see Matthew Rhys in something or other..."

"Nice! I love Matthew Rhys."

"So does your mother. He's not a patch on Daniel Evans if you ask me, but he's much better than what's his name, you know..."

"Who?"

"That scarecrow... the one off *Notting Hill*..."

"Rhys Ifans."

"Yes, him. That bloke needs a bath!"

I leave him to it and retrieve my supper, as well as Paddy's from the oven. My dinner looks very tasty – chicken casserole with red wine and tarragon – while Paddy's looks like over-processed guacamole.

We've settled into some kind of pattern ever since Paddy came to stay, and eat our dinner in each other's company every night. It relieves the pressure from my parents and it gives Paddy and me the chance to chat. I'm determined to make the most of our time together, so I load the crockery onto a tray, grab the Dixons bag and leave Dad at the kitchen table.

I reach the landing and place the tray and bag carefully on the chaise longue. I tiptoe to the attic to retrieve my favourite cardigan and notebook. Opening the door to Paddy's bedroom the cold and the smell hit me. A medley of farts, feet, antibiotic ointment, various mints and boiled sweets, ammonia, despair and lost dignity. The cold is the result of Paddy's insisting he has the window open at all times. He wants it this way because:

1) His temperature is so high that it makes him burn up "like a pasty Geordie on a package holiday in Hell";
and
2) He wants to hear the sounds of nature from outside.

Even though there are more Nissan Bluebirds in the vicinity than there are real birds, his wish is fulfilled. Unfortunately this means every visitor has to wear an extra layer. His personal perfume is potent and unpleasant but my senses adapt straightaway, and soon enough I'm eating my supper as though surrounded by freshly-cut flowers.

"Here's your supper, Paddy," I say, placing the bowl of green-brown goo on the table that bridges his legs. He moves his newspaper out of the way and lifts one side of his lips. He's not happy. As he prods the food with his spoon, I take the notebook from my back pocket and sit with the tray on my knees on the chair by the side of the bed. "Anything interesting in the paper, Paddy?"

"Nothing, just reading the obituaries…"

"Why?"

"Just checking I'm not dead yet. How was your day?"

"Fine, you know. The usual stuff, nothing major." I hate talking about my work as it's so routine and uninspiring, so I change the subject by giving Paddy the Dixons bag.

"What is it?" he asks, but he's already opening it. After taking the box out, he sucks his breath through his teeth. The sound echoes eerily somewhere deep within him, but I ignore it, as I'm just glad he seems pleased. "Al, Al, Al! You shouldn't have…"

"I didn't have a choice, did I, at least I can have my stereo back now!" I say nodding at the machine I lent him. Paddy holds the box in wonder, making me smile. It's the little things that bring most joy to someone in his situation. "Now eat your food, young man, or it'll be straight to bed with you!" He lays down the box on the bed and stirs his soup unenthusiastically.

"I can't eat this," he announces, furrowing his brow. "It's disgusting!"

"You have to. Energy, nourishment and all that…"

"What do I need energy for? All I do is lie here. And anyway, it's easy for you to say when you're sat there with your… what's that… what've you got tonight?"

"Chicken casserole with tarragon sauce," I reply, filling my mouth with a heaped forkful.

"Let's have some of that, Al, a bit of chicken?" he asks, his eyes wide, a little drool escaping from the corner of his mouth.

"You're not allowed solids, Paddy, you know that," I say, as I chew the meat and wash it down with a little squash. "You can have the sauce though, pour it on top of your supper…"

"What? You don't mean *sauce* with extra *sauce*?"

"Something like that…"

"Oh, thank you sir, you're too kind."

"Paddy, if I wan't sarcasm, I'll watch *Seinfeld*, so less of that, please, or you get nothing! This sauce is lovely mind, so you know, just enjoy it… and don't tell Mam." Paddy holds his bowl out so I can scrape some sauce into it.

He eats the lot without complaining for the first time since he got here. I put the tray to one side, unplug the stereo and fix the new one in place. I've bought him a midi-system – nothing flash, but perfect for him and this little room – and I'll be glad to have my stereo back too. I choose a live Donald Byrd CD from the pile, slot it in and check that the levels are OK for chatting and listening without disturbing Mam.

Paddy wipes his face with a Wet Wipe as I put his bowl on the tray. Turning back to the patient, I notice how he writhes in discomfort every time he moves. The bed sores are obviously bothering him even though his skin is under a sheen of ointment. But despite Paddy's discomfort, he never complains about it. The bedsores seem to bother Mam the most. She feels guilty because the sores appeared since Paddy came here.

We sit in silence being soothed by Byrd's harmonies. Paddy asks, "Is that what I think it is?"

I follow his eye-line to the notebook on the bedside cabinet. I haven't had the guts to share any work with Paddy until tonight. Fair play to him, he hasn't put any pressure on me, but he's clearly as excited as I am nervous.

"It is," I admit. My stomach starts a spin cycle in anticipation.

"Let's hear one then." Seeing me blush, he adds, "C'mon now, Alan, there's no need to be embarrassed. Remember, you're reading to a grown man who can't wipe his own arse."

"Patrick Brady, do you have to be so disgusting?" Mam asks as she enters the room in her glad rags.

"What? Just settling the boy's nerves before his reading…"

"Reading?"

"Aye, Al's reading me some of his poetry…"

"Poetry!" Mam exclaims. "I didn't know you wrote poetry, Al."

"They're not very good." I know my hiding this from Mam will hurt her a little. I usually tell her everything.

"Let us be the judge of that, now c'mon Al, read so your Ma can listen before she leaves." So Mam takes a seat opposite me and I try and calm my nerves and begin to read, keeping my eyes firmly on the paper.

"'Two People Looking Back At Me'."

Reflections in a looking glass,
Fifteen months since I looked last.
One year and a bit, am I still the same?
Have I suffered from playing this life, this game?
If I look beyond my pathetic frame,
If I look beyond my selfishness so lame,
I have something extra
A guiding light
Entwined within me
She shines so bright.
Back to the question
The change with time,

Not to develop is surely a crime.
I'm still the same
With subtle advances,
A little more thought
Take fewer chances.
Look after the body
The soul will be free,
Look after my brightness
She's now part of me.

I keep my head down: the silence says it all. Looking up, though, Mam is sobbing and Paddy's quieter than when he's asleep!

"What's the matter?" I ask Mam.

"That... that... was beautiful, Al. So beautiful..." I smile at her sheepishly. She apologises for having to leave. "I wish I could stay and hear some more," she says as she brushes past me, but I should be the one apologising for ruining her make-up...

"Very nice, son, now tell me, who was that about then?"

"No one. Not really..."

"Bollocks! Don't talk daft. It was far too passionate *not* to be about someone. And at the end of the day, all good poems are about shagging..." I almost choke. "Love is the purest emotion you see, Al, that's why it hurts so much when you lose it. But when you find it, well, when you find it, don't let it go." He pauses. "So who's it about then, Al, c'mon, you can tell me?"

"No one." I've never been in love... I've never even had a girlfriend... not a real one.

"Ah, c'mon, son, you can tell me. Who is she?"

"She's nobody," I say a bit too defensively, "She's imaginary." Paddy's eyes are full of pity. It dawns on me how sad my life is, how incomplete.

"Imaginary? Well at least she won't answer back!" Paddy is trying to steer my thoughts away from the shadows but I'm heading that way.

"Will you read it again for me, Al, can you do that for me?"

"Of course." I hear my parents leave the house and Paddy starts to snore, so thankfully I don't get much further than the first few lines. As Paddy's chest whistles its sad song, I listen to the rain attack the windows, collect my stuff and leave him to his dreams.

Returning the dishes to the kitchen, I load them into the dishwasher, open a can of tuna for Dwdi and return to my room to hook up the stereo. Connecting the speakers, I'm interrupted by the door bell ringing three times. I go down the stairs quickly and open the door on the best, worse and biggest surprise of my life.

It takes a few seconds for my eyes to adapt to the darkness and rain. I don't recognise the girl at first. The usual thick layer of make-up is absent. Here is the most naturally-pretty woman on the planet. Long blonde, natural hair pulled tight into a pony tail and bright training gear soaking wet after the short walk across the drive, she looks years younger than the woman I thought I knew. We stand there in silence for a while, and just stare at each other. She seems scared, but fear and excitement are close cousins. My heart beats a tribal rhythm. Her lips quiver and she looks as if she's about to say something but stays quiet. I say the first thing that comes to mind. "My parents aren't here."

"I know, I saw them leave about ten minutes ago."

"Are you stalking me?"

"Sort of."

And right then, without warning, she steps towards me, wraps her hands around my neck and pulls me towards her until our lips lock and tongues wrestle. My eyes are wide open in utter shock. I know it isn't right, it's against the 'rules', against the Word and commandments, but still, I can't stop. It seems that I, like every mortal man, am weak when it comes to matters of lust. Not that *anything* like this has ever happened to me during my twenty-nine years on earth.

We gorge on each other by the front door. It is a sweet thrill with a slight hint of sourness – as guilt reminds me who I'm actually kissing. Still, I'm harder than I've ever been. I close the door with my right foot as her hands creep inside my cardigan, bringing me out in goosebumps. Despite my lack of experience and my shaking hands, I manage to release the catch on the back of her super-tight sports bra. As I fondle her breasts, my sister-in-law purrs in anticipation.

Our breathing is full of forbidden desire. We both know that this is wrong, but there's no stopping it now. Mia leads me up the stairs, and I can't help but stroke her tight bottom and swollen lips through the skin-tight lycra of her cycling shorts.

On the landing she turns to face me. I see this as another opportunity to kiss her, but she stops me.

"Which one's your room? Unless you want to do it right here!" I regain some composure and lead her up to the attic. Breathing deeply, I make a beeline for the stereo and insert a Minnie Riperton CD, press PLAY and thank the Lord that everything seems to be working fine. Mia closes the door behind her and looks around.

"I love Jack Nicholson," she says, staring at the framed poster on the wall. "'Ever danced with the Devil in the pale moon light?'" I want to say, "Not yet; give me a chance" but as usual, I hesitate.

"Where's that?" she asks, pointing at the cross of Black Rock.

I tell her and ask, "What's going on, Mia?" A pretty lame question but I need an answer, since I am being seduced by my brother's wife.

"I want you, Al. I've wanted to do this to you for ages…"

"Do what?"

"This." She moves towards me and tears at my clothes. My cardigan, followed by my shirt and then the rest fall to the floor in thirty seconds flat. I'm naked now, for the first time in front of a girl – a woman – and I must admit that I'm not totally comfortable. Nervous. Confused. Paranoid. Excited. Ecstatic. Mute. Uncomfortable. Mia is stunning, but the reason I can't close my eyes when kissing her is because Will keeps appearing behind my eyelids. He's already haunting me.

I stand by the bed feeling completely self-conscious, skinny. I feel like cupping my testicles in mortification. Mia takes off her top, revealing a perfect pair of breasts. The first I've seen in the flesh! They're more than a handful but are still firm and pert, while her dark brown nipples are harder than a spear's tip. Instinctively, I take both breasts in my hands, lean towards them and suck passionately, using the sounds Mia makes as a guide to how well I'm doing. I look up at her face, which is frozen with desire, as I suck away enthusiastically. Then Mia opens her eyes and looks down at me – a goddess scrutinising her subject. We kiss again, bringing me to the edge of climax as her flesh massages mine, She suddenly asks, "Have you showered tonight?" I lie: "yes". In for a penny... Mia looks at me for a second; as if she knows I'm fibbing, but after a slight pause she kneels before me, taking my stiff little stump between her lips. She licks the length of my sword's fleshy shaft, teasing my bell gently with her teeth. Then, she wraps her lips tightly around it and vacuums the length slowly and deeply into her throat. She repeats the sequence and I look down at her naked back, desperately trying not to come too soon. As she sucks hard I watch her hands peel the lycra shorts over her beautiful behind. She's got nothing beneath them and I notice some faint stretch marks scarring her skin. This just adds to my craving, making her seem more real.

Her backside is revealed and I feel a tremor as I explode into her mouth. After a short pause, she gets to her feet and stands before me, swallowing. I examine her fine form and notice that Mia is completely bald... you know, down below.

"You could have warned me, Al!" She exclaims, while freeing her hair from its tight tail and letting it cascade over her shoulders. I'm not sure what she's talking about, preoccupied as I am with her smoothness.

"Sorry Mia, I didn't know I was supposed to... I've never... I've never done this before." She hugs me tightly, starting to tongue my shoulder, moving her lips towards my ear. Waves of ecstasy rush through me; soon we are lying on the bed pleasuring each other as the stiffness returns.

"Why are we doing this? It's so senseless," I say, exploring her body. But this sensation is stronger than 'morality'. Everything's so new to me and the sensation is greater than anything I could ever have imagined.

"I can't speak on your behalf, but I can tell you why I'm doing it."

"Please, go on." I hope that she can erase some of the guilt. Maybe Will's having an affair too?

"I like you, Al. And I'm fed up of how your brother treats me..."

"Does he beat you?" I hope he does too: then I'll be able to wave goodbye to all the guilt in the world...

"Nooooo, god no, don't be silly," she says, as she leans up on one elbow, inviting me to kiss her breasts. "He's an arsehole, yes, but he's no wife-beater. Look, all he wants is a trophy... mmmm, that's good... something nice-looking for his idiot mates to be jealous of when, on those rare occasions, he invites me out with him... mmmm... just like that... I'm fed up of it, to tell the truth..."

"But why me, Mia? I'm nobody, nothing... and I'm his brother!"

"Exactly. If he ever finds out about this... ooh! Watch it! Not too hard... he'll be so surprised he'll choke to death... hopefully... mmmm, that's better... He's not a very nice man, your brother..."

"I know."

"I know you know, I've seen how he treats you and that's how it is for me at home. I need to feel wanted, that's all, cos I'm... oh... that's it... I'm sick of being treated like shit. I'm not a piece of shit, Al!"

"I know you're not. You're beautiful..."

"So are you..."

"Shut up!"

"You are. You're the exact opposite of Will. You're kind, gentle, sensitive and you've got the sexiest eyes in the universe. Life's too short to be unhappy, don't you agree?"

"In theory, yes... but what about Will? This is wrong." I try to pull away from her, but there's some inexplicable force – or possibly sweat – which stops me from doing so.

Mia takes my head in her hands and kisses me slowly: "Will treats us both the same, Al. Like shit. So, for once, why don't we treat each other like we deserve to be treated?"

She rolls me onto my back and kneels on top of me, rubbing her clitoris with the tip of my rock-hard penis. It's quite obvious, even to me, that Mia's pretty experienced in this field, and she makes sure that I don't spoil her fun the second time around by guiding my penis in and out of her while holding the base between her thumb and forefinger and leaning as far back as she can go, to feel the full thrill of the act. Contradictory thoughts fly through my head as we make love – Will is a constant presence, as well as the guilt of betraying him and God's word. I'm lost in complete confusion, but as happy as I've ever been. Although I know what we're doing is very wrong, I don't want to stop...

"Feel my tits!" Mia demands, as her skin glistens under a layer of sweat. I squeeze them hard. I haven't got a clue what I'm doing, but Mia's appreciative shrieks – which grow louder and louder with every thrust – prompt me to carry on. She bends ecstatically backwards, her head is almost touching my feet in an arch of pure pleasure. Her enjoyment reaches such a cacophonous crescendo that I have to tell her to keep the noise down in case we wake Paddy.

"Sorry," she says mischievously, "I forgot about your grandad."

"That's OK, I think he's asleep..."

"Probably not anymore though, right?" And she kisses me hard before regaining her rhythm and riding me down the home straight *ummming* and *ahhhing* and biting her lips seductively. As my platoon threaten to burst through the barrack walls once again, I warn her.

"I'm gonna *cummmmmmmmmmmmmmmmmmmm*!" I scream, louder than any noise Mia made. Only then do I notice the tattoo on her taut stomach. As Mia steps up a gear or two, I'm hypnotised by the cross lying about three inches to the right of her pierced belly button. Even though it's a Celtic cross, the symbol shakes my conscience. I close my eyes and see images a hundred times worse than Will's face. Blood-soaked stigmata on open palms and a crown of thorns penetrating the flesh of a faceless martyr. There's no hope of ridding the image from my mind now, so I open my eyes and concentrate on Mia's fantastic figure.

Mia brings herself to the edge of climax by stroking her clit and rowing her hips to some unseen rhythms. But my experience is spoiled by guilt. And as we both come as one, I know that once the mess is mopped up, this, or anything like it, will never happen again.

Regaining our normal breathing patterns, we bask, kiss and cuddle like true lovers, as opposed to the pair of traitors we really are. Personally, I can't wait for her to leave, even though I've just experienced heaven on earth in her company. Even though Will and I aren't good friends, my guilt is intense.

"What now, Mia?"

"What do you mean? Am I gonna leave him?"

"I s'ppose, although I'm not sure if that's what I mean either."

"It doesn't matter anyway, 'cos I can't leave him. Not at the moment anyway. You see, although that man, your brother, blatantly uses me, it's not all one way traffic. I mean, I use him in many respects too…"

"Don't tell me, Mia. I don't want to know." Unfortunately I already know: she uses him for his money. Without Will, Mia and Sophie's lives would be much tougher. But, in my opinion, Will deserves everything he gets…

Minnie Riperton's sweet voice fills the room, and Mia says, "I never thought you were gay either, Al. That was just your brother shit stirring…"

"Well, now you know for sure. Maybe you can pass the information on to him."

"I'll keep that information for another day; you never know when it'll come in handy… And anyway, you could still swing both ways!" And I look at her; eyes wide, feigning hurt. "I'm only joking, Al… I know you're *all man!*" She climbs back on top of me, kissing me on the lips and rubbing her breasts on mine. Then she dismounts and starts to get dressed.

"I told Will I was going circuit training."

"Do you think he'll fall for it?"

"No reason not to. After all, I do look like I've just had a hard session." The cheeky smile returns again, and I get up and dress as well. As she covers her breasts with the sports bra, she steps towards the window and looks out into the dark. "I saw you looking down that Sunday, you know."

"What? Really? You can see through the blinds?"

"Yes, you can see through the blinds. I could see your shape, your shadow… unless it was a ghost."

"I don't believe in ghosts. I've never seen one anyway…"

"I hated Will more than ever that day, he was such a bastard to you…"

"And to you."

"Yeah, well, I'm used to it and I've learned to deal with it… but

107

that day it really got to me. I wished I was somewhere else, you know, with someone else…" And it's then I realise that Mia has just used me in a similar way to how she uses my brother. Revenge. That was the purpose of tonight's visit. Revenge for the way Will treats her, and with his naïve little brother too… I just hope that telling him is not part of her master plan.

After Mia's finished dressing, she ties her hair back tightly and we go downstairs. After an uncomfortable moment when we're both unsure of how to say goodbye, she pulls me close and kisses me.

"You're not going to tell him are you, Mia?"

"I'm not planning on it, but you never know."

"Don't say that!" Seeing the panic in my eyes, she starts to laugh.

"Don't be so soft, Al. This is our little secret. OK?" And that's it: it's happened, it's over, she's gone.

I find myself in the kitchen. The kettle's boiling, the lights are low and Dwdi's scratching at the back door. He's on the other side of the cat-flap moaning, but like every cat I've ever met, he refuses to use his private entrance when he knows there's someone nearby who can help. I open the door and let him in, ignoring his plea for food as his bowl's still half full. Dwdi has a strop but I take no notice of him tonight. I pour boiling water over the camomile teabag and spoon some honey into the mug, sit down and try to read the paper. But I cannot concentrate.

I think back over the past few hours and I know that life will be very different now. My innocence has just been taken from me – stolen as part of my sister-in-law's game. I hope and pray that Will will never discover the truth. It's going to be hard enough living with my own conscience, never mind an angry brother hell-bent on revenge.

While sipping my cuppa, I consider my performance. Not bad for a virgin. I've been hoping for and dreading this moment for years, thinking that the day would probably never come, but when it did, it went much better than I could have imagined. Except that it happened with my brother's wife. I'm glad to have finally graduated as a proper adult, although now I must have sacrificed my place in Heaven. What worries me most is that this will come back to haunt me… and…

and... oh no... condom, no condom, I didn't wear a condom! I get up and pace the floor as the panic engulfs me. But, after some serious contemplation, I take another sip of tea and calm down. I mean, Mia – as a young mother in a long-term relationship – must use some serious contraception. She must...

I'm not sure Will entirely deserves this either. The details become cloudy: the whole episode seems so surreal that I start to doubt whether it happened at all. But I can smell her on my hands.

I leave the kitchen and climb the stairs, hoping for an uncomfortable night's sleep at best, but as I reach the landing I see a light on in Paddy's room so pop my head round the door to check that the old man's alright. I hope to God that he slept through the commotion, but when I see the look on his face, I know my luck's run out. Paddy's sitting up in bed, sipping a huge whiskey, with a sly little smile dancing on his face.

"Everything ok, Paddy?" I ask, hoping I can keep this visit short and sweet. Paddy takes a sip of his tonic before answering.

"I'm not sure really, Al. *I'm* fine, but something disturbed my slumber earlier on..."

"Sorry about that, I had a visitor." He laughs out loud, spilling a little malt on the bedsheets.

"I know. In fact I know quite a few things..."

"What do you mean by that?" Too defensive, Al!

"Well, for a start, I know now that your imaginary muse is real..."

"And..."

"And I also know why you want to keep her a secret." I want to deny it all, but it's as if God himself is preventing the lies. "I wasn't joking when I told you I can hear *everything* from this room here." I just stare at him now, with no hope of retrieving the situation. "Now we've all done some stupid things in our lives, but Alan, tonight's foolishness takes the biscuit, it really does..."

"It wasn't my fault!" I manage to blurt, which makes me sound like a petulant child.

"Let's say I believe you, but even if it *wasn't* your fault, it still happened and it's not right..."

"But…"

"Don't but me now, son, just remember how ironic it is that you found my swearing offensive a few weeks ago." I look at the floor as the humiliation sweeps over me. I've got nothing to say now."

Chapter 9: A WALK ON THE DARK SIDE

After an uncomfortable night, my first ever hangover thunders between my ears. I lie naked in bed like a newborn baby, both hands on my head in an attempt to stop the ringing. The door's wide open and a pleasant breeze blows between my legs. My mouth's as dry as Jack Dee's delivery, and my head bangs like a samba band in full swing. I reach for the glass of water and, like a Bedouin who's just discovered a stall selling Brecon Carreg next to a palm tree in the desert, gulp it down greedily. I realise that last night is a complete blur, though I *do* remember being sick over my bike.

I get to my feet and sway like a well-developed Jenga tower for a few seconds as my head rushes and the back of my eyes throb. Refilling the glass, I sit down in a chair already occupied by Paddy. He leaves the shed, lighting a Woody and disappears into the netherworld.

My head rumbles as I remember that I'm supposed to be starting my new job at the Arches in... half an hour! Right then the alarm clock crows. I turn it off and two hideous thoughts occur to me:

1) I've never felt so rough;

and

2) I've never worked in a pub before.

I recall Floyd's big talk about me being an experienced barman... and did I say something about a double shift?

I manage to get up again and splash cold water on my pits and face. This stings a little to start with but is quite refreshing and after a while I sort of feel a bit better... sort of... not really.

Without any warning, grief hits me like a below-the-belt blow from a heavyweight boxer, and I find myself in the chair again, naked and sobbing uncontrollably. My loss is colossal. As I recall my parents, I also remember that I have a brother who I haven't seen for years. Will and his family live less than a mile away from here, but that mile seems like a million. After a lifetime of bickering, bullying and betrayal, it's as if I've brushed my brother under some carpet. The smell of the local pub's greasy microwaved meals and Wedal Road's rotting waste makes the bile rise and I rush to the door in time to pebbledash the front step with parmesan, Stella and the obligatory carrots. I lean on the doorframe, breathing deeply as the saliva and snot hangs from my mouth and nose. The tears cease but the emptiness remains, so I wash again in the sink, get dressed, lock the door and wipe the bike's saddle before setting off for the Arches and my new career.

As I battle weakly up Allensbank Road, the sweat pours off my body, and my head continues to throb. I stop at Londis for breakfast – Lucozade and a Cornish pastie – and after devouring my meal in the shade outside the shop, continue on my way and reach the pub two minutes late. Dad would be disgusted by my lack of promptness. I try to cool my body under my white polyester shirt by blowing on it, but it doesn't seem to work, so I introduce myself at the middle bar, sweating like a fat man at a cake stall.

"Can I help you, mate?" the barman asks, with more than a hint of resentment in his voice.

"I hope so. My name's Al. I start work here today." He just looks at me. I try to remember the manager's name to back up my claim by clicking my fingers and tapping my head, which I must admit, is a bad idea. "John!" I exclaim at last. "John, the bar manager... he *is* the bar manager, isn't he?"

"Yeah, John Smith, just like his favourite beer."

"I talked to John yesterday, I start today. Double shift. Is he around?"

"No, he'll be in tonight."

"Oh. Did he tell you about me?"

"No," but after a few uneasy seconds, the barman's serious look disappears and is replaced by a broad smile. "Only jokin' bro! He did tell me about you, in fact, he introduced us last night..."

"Did he? I don't remember. Sorry."

"Don't be, you were wrecked. Anyway, I see you're a bit hungover..."

"That's an understatement, I can't stop shaking or sweating. It's a nightmare."

"Well, before we get you started, I'll fix you a cure and you'll be right as rain. Pull up a stool, I'll be back in a minute, bro."

"What's your name, by the way?"

"What, you don't remember? My real name's Michael Knightbridge but everyone, apart from my pares like, call me Hoff... or bro... or whatever really... anything 'cept Michael, OK?" And off he goes towards the bottom bar to fetch me some Alka Seltzer or something similar.

While he's gone, I start feeling a bit faint. Then the tremors return in my stomach so I dash to the toilets just in time for an unexpected chunder. I thought that business was done with, and after saying farewell to the Cornish pasty, I think the tempest at my core has calmed.

I return to the bar, where Hoff awaits.

"You all right, bro? You seem to have turned green."

"I'm OK," I lie. "But I hope that hangover cure of yours really works."

"It does. Every time, bro," and he pushes a glass of reddish liquid across the bar as he explains: "Bloody Mary, the original and *still* the best hangover cure since thirteen twenty-nine, or something like that."

I lift the glass and smell the concoction as he runs a hand through his greasy mane.

"What's in this, Hoff? It smells... it smells nasty."

Hoff smiles and nods. He's much younger than me, ten years at least I reckon if his acne's anything to go by, but clearly Hoff's already an experienced drinker.

"Bloody Mary, Al! You don't know what's in a Bloody Mary? Bloody hell and Jeezus fuck, bro, where've you been and what the fuck have you been doing? Vodka, double; tomato juice, bottle; Tabasco sauce, dash; ice, shitloads. It'll bring you back to the level and sort the DTs out in an instant. Don't think about the contents, bro, just guzzle the fucker and let's go to woik!"

And I must admit it seems to work. The involuntary shaking ceased within ten minutes, as well as the sweats and the sickness.

After being introduced to the rest of the staff, I find myself behind the middle bar, learning how to pull pints as there aren't many punters in yet, I can only agree with Floyd's claim that barwork is easy. Under Hoff's leisurely tutelage I'm actually starting to enjoy myself by the time the lunchtime trade starts.

I've got my back to the bar, inserting cash into the till after pulling a perfect pint of IPA for some old bloke with a Hitler moustache, when I hear the chatter of a group of young girls. I feel Hoff's hand on my shoulder, inviting me to turn around and face the scene, and when I do, I thank the Lord for the heatwave we're experiencing at present.

There are four of them. They strut towards us like models on a catwalk during London Fashion Week – all legs, breasts, tiny vests, massive shades and borderline-legal Daisy Dukes. Hoff rubs his hands together and licks his lips.

We both ignore a middle-aged couple awaiting their Pimms, preferring to serve this gorgeous foursome, when a cruel voice calls my name from the bottom bar. I ignore it to begin with, as I know that I won't have to budge if I'm in the middle of serving someone. But it comes once again, more forceful this time.

As Hoff offers his service, I turn away and curse my bad luck. Maggie – an experienced barmaid with a face like a stained beer mat – welcomes me when I reach the bottom bar.

"Thanks, luv, it's gettin' a bit 'ectic down 'ere. Can you serve this gentleman for me." I want to point out to her that this bar isn't half as busy as the one I've just left, but a coward never bites at times like these, so I turn to the 'gentleman' and realise he's nothing of the sort...

"Whatsssssappennin, Al, how was the head this morning?"

"Don't ask, Floyd, I was a complete mess until Hoff introduced me to his friend, Mary."

"Good old Mary," he says, sucking on a cigarette and blowing the smoke towards the ceiling. "Can you do me a lager top please, mate?"

"Of course I can," I say as I pour a little lemonade into the pint glass. "Early start today?"

"Aye, I'm here all day Saturday. What you might call my weekend job," he winks conspiratorially. "Except I'm on this side of the bar getting pissed while earning a little more than five twenty an hour if you knows what I mean?"

"I do. Stella is it, Floyd?" But my friend's response catches me by surprise.

"Fuck no, not at this time of day," he explains his tactics. "After three, Stella for me; around midday, something gay."

"Something *gay*, what, like Babycham?" Which makes him laugh out loud.

"No, no, no. Carling or Fosters. Something like that..."

"Why d'you call them gay?"

"Cos they're weak as piss, that's why," and after taking that nonsense on board, I fill the rest of his glass with the amber nectar and exchange it for a crisp twenty. As I fish in the till for his change, I hear Floyd say "leave the change by my pint Al, I'll be back in a minute" and turn to watch him leave the pub in the company of a huge blond body-builder in a vest. Business must have started early today.

Nobody seems to take any notice of what Floyd is up to. It's as if he's got some kind of freedom to do as he pleases. Dopelomatic immunity maybe...

As the hours pass, it becomes apparent that working behind the bar is hard going. I spent most of the day in the bottom bar, packed full of male residents mainly from the nearby Crystals estate, and by now I'm well acquainted with the spirits, a master of the cask ales and a dab-hand at pouring the Artois. Although I'm enjoying myself, I'm tired. I'll never offer to do a double shift again…

But one good thing about continuous work is that time flies, and even though I'm dying to sit down, the monotony and the constant socialising makes me forget my aching feet.

By now, Floyd has graduated to Stella and the bar's still full of men… just men. It's like the Masons for the working class in here. Now and again, I hear female voices coming from the middle bar, and even though I can't hear or see him, I know that Hoff's there somewhere, winking and flirting and 'laying some groundwork' as I heard him say earlier.

Even Paddy's here this evening. He came in about half-past five, bought a pint from somewhere, from someone, and has been sitting in the corner in quiet contemplation ever since.

A lot of people are taking the mick out of me for being drunk last night. Many of them seem to know my name even though I don't remember laying eyes on them. Jase is still telling everyone within earshot that he's thick and I've watched Floyd visit the car park at least twenty times over the course of the day. I'm not the only one working a double shift today.

As the clock tick-tocks towards ten, I'm leaning against the bar every chance I get. Remembering people's orders is difficult, and keeping my eyes open, harder still. The heat of the day has turned into the stickiest of nights and my own sweat has dripped into many a drink I've served. Lager dash, did you say? Out of the chaos comes a threatening voice. I look up and see the blond body-builder standing by the door.

"You fuckin' skanked me, yuh short assed fuck!" He bellows at Floyd; his tight white jeans and loose black vest exhibiting his sculpted form. No one takes any notice of him, so he marches towards Floyd and taps his shoulder. Floyd − red of eye and worse for wear − turns slowly on his stool.

"Are you shouting at me, Fabio?" he asks, staring daggers at the hulk before him.

"Too fuckin right I am, short stuff," he retorts, seeming a little uneasy about Floyd's lack of fear. "No one fucks me in the ass and gets away with it!"

"What?" Floyd asks in mock-surprise, before turning to the faces that surround him with a smile. "Not even your boyfriend?" The whole place erupts with laughter in respect for the size of Floyd's testicles. Fabio's nearing boiling point, a purple vein appearing on his forehead. His eyes blaze and his hands are clenched tight. "I want you," he points straight at Floyd, holding his finger about an inch from his nose, which in turn draws a chorus of 'Wwwwwwwwwwwwwwww' from the audience, "outside, now! I'm gonna teach you a lesson, you skankin' son of a cunt! No one takes the piss out of me, no one!"

Fabio is almost twice Floyd's size and is obviously on a steady diet of self-prescribed steroids: the last time I was in such a grave situation was when Knocker and Edwyn Tripple Nips went for each other's throats after the prison's ping-pong final. Floyd examines Fabio closely, studying his nervous steps and the horror in his eyes.

"You should leave, boy, before you regret comin' in 'ere."

"Fuck you, pygmy! C'mon, outside now!"

"Hang on," Floyd insists, holding his palm up in front of him like Sitting Bull chairing a meeting outside his tepee. "Hang on a sec now, Fabio, let me get this straight. You're accusing me of skankin' you, of professional malpractice in other words, am I right?"

"You sold me shit; it wasn't even green."

"Shit is usually brown, you do know that?"

"Fuck you!"

"Fuck me? No, fuck *you*, Fabio! You're accusing me of selling you some bunk gear, something I find both offensive and perverse. Offensive because I've been doing this for twenty years and never have I skanked anyone in that time. Fuckin' nobody, ya here that you little prick? And perverse because here you are, Mr Muscles, obviously off your fuckin' head on something, offering me out."

"I'm not off my..."

"You must be if you want a piece of me, son. You fuckin must be..." The tone of his voice softens a little as he continues. "Now seriously though, as I'm a reasonable man, if you turn around and walk out of here right now, we'll forget all about this little episode. What d'you say, Fab?"

Fabio is trembling with rage, and walks backwards to the door, gesturing for Floyd to follow him. Floyd gets down from his stool slowly, turns to me saying, "Bring my pint, Al," and marches towards the car park with the whole bar following him. Floyd's drunken merriment has been replaced by a wildness behind his eyes.

A circle of sweaty bodies forms outside the pub, penning in the gladiators between Jack Brown the bookies and the undergrowth over towards the arched bridge.

As the testosterone surges, Floyd turns into some kind of demon, rolling his head and loosening his muscles. John the manager appears at my side holding a pint of Smooth in one hand and a fag in the other.

"I love the smell of brawling in the evening," he says with a wicked smile.

Floyd and Fabio eye each other up like two bulls in a room that's painted red. Sweat glistens on Floyd's forehead; Fabio's desperate to land the first punch. And when one of his friends throws him a baseball bat, Fabio has the upper hand.

"What the fuck you gonna do with that, boy?" Floyd asks, his expression still stern and serious.

"I'm gonna teach you a lesson, short ass, like you fuckin' deserve."

And with that, the battle commences with Fabio rushing towards Floyd and striking him on the side of his stomach. But, instead of recoiling in agony as you'd expect, Floyd takes the pain and breathes deeply, not once taking his eyes off his opponent. Purposefully, he takes off his shirt to reveal his muscles which form a suit of armour.

"Try that again," he suggests casually, and Fabio does just that, except he aims for Floyd's head this time. The crowd close their eyes, but Floyd stops the bat a few inches from his face with his right hand before counter-attacking his opponent by concentrating on the pressure points around his lower back. After disarming Fabio with a nasty blow to his stomach, Floyd throws the bat away and locks his opponent in a half-Nelson. Floyd attacks his nemesis with gusto; striking him in his kidneys, the ribs, his spine, his bladder and every other weak-point on his upper-body. The man mountain becomes weaker with every blow and the crowd show their appreciation.

Floyd's face is halfway between pure chaos and calm, and even though Fabio's at least a full foot taller than him, the contest is as one sided as Action Man teaching Malibu Stacey a lesson. After another blitz of merciless jabbing, with Fabio's arm still locked behind his back, Floyd reaches up and sinks his teeth deep into the big man's bicep. In a shower of blood and a shriek of pain, Floyd ruins Fabio's meaningless tribal tattoo and finishes him off with a flurry of kidney punches. Fabio kneels defeated in a pool of blood, holding his torn skin and coughing a crimson liquid all over the car park. Floyd kicks him in the jaw: Fabio falls lifelessly to the ground. Floyd stands over his victim's still body, breathing deeply and wiping blood from his mouth with the back of his hand. I half expect him to keep on going, finish the job and stop Fabio from breathing. But thankfully he spits at Fabio and faces the hushed crowd. Stepping out of the shadows with his opponent's blood all over his face, Floyd looks like a cannibal.

Fabio has started moving again at last; his white jeans darken as the contents of his bladder, urine and blood, empty all over the denim and fill the air with ammonia.

The crowd parts to let Floyd through; he struts towards me and grabs the pint I've been holding for him all along. He downs the contents in three seconds flat and turns to his audience.

"That fucker better not have AIDS!" he exclaims, handing me the empty and strutting back to the bar. Fabio's friends retrieve him from his resting-place and put him in their car, heading for the hospital if they've got any sense. They wheelspin away, leaving a cloud of dust hanging in their wake. I look back on my first day in my new job. My feet are killing me and what I've witnessed borders on the barbaric. But all I can focus on is how glad I am that Floyd's on my side…

Chapter 10: JUDGE NOT...

It was a stressful Wednesday. An important deadline and a faulty computer system conspired to give ENCA a bad name. But things were about to get worse. I'm crouched staring into an empty oven in my home's empty kitchen. My thoughts are dark. Perversely, I welcome them: they make a change from the constant guilt since Mia's visit last week.

I put my shoes in front of the Aga and go up to Paddy's room. Death won't stop preying on my mind. With one hand on the brass door knob, I am rehearsing the opening line of Paddy's eulogy in my head. I open the door slowly to avoid creaking and take a peep. My teeth are chattering. The three people in the cold room are alive, but they seem to be in a kind of hell. Paddy lies on the bed completely naked. The old man, who lies on his right side facing the window, slides helplessly on a plastic sheet. Paddy cries quietly; his sobbing haunts the room like a theramin's echo in an empty concert hall.

My parents bend over Paddy's shipwrecked figure. Mam concentrates on his upper body, while Dad's in charge of down below. I am desperate to walk away, but I can't move. Bed sores have colonised

Paddy's back, from his stooping shoulders to his backside's limp butt-cheeks. His legs are a pair of chicken drumsticks and his whole body trembles. I watch from the shadows, feeling the guilt of being almost thirty years old and still living at home; over not helping them nurse Paddy; and over Mia. But seeing Paddy being bathed like a newborn baby breaks my heart.

"After three now Patrick," Mam says, her voice calm. She grabs hold of Paddy's left arm while Dad does the same with his leg. They turn him over carefully towards me and the door. Paddy's ribcage is trying to rip through his skin, which is loose and transparent.

"Get out!" Paddy spits across the pile of books by his bed. Our eyes meet and I feel how his lust for life is waning. I can't stop looking. My parents glance at me over their shoulders, exhaustion showing in their eyes. "Out!" Paddy repeats, and this time I obey.

"Not going to the golf club tonight then, Dad?" I ask him in the kitchen. I'm eating a bowl of chilli con carne and rice that I found in the freezer. Dad's expression tells me no. My parents' social lives have been put on hold until Paddy's situation has 'resolved' itself.

"Where's Mam, still with Paddy?"

"No. She's gone for a lie down…"

"Again?"

"Again." Dad sighs.

"She *did* look tired earlier."

"She's not the only one…"

"I know. I'm sorry Dad…" Dad grabs a tea towel and faces me.

"For what, Al, why are you apologising?"

"For still being here and not helping with Paddy…"

Dad looks at me and shakes his head slowly, making his chin wrinkle.

"Don't talk rubbish, son. And don't ever apologise for living here. You can stay forever, you know that. Don't you? This place wouldn't be the same without you…" Finishing my dinner, I consider Dad's kind words. I know my parents love me and are happy to have me around, but I can't ignore that there's something pathetic about a man on the verge of turning thirty still living at home with his parents.

"And don't think for a second that you don't help us with Paddy. Maybe you don't wash him or nurse him, but all he goes on about is 'Alan this' and 'Alan that' every time I go to see him. You're a huge help spending time with him every evening. We're very grateful for that, Al, and don't you ever forget it…"

"Ok," I say and get up to help with the dishes. Then I leave Dad to his fresh coffee and newspaper and make my way to Paddy's room to see how he's doing.

Straight after Mia's unexpected little visit last week, I tried to avoid Paddy. But within a day, I was back by his bedside, reading poetry and discussing everything and anything that came to mind. I decided to tell him everything. After he listened in silence to my tale, he said, "Make sure it doesn't happen again". That's it. No judgement. No lecture. Nothing. He knows that I know I've done something terrible. And he also knows that no preaching on his behalf is going to change a thing. He's as wise as Solomon. Our relationship is as strong as ever. As his condition deteriorates, I treasure the time I have in his company and try to absorb his wisdom.

I knock quietly on the door and push it open. Paddy sets aside his book by Harry Webb and I smile weakly.

"Sorry about earlier, Paddy, I was just…"

"Don't mention it, Al. I shouldn't have shouted at you either."

"It's ok, I should have…" Somehow we both crack up laughing. Even though Paddy's grin ploughs deeply into his cheeks, I can still see traces of tears. He crosses his arms, rests them on his belly and sighs.

"What's the matter?"

"I'm not sure how to say this… so I'll say my piece and see what you think, ok?"

"Of course."

"I want to die, Alan, and I need your help." Silence. "Are you shocked?"

"Nnn… nno… not about the first part anyway…" I regain my composure. "I've known that you want to die ever since you arrived. I mean, you told me so yourself. But… me… help you? I can't, Paddy. Sorry…"

"It's ok. I understand," the old man nods. "But if you could just live one day in my shoes... in my pyjamas more like... then maybe you'd understand."

"I can see what you're going through..."

"Seeing's not enough, Al, you need to *feel* this pain, *live* this life. Not even Joyce could imagine the indignity I felt this afternoon, hell, the indignity I feel *every* day. And after you've lost that, there's not much else left." His eyes cloud over. We sit looking at each other. Paddy's request for assistance with the final deed, the final act, fills my head to bursting point. Could I do what he's asking? "It's gone now forever of course, there's no getting hold of fresh dignity. It's not like fruit or veg, you can't just go down the greengrocers for a half pound of dignity and a bag o'grapes..."

"If only it was that simple."

"If only, yes... Everything that defined who I am, who I was, has gone. I'm left with nothing – no belongings, no wife, no future. This is it for me, Al. This bed *is* my life. My legs don't work, my lungs are packing up, I've got a lump on my oes... oeso..."

"Oesophagus."

"That's right, on my oes-oph-a-gus. And on top of all that, I've got a buggered bladder and bowel combo to boot! Even an idiot can tell that that's not an impressive haul for anyone's lifetime. Every hour, every minute, every second of my life was leading me here to this bed." He shakes his head. "I wouldn't have worked so bloody hard if I'd known. It's such a disappointing destination. No offence, but it's like being promised Barbados and ending up in Bognor Regis. I mean, I might seem full of beans but that's just a façade. You see, Al, I *know* I haven't got long left on this earth. It's just a question of whether I leave this land with or without some pride. If you don't help me, there won't be any dignity left, no pride or anything else I value."

"Don't say that..."

"Why, are you scared of the truth?"

"No, but I do know it hurts..."

"You're right there, Al, you're right..." A tear slides from his left eye, down his cheek and lands on his pyjamas.

I can see how fragile and hopeless my hero Paddy really is. At his core, Patrick Brady is simply a man. A man who is clinging on to self-respect. A man full of uncertainty and doubt, who needs help and support. A man like me.

"Excuse me up there," Mam's voice breaks the silence through the baby monitor. "Can you come down here please, Al. We've got a visitor." On hearing this, Paddy raises his eyebrows and smiles slyly. Is it Mia? I hope not. What'll I do if she's sitting in the kitchen waiting for me?

"I'll be back in a minute, Paddy," I say and leave him to his morbid thoughts. He comes back to life for a second.

"Have you seen my shoes, Al, I haven't seen them for weeks now?" I look at him in confusion.

"No, I haven't, but I'll have a look for them down stairs, ok," I promise, but I forget about his shoes as soon as I'm on the landing. I've already decided not to help him die, and hope that that'll be the end of it. As I go down, I whisper a little prayer, asking the Almighty for a little help and guidance.

In the kitchen is my brother, chatting quietly with my parents. My cheeks blush deep crimson. Will looks at me and I'm sure the game is up, but he doesn't seem to notice. He smiles warmly at me and asks how I'm doing. I'm caught off-guard. His confidence and cockiness have gone: my brother almost seems 'normal'. He is either growing a beard or hasn't shaved for a week. I've never seen him look so dishevelled, and his eyes – usually sparkling – seem tired and bloodshot. He stares down at his coffee, as though hypnotised.

Mam asks, "Is everything ok, William?" And steals a glance at Dad across the table.

"Aye, everything's ok, Mam. Nothing to worry about, honest."

"And the girls are ok too?" Dad adds, blowing impatiently on his drink.

"Everyone's fine, Dad, and they both send their love. Sophie's staying with Mia's parents for a few days…"

"That's nice…" Mam smiles, but I conclude that Sophie's with them for a reason. I'm desperate to leave but can't, so pull up a chair and sit opposite Will so I can face my fate like a man.

Something grave must be on his mind to make him choose to come and see his family.

"How's Paddy doing?" Wil asks.

"Not brilliant," Dad answers.

Mam adds, "Why don't you pop up to see him? He'd be over the moon to see you…"

"I don't know if it's a good time at the moment actually, Mam…" I say, recalling what Paddy asked of me a few minutes ago.

"Why? What's wrong?" Mam asks, full of worry.

"Nothing, really. He's ok. Just a bit down in the dumps, that's all…"

"So seeing Will might lift his spirits…"

"Actually, Mam, I'm not too good myself either. I'll come back in a few days…"

Now it's Mam's turn to read between the lines.

"I knew it! I knew something was wrong! What is it, Will? Can we help at all?"

"Mam, please, stop fussing, would you! I don't want to talk about it right now, ok?" Will slurps the thick dregs from the bottom of his mug, gets to his feet and puts on his leather long-coat. "Right then, thanks for the coffee, but I've got to go. Al, fancy a pint? I want a chat…"

Any hope for escape disappears. Refusing is not an option, and I can't even think of a good excuse. I get my coat. The drive is shining under the first frost of the year and the full moon is on full beam. We walk towards the car blowing on our hands. Will actually puts his arm around me and gives me a hug without pulling any underarm hair or pinching any flesh. He misses me, apparently: I feel guiltier than ever before.

In the car, Will treats me like an adult and by the time we reach the pub, the nagging distrust has retreated a little. I haven't been in a pub for years. I don't like them. Never have. But I follow Will past the first two bars in the Three Arches to the grottiest one with no carpet nor cushions. The bare strip-lights above hurt my eyes. The place is pretty full. Dad would call this the 'People's Bar'. Will calls it 'Gippsville'. I try and persuade him to return to the middle bar and its comfy seats and carpet, but as we stand at the counter I notice Will eyeing one of the locals, trying to get his attention.

"What's your poison, Al?"

"Orange juice please," I answer. Will looks at me for a split-second, but instead of mocking me, he just orders the drinks.

"Pint of Stella and a couple of bottles of orange juice, please Maggie," he asks, smiling broadly at the middle-aged woman and unconsciously rolling a tenner between his forefinger and thumb. Maggie places the order on the bar. While Will waits for his change, I take my juice and head for the corner furthest away from the Bandits and the three drunken fools playing pool.

Will approaches, nodding and acknowledging a few familiar faces along the way, before insisting that we swap seats so he can 'keep an eye' on the bar. Very strange behaviour, but I do as he wishes. He continues to stare past me, at the bar beyond, and takes a long swig of his beer. After a long silent pause, for some stupid reason I ask, "So how's Mia doing?"

I look at Will, swallowing dry spit. His eyes cloud over and he fingers his glass.

"I don't know how to tell you this, Al, but I didn't know who else to turn to…"

"Say what?" I panic.

"Em… well… we're having a bit of a bad patch at the moment… you know… Mia and me, that is…"

I nod and hope I show compassion rather than pure guilt.

"I'm not sure what's going on to tell the truth… I'm in a right mess if you want to know… I couldn't live without her… without *them*. They're my life, Al." I smile weakly and strip the label from my bottle of juice.

"Sexually frustrated, are you?" Will says, looking at the mess I'm making on the table.

"What?"

"Nothing, it's just that they say doing that to your bottle of beer, juice, whatever, is a sure sign of sexual frustration, that's all." I nod and try to ignore the irony of his statement. "Thanks for this, Al, I appreciate your company… your ears."

"No problem. I'm just a little shocked, that's all."

I now know that the pearly gates will be locked against me. There's only one place for people like me in the long run...

"I'm sure you are. I mean, I was too. I don't know where it all went wrong..." I have to fight the urge to suggest a few things that might have helped over the years – listening to his wife for example, respecting her and appreciating her now and again – but I keep my mouth shut. "I'm determined to put things right though. They're both too important to even think about losing them."

"Why me though, Will?"

"What d'you mean?"

"Well... I don't understand why you're telling me this, instead of one of your other friends. I mean, we've never been very close, have we?"

Will considers his words carefully before answering. "You can only discuss some things... some problems... with family – blood's thicker than water and all that – and I didn't want to share this with Dad, knowing what he's going through with Paddy at the moment. So here we are, you and me, sorry if it's all a bit heavy, but I had nowhere else to turn..."

My brother's persistent apologising makes me feel quite sick. I want to admit everything to him. Get it off my chest. Take my punishment. Erase the guilt. Or at least alleviate it a little. But I don't do anything of the sort, just listen to Will.

"I think she's having an affair," he says, which makes me choke on my OJ and cough some juice out of my nose.

"Why do you say that?" I manage to ask after a proper coughing fit.

"Nothing specific. More of a hunch really... are you ok – d'you want some water?"

"Yes, yes. No thanks," more coughing, some tears. "A hunch?"

"Yeah, as I said, nothing specific, but she's changed recently. She's more... what's the word... challenging... no... disobedient... fuck, that makes me sound like a Victorian dad or something. She's just different, that's all. Distant. Definitely. Jesus, Al, I don't know, seriously, I've never been so scared in my whole life. I don't want to lose her, you know…"

"I totally understand, Will. But what can you do?"

"I have absolutely no idea…" He smiles. "Change. Be more understanding. Less impatient. We've already discussed the situation. Couple of nights ago. She's not happy, that's for sure, but we've agreed to work at our relationship, for Sophie's sake, that's the official reason anyway, but for me, Mia's the priority. I mean, loving Sophie and being loved by Sophie is unconditional, while Mia's love… I've never wanted anyone else. Just Mia. Just Mia…"

"I hope you sort it all out, I really do…"

Instead of the ogre, the bully, that's usually present, I see in Will a simple man, an insecure one who just wants to please his wife and raise his child.

My brother's eyes dance across the bar behind me: without warning, he gets up and mumbles that he'll be back in a sec, and leaves the pub accompanied by a short bloke with a blonde flat-top. I've got a pretty good idea of what they're up to, but I follow them just to make sure. Through the open door I watch my brother buying 'something' from the car-park-chemist over by Jack Brown the bookies. It appears that they know each other quite well as they chat and laugh comfortably in each other's presence. Will hands him some money before they touch fists like a couple of Boyz 'n' the Hood. I'm well aware that Will has 'seen it all and sampled everything' but I still don't understand why a thirty-three-year-old surgeon is still buying drugs in a car park off some Flat Top McReefer.

I sneak back to my seat and sip my orange juice, but when Will returns the scorn must be plastered across my face.

"What's the matter with you?"

"That's not the answer to your problems," I hiss. He looks at me and takes a swig of Stella before answering.

"You're right. And I've known that for years. But you see Al; I'm not looking for the answer because the answer doesn't exist. I know this because I've been questioning everything for most of my life…"

I stare back as I consider his answer. "But why, Will? *Drugs*, Will?"

"Don't be so fuckin naïve, Al!" It's his turn to hiss now. "It's just a bit of ganja, that's all. Not every drug's the same, you know. And my fondness of the herb has never led down the path to smack, crack or anything else, and it's not going to happen now, ok. I'm no junkie, Al, just a man who enjoys a little smoke. It doesn't interfere with my work or any other aspect of my life. I work extremely hard, under constant stress, every day, and I just like a little smoke of an evening, that's all. Something to help me unwind, to relax – like a glass of wine or a pint of bitter... and I'm not apologising for it either – everyone deserves a little pleasure in life if you ask me..."

"But it's against the law."

"Who are you, my mother? And anyway, Mr Religious Studies, how can something that grows naturally on earth truly be considered illegal? It's like outlawing daffodils, roses or lilies."

"What do you mean?"

"C'mon Al, you know what I'm saying. How can something "God" has "put" on this earth, something which grows wild without being touched by man, be considered illegal? I'm not sure who said this... some judge if I remember correctly... but I've learnt this little quote which says it all I reckon," Will takes a swig of beer. "'How absurd is a law that seeks to classify a plant as a crime; as if there's something feloniously wrong with nature'. The law is certainly an ass in this respect, wouldn't you agree?"

But seeing I'm unconvinced, his voice softens. It appears he just wants to stop all the bickering.

"Sorry, Al."

What right have I got, Judas MkII, to sit here judging him over what he chooses to help him relax, when I've got my own dark secret?

I smile, and as the guilt settles once again, we return to small talk and newfound friendliness.

Chapter 11: DRINKING IN THE SECOND CHANCE SALOON

I put down the customer's overflowing pint of Bow on a tatty beer towel. He is Coxy; an ex-copper from Llanishen with an unforgettable silver-grey handlebar moustache. He has long-since retired to concentrate his efforts on drinking his way through his pension. I pause for a while and watch the bubbles rise towards the surface.

"Two-twenty please." Coxy rummages in his pocket; I lean on the lager pumps and wipe the sweat off my face with the back of my hand. Cardiff's heatwave continues but all I hear is people moaning.

It's Friday today, and I've settled into a nice little routine over the past week. I work the eleven-till-six shift, seven days a week. Initially, John wasn't too happy with this because of the 'health and safety issues' connected with working every day of the week. But I remind him that I'm employed illegally anyway since I get thirty pounds, cash in hand at the end of every shift, no tax paid, no questions asked. Even though the work can be hard, I enjoy the monotony and the order. I make little money, despite all the hours, and I'm grateful Floyd doesn't charge rent. It'll take a year and more for me to save enough cash to put down a deposit on a bedsit or flat...

My salary has led to an unexpected union, full of exciting possibilities: my relationship with Lidl. There were a few of them around before I got sent down, but Lidl, as well as Aldi, were ridiculed back then. Shops for the poor, that's what people believed. The snobs especially. I know I did, without any kind of evidence to back up this claim. The truth is their produce is as good, if not better, than anything Tesco or Sainsbury's have to offer. The only difference I can see is that the product info's in a foreign language... and of course, everything's roughly half the price too! I spend twenty pounds there every week, and for that amount I get to breakfast like a king on a daily basis. That's the only meal I eat at home, as I get a sandwich from the kitchen at lunchtime and join Floyd on the other side of the bar for supper every night. I'll never be a rich man but right now I'm content with life.

Except for Coxy's lonely presence, the bottom bar's lifeless. The Brain's Dark clock hanging next to the Gordon's Gin and the collection of random postcards that have been sent here by some of the regulars – Birdlife of Benidorm, Full English Breakfasts of the World and the 2001 Nimbin Cannabis Cup among them – tells me it's just gone midday. There's no sign of Floyd yet, which is odd.

I bend down behind the bar to fill the dishwasher to make the minutes tick by a little quicker – when I hear voices. My broad smile welcomes the foursome in a professional and friendly manner. Textbook stuff. But nobody notices. Mainly because three of the four are hanging on every word the other one's saying. I join them and listen as the well-tanned local, wearing a white T-shirt sporting the Golden Arches and the word McShit beneath, recounts a tall tale about a prostitute, a hammock and a hamster. I patiently wait for him to finish his story before offering my assistance.

"What can I get you, gents?

"Two Fosters, one smooth..."

"Brains or John Smiths?"

"Brains, please."

"...and a Guinness for me,"

"Extra cold?"

"Too fuckin' right, *extra extra* cold if you can," the stranger says, before turning back to face his friends. "I'm telling you boys, three weeks in Thailand and it's hotter in Cardiff than it was on Ko Samui!" That explains his complexion anyway, which, together with his whitewashed locks makes him look a little like a pint of his favourite drink.

As he tells more tales about opium dens, corrupt policemen and Pat Pong's infamous pingpong-popping residents, I concentrate on completing the order, starting with the perfect pint of Guinness.

I hold the glass at a forty-five degree angle and fill two-thirds with the dark liquid. Then I let the clouds settle and turn my attention to the lagers and the smooth. Pouring Guinness is one of my favourite parts of the job. The guidelines – step one to four – are glued to the back of the pump, so that the new worker can learn the fundamentals without revealing the 'secret' of the perfect pour and ruining the mystique that's attached to the Black Stuff. The only advice I got on my first day from Hoff regarding Guinness was "Read that, copy it, voilà." Those who can, teach. Those who can't, work in a pub.

I place the Fosters and smooth on the bar before going back to the recently-settled stout. I lift the glass to the pump, holding it completely level under the flow until there's about a centimetre of white resting on top of the dark body. I complete the ritual by drawing a perfect shamrock on top of the cream, and place the pint with the rest of the drinks on the bar. There are only three things that could make the pint even more perfect, and that's a personal appearance by Rutger Hauer... on a white horse... accompanied by the sounds of Leftfield.

I stand there listening to yet another story about Thailand's prostitutes and their seemingly magical powers – laughing in all the right places, although I'm a little confused by some of what I hear, and pretty disgusted by the rest. But then Randy, the man who's recently returned from the far east, falls silent and does a double-take when he spots his Guinness.

"What the hell is that?" he asks, as his eyes dart back and forth incredulously between the glass and me. "Where's the rest of my head?"

"Easy now, Randy, you're not in Patpong now, mate!" says one of his buddies, but it appears that Randy's quite serious. It also seems Randy is quite possibly insane.

"What's that?" he repeats, and this time I have to say something.

"It's a perfectly-poured pint of Guinness," I announce, shrugging my shoulders in disbelief. Randy's eyes are staring straight at me, so I smile weakly.

Randy places both his hands flat on the bar between us and shakes his head slowly.

"No–no–no–no–no–no–no," he says, and I look from the glass to his face and back again. Now I know that people can be extremely fussy about their drinks, after all, that's part and parcel of being a barman. I have to deal with one local who drinks bitter shandy with soda water instead of lemonade and accompanies every order with a huge amount of fuss, but that's nothing compared to this madness. As the silence becomes uncomfortable, it dawns on me that this could be a joke... or a despotic conspiracy... or maybe even a quantum leap...

"How long have you worked here, son?"

"Three weeks tomorrow."

"What! And no one's told you how I like my Guinness?"

I shake my head at how self-important some people can be. Randy starts shouting for John to come and join us. After waiting for another excruciating minute, John saunters over and greets Randy like an old friend. As he reaches across the bar to shake his hand, John says, "Welcome back, Randy, how was the whoring?"

"Fuckin' marvellous, as usual," he says, before returning to the matter in hand. "But forget that for now, why don't you show this young buck by 'ere how to pour me a proper pint..." I watch John go to work on the worst pint of Guinness in the history of the world. He catches my eye when Randy's attention is drawn away for a second and gives me a little sly wink and a silent sigh, as if to say "the customer is always right, no matter how mental they seem to be". John, who's worked in the industry for almost thirty years has long since perfected the art of customer relations. Grin and bear it, that's his secret. John stands the glass on the flow tray directly under the tap. I watch the process and can't quite believe what he does next. John opens the tap and fills the glass right to the top. This is completely at odds with the guidelines and leaves a two and a half-inch head at the top of the glass. John hands Randy his drink. Randy smiles and takes a huge gulp, covering his top lip with froth and foam.

"Ahhhh! That's more like it!" he exclaims, licking his lips and handing John a ten pound note.

John apologises to Randy for my 'mistake', leans on the bar and starts swigging the perfect pint I pulled a minute ago. Randy repeats one of his earlier stories for the manager's amusement.

Floyd arrives just after one, dripping with sweat and still in his work clothes. He complains for half an hour about his morning cleaning anti-Semitic graffiti off some of the cemetery's graves, then settles down to an afternoon of drinking and selling, selling and smoking. His business appears to tick over nicely as his customers appear wearing less and less as the temperature reaches towards the mid-thirties.

Once when he returns from the car park, he's so hot that he orders a bottle of house white from the fridge, pays for it and proceeds to hold the bottle against his face to cool down a little. He keeps the full bottle in the fridge and uses it as an ice-pack as the day unfolds.

It's pretty hectic by three o' clock, although the bar is empty, with most people outside enjoying the weather. Floyd sits alone at the bar, while John and myself are on the other side, watching Hoff through the window smoking a cigarette and having a good perv at the sixth-form girls drinking their Bacardi Breezers under a parasol.

Hoff's sleeves are rolled up and his long hair is pulled tight in a tail. He inhales deeply before spewing the smoke out once again.

"How many breaks has he had today?" I ask John out of interest as opposed to wanting to stir up trouble.

"Dunnow, four, maybe five."

"Fuckin' hell, John, are you serious?"

"Yes, Floyd. Why?"

"Seems like a lot of breaks, that's all. What d'you reckon, Al?"

"It does seem excessive, but I don't smoke, so I really don't know..."

"How many staff members smoke, John?"

"Everyone, apart from Al by 'ere."

"And does everyone have four or five breaks per shift?"

"It varies. Some do, some don't."

"I don't even have *one* break during my shifts!"

"Seems a bit unfair on Al to me, John..."

"How d'you mean?"

"Well..." Floyd starts, but I cut him off mid-sentence.

"I don't take one break during my shifts. Apart from toilet breaks of course..."

"And?"

"How long does it take to smoke a cigarette?"

"I don't know, ten minutes, probably less."

"We'll call it ten minutes then, to make it easier. So, if everyone who smokes takes four breaks during a shift, that means you're losing forty minutes of everyone's shift except for me, who slogs through 'til the bitter end. That's forty minutes you lose, possibly more, for every six-hour shift..."

"How?"

"'Cos you're paying the fuckers to do nothing, that's how, John!" Floyd explains, in layman's terms.

"Exactly," I add, not knowing where this conversation's leading. As well as the smoking, I've also noticed that older members of staff for some reason are 'excused' from doing certain chores like cleaning ashtrays. This really winds me up, but I decide not to bring this to John's attention. One thing at a time...

"So what's your point, then?"

Good question. I look to Floyd for back-up, but he shrugs his shoulders in response.

"I want a pay rise..." I say, full of unexpected confidence.

"You *deserve* a pay rise, mate," Floyd, holding his Chardonnay to his forehead.

"Cheers, Floyd," John is derisive.

"Listen," I continue, as John leaves me behind the bar, lights a cigarette and sits next to Floyd on the other side, "I work six hours straight every day here. I eat a good breakfast before coming, have a quick sarnie for lunch, and apart from when nature calls, I don't stop working until my shift ends. I think you could show some appreciation by giving me, oh I don't know… an extra pound an hour…" John stares at me as he pulls hard on his Benny lungbuster.

"You've got some big balls there, Al, I'll give you that," I smile, "but the answer, unfortunately for you, is fuck off!" John and Floyd laugh together, enjoying their smoke.

But before I have a chance to catch my breath and argue further, Will walks in. My brother's come straight from work and he stops dead when he sees me. He's paralysed and mute. So am I. He steps towards Floyd, holding my gaze, and they greet each other by touching fists. Why they do this, I have no idea…

"Whatsappenin' Will?"

"Not much, Floyd," my brother answers, still staring straight at me.

"You wanna step outside for a second, or have you got time for a pint?"

"I'd love to have a beer, but no offence to you here Floyd, I'd rather share it with my brother. We haven't seen each other for a long time…"

"Your brother?" Floyd asks, turning to look at me as well. "Brothers! Jeezus H Cribbins, you never told me any of this, Al!"

Suddenly, Floyd's all excited, but Will is silent. We haven't been face to face like this for over three years. His grey-blond hair's cut short, but his eyes are as alive as ever.

Although our relationship got much better during the months leading up to what happened, I have no idea how he feels about me now.

"Can I take ten minutes to talk to my brother, please John?" I manage to ask.

"I can hardly refuse after what we talked about just now, can I!" He gets up off his stool and returns to the other side of the bar to cover my absence. His first task is to serve Will.

"What can I get you then?"

"Pint of Stella for me and…" He looks at me, awaiting an answer.

"I'll have the same, please."

"Two Stellas then, please John."

Will waits for the drinks by the bar, chatting to Floyd, as I make my way to the far corner, preparing myself.

I sit with my back to the bar and absent-mindedly peel a Brains SA beer mat as I wait for Will to join me. Outside the window I can hear voices and laughter as the crowd enjoy the sunshine and hops.

"Déjà vu," Will says, as he places the beers on the table and takes a seat next to Paddy, who's just appeared holding a pint of Dark. Will smiles and offers me his hand to shake. "Well, this is a bit of a shock, Al. And sorry if I looked like a total spaz just now, but this is the last place – you know, a pub – that I'd expect to find you…"

"Well, a lot's changed since you saw me last…" I manage to mutter without emotion. We both take a swig of ice-cold Stella, replace our glasses and continue to stare. Will's eyes are glazed after a long day of saving lives, but behind the lethargy lies something else.

"I'm sure they have…" he agrees. "You've been through a lot…" he adds, and once again the guilt catches me with a sucker punch as I realise I'm not the only one who's been to hell and back.

"So have you," I retort. I keep looking at him, but no matter how hard I concentrate, all I can see is Mia staring back.

Will attempts to break the awkwardness.

"When did you get out, then?"

"About a month ago."

"A month! You've lost some weight, but you're doing well, I can see that…"

"I'm ok. Just getting on with it… a new beginning and all that…" Although my curt answers are sure to annoy my brother, I'm finding it difficult to explain. I'm happy to see Will on the one hand, but feel like I'm talking to a complete stranger on the other.

Will smiles again and lifts his pint. But, instead of taking a swig, he asks, "What's wrong, Al, aren't you glad to see me?"

"Of course I am," I smile back. "But…"

"But what? Come on, spit it out!"

"Well…"

"Yes?"

"Well... why... didn't you – or anyone else come to that – visit me in prison?" And there is the question that's been gnawing away at me. Though I'm not so sure I want to know now... I swig vacantly at my pint, cringeing as the smile disappears from Will's face. Then he starts to answer, choosing his words carefully.

"Well, and obviously I can't speak on anyone else's behalf, but the reason I didn't personally come and see you was mainly due to the fact that you fucked my wife..."

Spitting and spluttering on my lager, I glance towards Paddy who is looking incredulous. At times like these, I'm sure he can hear. I turn my attention back to Will. I expect him to take his revenge now, but he shrugs his shoulders and smiles, making me even more confused.

"How did you find out?" I manage to ask at last.

"Mia admitted everything to me, Mam and Dad the day after you... you know."

I nod.

"Sorry Will. Seriously now. Sorry." And I mean it too. What happened between Mia and I has been such a burden.

"Thanks," he says flatly. "We were having a pretty rough time of it during that period, if you remember, and I wasn't innocent of playing away from home myself... more than once. Look, I'm no angel, but you know that already. Mia found out about one of my affairs, not that you can really call fucking a student at work an affair. It's just exciting at the time but leaves you feeling empty, unsatisfied and exhausted. Anyway. What I mean is, it was just sex. No dining out, no gifts, no romantic walks. Fuck all except for, well, fucking. Anyway, she found out and took her revenge." He points straight at me. "The important thing is that what happened made us realise we had to work at our relationship, for Sophie's sake if nothing else, but also because we love each other and we're determined to stay together..." Will's confession of infidelity is a relief, I must admit. Not that it changes anything, but he seems to be over what I did by now. His good mood certainly soothes my conscience. "Things are better now than they've ever been, and our relationship's stronger than ever..."

"Of course. Sorry, I forgot. Congratulations!"

"For what?"

"Another girl. You've got another girl haven't you?"

"Yes. Yes we have. Shit, I keep forgetting that you've... you know. Whatever..."

"What's her name?"

"Lauren."

"Lauren?"

"I know, I know, another English name! Mia insisted. Her Gran's middle name or something..."

"It doesn't matter. I'm just glad you're all ok. Happy. You know..."

"Cheers. We are. It's good to see you..."

"You too."

We fall silent. Sip our Stellas. Stare at each other. I don't know what's on his mind, but I can't help thinking of our parents and how they found out about what their youngest son did with his brother's wife. The happiness disappears as I realise that I let them down, not once, but twice.

"You ok, Al? You're miles away..."

"Just thinking of Mam and Dad, that's all. I know now why they didn't come and see me..."

"Try and forget about it. Seriously, they'd forgiven you before they... you know..."

"But why didn't they..."

"It took them quite a long time to forgive you for everything, Al. Mia and... you know, but I know for a fact that they were meant to visit as soon as they came back from whatshamacallit, the passion play thing..." I know that Will is trying to comfort me but I'm gutted that that I'll never see them again, never have the chance to explain myself.

"Al!" Will drags me back from the darkness. "You've got to believe me, that's the truth."

"But I didn't get the chance to explain..." I blurt, while struggling to keep the tears at bay.

"You didn't need to explain anything. If you ask me, it was only a matter of time before you regained your rightful place as their favourite son. Numero uno, so to speak. They *had* forgiven you, Al, that's the truth whether you choose to believe it or not."

"I *do* want to believe you..."

"Good."

"Bu-bu-but... I miss them, Will, more than anything."

"So do I, Al. But I've missed you too..."

"Even after..."

"Even then. You're my only brother, my only living blood relative, except the girls of course..." And he reaches across the table and holds my hand tightly before we both grab our pints and start drinking in an attempt to control our emotion. "I was worried about you, you know."

"What, in jail?"

"*Yes*, in jail! I mean, you hear all sorts of stuff... what was it like, how did you... you know... cope?"

"Some other time, ok? Not now..."

"Of course, no worries. Listen, Al, about the inheritance..."

"Don't worry about it."

"I just want you to know that everything's in my name at the moment, but if you need any kind of help, or just some spending money, just ask. Ok? Do you need some cash?"

"No thanks", is my answer, although I'm not entirely sure why. Something's holding me back – new found independence, maybe. "I'm ok at the moment. I've got a full time job..."

"Where are you living?"

"With Floyd." Bad answer. "Up in Thornhill. Temporarily, you know, until I find a place of my own..."

"Alan, time's up buddy, I need you back here." John cuts the conversation short. Will gets to his feet and I follow suit. We embrace, and then I apologise.

"Al, don't *ever* apologise again, ok. I forgave you a long time ago, and although I'll never be able to forget what happened – I'll never mention it again, as long as you promise not to. I love you, Al. I've missed you..." The tears well, Will holds me in his arms and I'm at peace.

"Where d'you think you are, boys, the fuckin' Blue Oyster Bar or what?" Floyd bellows.

I return to my duties and pull another bad pint of Guinness for Randy who's been tanning himself even further in the beer garden, and watch Will and Floyd make their way to my friend's open air office. Before leaving, Will turns to me and says, "I'll see you soon, ok?" and I really hope that I do.

Chapter 12: FEEDING TIME AT THE ZOO

Why am I still wearing these blinking shoes? I think during the final quarter mile of my journey home. It is cold, damp and dark – just how I feel. I pull my duffel coat tight around my neck and feel hard leather burrow into my heel's soft skin like a plough's blade through a potato field.

Returning home at the end of the day is becoming ever more depressing as the weeks since Patrick Brady came to stay turn to months. Dad, after years of nagging on Mam's behalf, is losing weight without even trying. The physical exertion of looking after an invalid twenty-four hours a day, as well as the mental trauma of nursing a relative towards certain death, is doing wonders for my father's waistline. Strong coffee is his main nourishment these days, which is something else for Mam to worry about as Dad is slightly manic one minute, totally spent the next and in a dark mood on every other occasion.

Mam on the other hand is sleeping as much as a new-born baby. Her days consist of nothing more than waking, nursing, cooking, sleeping, before the cycle starts once again later in the afternoon.

I'm sympathetic towards Paddy, and although it is their choice, I feel worse about my parents' sacrificing their retirement to look after the old man.

I say a prayer as I open the back door. I wish for a painless end to Paddy's life, a long and happy retirement for my parents and total forgiveness for betraying my brother. My guilt is worsened by seeing Will more often lately. My brother has changed, from a self-important, smug and selfish man, to a more mature, considerate and amiable being. Although Will's been here on an almost daily basis recently, Mia hasn't returned since the night in question...

Paddy was taken to hospital yesterday morning for a biopsy on his oesophagus, to see if it's developing into anything more serious. They also needed to decide if it's time to start feeding him through a tube as the growth is causing him difficulties with swallowing.

So, with Paddy in hospital overnight, it was an opportunity for my parents to relax. But after they cleaned his room they didn't have any energy left to do anything other than sleep. And that's where they were when I got back from work yesterday, and when I left for work this morning. There's got to be more to life than this...

Paddy should be back by now, so I've bought him a bag of goodies which may help lift his spirits. Mam has actually got dressed. She is sitting at the kitchen table with Dad and a young woman. Even though they must have slept for almost twenty hours, my parents still look as tired as ever. I greet them all, and the stranger's kind smile that greets me in return dries a little of the dampness that envelops me.

"Alun, this is Anna; she's a dietitian who's been to see your grandad," Mam explains.

"Nice to meet you Anna. How's he doing?" I ask, noting the health worker's striking features. Although her skin is pretty pale, her hair's as curly as an afro and her toothy smile could light up the heavens. I take off my coat and watch from the corner of my eye as she lifts her mug to her voluptuous lips, revealing a wedding band on her left hand. I seem to be more confident with women since Mia's visit, though perhaps 'horny' would be more accurate. I've tasted the honey and now I'm constantly searching for the hive...

"Not brilliant," is Dad's answer. "We'll get the biopsy results in a fortnight..."

"And he's a bit traumatised by the whole thing," Mam butts in, adding, "There's some soup in that pan by there and some fresh rolls in the Aga."

"Lovely, I'll have it later…"

"I'll make you a bowl now." Although Mam's struggling, she still can't help but fuss.

"That's all right Mam, I need to get changed first, I'm soaked, and I want to give these to Paddy before he passes out for the night," I hold up the plastic bag.

"What have you got him?" asks Anna.

"Just some spoken word books on CD. He gets tired holding a book these days."

After a quick change I head for Paddy's room, knock quietly and open the door without waiting for an answer. The old man uses his oxygen to breathe between almost every sentence these days, so I don't want him to waste his efforts answering the door to me. What I see is close to repulsive, but I bite my lip and take my seat in silence.

Paddy is propped up on his pillows with his oxygen mask over his mouth and nose. He is staring down at his stomach, on show above his pyjama bottoms. Protruding from the loose, translucent skin is a tube, and from the tube a pipe, which in turn is attached to a feeding device by the side of his bed.

"Well, that explains the dietitian downstairs," I say to break the silence, but Paddy takes absolutely no notice. He just keeps on staring – past the silver cross that hangs from a chain around his neck, at the PEG that penetrates his skin. He is wheezing heavily through the mask.

"Look what I got you," I say, and place the CDs and a poetry magazine on the bed beside him. Paddy turns his head slowly and looks at me for the first time. The effort's magnified in his exhausted eyes as he moves the mask to free his mouth.

"What have you got there, Al?"

"I got you some spoken word books and a magazine. Look at this one," I exclaim rather excitedly. "I couldn't believe it when I

found this – it's Bono reading *A Portrait of the Artist as a Young Man.*
It's his favourite book too, apparently!"

"Who the hell is Boner and what sort of name is that supposed
to be?"

"*Bono* is a very famous singer. Haven't you heard of U2? Anyway, I
thought you'd like this. He's Irish, from Dublin, so it'll be like listening
to Joyce himself reading…"

He replaces the mask over his mouth and fills his lungs before
replying. "That's very kind of you, it really is. You're a good boy
and I'm very grateful," I smile, "but there's only one thing I want…
one thing I *need* from you now… have you thought any more about
my request?"

"No." I am lying, although other worries – not least Mia and
Will – have pushed this question into the background lately.

"Well I wish you would. Look at me Alan. I get fed through a tube
now, and they're testing me for cancer which I know I've got…"

"Don't say that!"

"Why not?" He gulps hungrily from his oxygen tank. "I can feel it
in my bones. My dignity's fast disappearing, my pride's been pulverised
and now I can't even taste my food."

"Hang on a minute now, Paddy; if you're so desperate to die, why
did you agree to be fed through a tube?"

Paddy looks at me, shamefaced.

"Like many a man, Alan," he sucks air, "I'm a coward. Simple
as that. A coward. I'm scared and I didn't fancy starving to death."
Another lung full. "Now that might sound completely ridiculous,
contradictory even, but that's the way it is. I need your help. You're
the *only* one who can help me."

"What do you mean by that?"

"Well, your parents won't have any of it…"

"You asked them?"

"I'm desperate here if you haven't noticed." He sucks hard through
the mask to regain some composure.

"What did they say?"

"Well, your Ma was not impressed and made her feelings quite
clear."

"What about Dad?"

"He did what most men would do in such a situation."

"What?"

"He kept quiet and let the woman do the talking. They won't have any of it is the bottom line. It's against their religion apparently..."

"Mine too, I think..."

"...I didn't realise Christianity was so sadistic... no, that's not true, I *did* know that except I've never suffered at its hands like this before. Only God has the power to take lives, so *they* say, but I reckon he'd appreciate a helping hand now and again." I look at him and must admit I tend to agree... to some extent anyway. Paddy isn't *living* life anymore, he's *suffering* life. Paddy turns the screws a little tighter. "You're my only hope now to salvage any dignity. I'll even write a letter explaining the circumstances and how it was all my idea..." A knock comes at the door.

I hope it's Anna returning to see her patient. But Will walks in and takes a seat opposite.

"How's it going, Pad?" he asks the old man, nodding his head in my direction. Every time I see him now, I'm terrified he knows the truth, but so far – touch wood – Mia hasn't told him anything. In a way, I want him to find out. On the other, partly for his sake, but mainly for my own, I hope the secret stays safe. The uncertainty is certainly exhausting.

"How you feeling, Paddy?"

"Shite," comes the retort, as he nods towards the PEG and breathes through the mask.

"They did a good job there," Will adds, gesturing towards his belly.

"You think so?"

"I *know* so. Does it hurt?"

"Everything hurts, William, everything hurts..."

"Feeding time at the zoo, is it?" Will adds. Paddy smiles and falls asleep, his chest rattling loosely as he snores quietly between us. "How about you, Al – all good?"

"Not bad, you know. Same old same old..."

"Aye. D'you reckon I can close the window – it's so cold in here."

"But Paddy's burning up. Look at the sweat!" And Will examines Paddy's naked chest as I absently close the zip of my cardigan.

"You're right. Jesus Christ." He buttons his coat right to the top and whispers conspiratorially, "Has he asked you to kill him yet?"

This catches me unawares as Will's only been coming to see Paddy during the past month or so. I'm actually a bit jealous, but maybe I underestimated just how desperate Paddy is...

"No, he hasn't," I lie. I find lying has become easier recently.

"Well, I'm sure he will..."

"He's asked you?"

"Aye," Will admits reaching for the CD.

"What did you say?"

"I told him to forget it! I'm not prepared to lose my job, or my freedom for anyone, I'm afraid."

"But he's so ill."

"My heart bleeds for him, it really does, but if I'd help him that would be the end of my career, simple as that, even if I didn't get sent to jail..."

"Jail?"

"More than likely. They're still pretty strict about euthanasia and assisted suicide in this country. Where did he get this?" He holds up the CD.

"I picked it up for him today..."

"Fuckin' hell, you'd think Bono had enough cash without needing to resort to reading this kind of crap!"

Crap? Crap! My blood boils but my lips don't move... I change the subject...

"So... how's things at home by now?"

Will looks at the floor before answering.

"Alright, I suppose. At least we're talking, which is a start..."

"Good. I'm glad."

"That's all we're doing – and I mean *all* too... it's very tiring, draining even, between you and me. It's exhausting. I'm bloody knackered by the time we go to bed at night. We're having a trial run for three months, to see how it goes. Our relationship's a mess, but we're determined to work it out. Well, I am at least..."

"What about Sophie, does she know?"

"She's a bright kid so I'm sure she knows something's going on – I mean, I'm sleeping in the spare room so it's obvious that something's wrong..."

"Really?"

"Really. Mia's being a bit weird about that side of things. She says she can't trust me..."

"Why?"

"I don't know, but I'm going to be as patient as I need to be with her. There's no way I'm gonna lose her."

Silence descends, although it's never completely silent when Paddy's present. Will seems to fall into a trance.

"What time is it?" Will asks suddenly.

"Ten to seven," I say.

"Shit, I've gotta go..."

"What's the rush?"

"I'm picking Mia up from circuit training at seven."

Will gets to his feet, kisses Paddy on his forehead and offers me his hand.

"I'm sorry," he says, as we touch palms.

"For what?"

"For many things. But mainly for being such a twat over the years. I'm trying to change, Al, so bear with me, ok?"

Only one brother should be apologising here...

"Don't ever apologise to me again, Will? Never."

"Ok," he nods, "it's a deal." He moves forward and holds me tight. After he leaves, I sit down again in astonishment.

"He doesn't suspect a thing then..." Paddy's voice drags me back to the here and now.

"What are you talking about?"

"Don't play daft, son. You know what I'm on about. Your brother, he knows nothing of what happened here with you know who..."

"No. No he doesn't. Not yet anyway... Is there anyone you haven't asked to help you die, Paddy?"

But Paddy's eyes close and the snoring starts over. Although I doubt how genuine his slumber is, I leave the room in darkness, just in case.

Chapter 13: COMPLICATIONS

As I freewheel down Allensbank Road on my way home from work, the cool breeze somehow reminds me of school holidays. I glide towards the cemetery, past prematurely-peaking sunflowers and scantily-clad gardeners tending their front gardens.

I've taken this route home from work which avoids passing Will's house every day since I saw him last week, even though we both were glad to see each other. Maybe it's the white lie I told him about staying with Floyd which is making me guilty now.

My life is so uncomplicated at present that I'm enjoying myself and don't want to re-open old wounds by depending on Will too soon. I need to find my feet and anyway, he knows where to find me…

My life follows the same pattern every day, and that's essential for my wellbeing. I get up, get dressed and eat my breakfast in the company of my neighbours, the squirrels and birds, before cycling to work by eleven. I work until six before eating my supper and having a couple of pints with Floyd, return to base around seven to read and sleep and start again in the morning. Apart from a few necessary detours, I stick to my routine religiously. Every day I wake up with a smile on my face; a contented, free man's smile.

Absently watching three young nurses on their way home from the Heath, I snap back to life just in time to avoid an illegally-parked car on the bridge that crosses the dual carriageway. The Mac's greasy kitchen continues to spew its hideous odour into the air. Regardless of this, the pub car park is full.

Following the short cut through the woods, I lean my bike under the shed window and unlock the door. The day's heat gushes out as soon as I open it and I see Paddy sitting in my comfy chair reading an untitled, ancient-looking book, with one of those little battery-operated hand fans held to his face. I haven't got a clue where he gets hold of such things, but he must have a pretty good network of connections in the land of limbo…

Like me, Paddy spends the best part of every day in the pub. But he drinks beer all day and still manages to get home before me every night. There are some things in life that there's no point even trying to explain.

I've given the shed a good spring-clean by now and Floyd's removed a lot of his stuff. There's a carpet on the floor – nothing fancy, just some offcuts that Floyd had in his attic – which seems to keep the dust under control. Floyd's tools are still here, but they're stacked in one corner, while all his electrical equipment and designer gear has disappeared. In their place, there's a wardrobe, a comfy leather chair from Floyd's house, a camping stove, a fridge packed with food and drink and a stereo to play my CDs (which I borrow from the library). I even have a Jar-Jar Binks lampshade and a goldfish in a small tank I found while helping Floyd clear his stuff. I call him 'Joyce', and he greets me with a chorus of bubbles as I go to feed him. The place is quite cosy, like the home of a retired CDT teacher who's recently lost the plot. I still sleep on the camp bed, mainly because of the lack of space, but I often wake up at dawn curled up on my comfy chair.

Paddy ignores me as I take off my daps. My socks stink of mature cheese following hours of captive torture, and the trees beyond the open door whisper quietly in a soft breeze. I open the fridge and reach for a shocking red Bacardi Breezer, watermelon flavour, before pressing PLAY on the stereo, opening the blinds, kicking back in my comfy chair and quenching my thirst. Alcopops are the best kind of booze if you ask me. And *I know* that they're bad because they're aimed at youngsters blah blah blah, but as a latecomer to the whole scene I must admit I'm not overly keen on the taste of lager, bitter, stout or any kind of short. I could never admit this to my new drinking buddies down the Arches though. It's not that I'm scared of what they'd think of me either, it's just I don't want to draw attention to myself... I want to be accepted, not insulted, or yet worse, ignored.

I relax to the sounds of Gil Scott Heron. After absorbing some of the eternal wisdom of *The Revolution Will Not Be Televised*, I turn my attention to the pile of library books next to my half-empty bottle. Still being officially homeless, I had to persuade Floyd to join the library on my behalf.

"I've never joined a fuckin' library in my life and I don't want to start now" was his initial reaction, but it didn't take much to change his mind. Although it doesn't boast an impressive stock (the one in prison was better!), the library's an improvement on nothing, since Will stored all my belongings at the Big Yellow Storage on Penarth Road after our parents' house was cleared.

I'm reading *Brave New World* by Aldous Huxley at the moment and his foresight and vision is both amazing and ridiculous. So many of his predictions have come true by now that it's a bit like reading a novel written by Nostradamus. I'm fully engrossed so don't look up when I hear a sound like someone coughing nearby. Random noises are part and parcel of living in a battered old shed... in a cemetery... by a dual carriageway... in a city.

But when I hear a knock on the open door, I look up and almost faint. Mia! Make-up-less and completely stunning. She's a horrific flashback and all my fantasies rolled into one. My head's spinning and my heart's doing the Mashed Potato in fast forward. With a shaking hand I put the book on top of the pile and slowly get to my feet. Mia's wearing a tight white vest which emphasises her deep tan, and a long loose pink coloured skirt with a dark flower on her left thigh. Her clothes and the way her her hair cascades naturally over her shoulders give her a gypsy look, or that of a Southern Belle. She has transformed her style but not her ability to turn me on.

"All right, Al, I brought you this lot," she says, dragging a bulging black bin bag into the shed. "It's your post, three years' worth, probably more. It all gets forwarded to us…"

I attempt to swallow some dry spit, and hoarsely whisper my thanks. I struggle to make eye contact with the only woman I've ever loved physically. Unfortunately, Mia misinterprets the situation, believing that I'm being a bit off with her…

"Bollocks to this, Al!" she exclaims, looking at me with hands placed firmly on her hips. I grab my Breezer and take a gulp, which lubricates the larynx and liberates my vocal chords.

"What?" I manage to ask.

"This! This… I don't know what to call it. Awkwardness, I s'ppose. I won't have it, Al, not now. Come here." But when I don't move an inch, mainly due to my legs not working properly, she glares at me, her eyes ablaze. "Now!"

I eventually step towards her and we hug like long lost friends. Being this close to Mia feels both uncomfortable and completely right. I'd forgotten how different girls, women, smell – like a Timotei advert crossed with a box of Jelly Babies – especially after smelling nothing but beer and fags for the past month or so. But although I still feel *something* for Mia, I don't think it's a physical thing anymore.

After unlocking from the embrace, we stand there in silence just staring at each other. Something subtle about her has changed since I last saw her this close. Maybe she's matured from a girl to a real woman during the years I've been away. She's certainly more comfortable in her own skin, and 'natural' is a vast improvement on the 'high class hooker' look she was sporting a few years ago. Suddenly she holds my sweaty hand.

"It's good to see you, Al, it really is." With a beautiful smile, she adds, "You look well. A bit skinny, but better than I expected…"

"What did Will say about me?"

"He said, and this is word for word: he's seen more meat on an Englishman's cock."

"Well, there's no point denying it," I say, looking down at my lean arms and skinny fingers.

"I've wanted to come and see you, to explain, since I saw you watching us by the lake that night..." I snatch my hand from her grasp, which wipes the smile form her face. Now it's her turn to be confused.

"I thought things were good between you and Will?"

"They are." She scrunches her forehead. "What the hell are you on about?"

"I don't know... what do you *want* then? After last time, I don't think it's a good idea for you to..."

"I haven't come here to fuck you, Al! Jeezus Christ, what's wrong with you? You're all so fuckin' clueless!" She shakes her head and adds, "I've got something to tell you." She looks away as I struggle with my embarrassment. "Does that thing work?" she asks, nodding at the behemoth of a television which dominates the room. I shrug my shoulders.

"I have no idea, actually, I've never even turned it on."

"Are you serious? Why not, I mean, you can hardly ignore it in here."

"Well, that's pretty much what I've done. There's more to life than television..."

"Try telling that to my kids – I don't know what I'd do without the Teletubbies and Thomas the Tank. I'd probably have to drug them or something."

I offer her my chair and grab a couple of Breezers from the fridge, before sitting on the chair that Paddy's recently vacated.

"Bit girlie isn't it, Al?" She giggles as she accepts the bottle and takes a swig.

"Maybe, but it's better than a can of bitter or Bow, isn't it?"

"You're right there. Cheers!"

We raise our bottles in a toast.

"How did you find me then? I lied to Will about where I was staying..."

"I know you did. And you know you can stay with us..."

"Thanks, but I don't... I feel... you know..."

"I do, but all that's in the past now... ish."

"So tell me then."

"Oh, yeah, of course. Well, you told Will you lived with Floyd, it is Floyd isn't it?"

"Yes."

"So I went to the Arches looking for you first, but thought if I didn't find you I'd ask him. Will reckons he's in there every day..."

"Pretty much."

"Anyway, I ask the barman, some fat middle-aged slimeball..."

"John, the manager."

"Really? God, you'd have thought he'd never seen a woman in that place..."

"Half of them haven't, not one like you anyway," and I blush as I blurt this out.

"Don't be creepy, Al, you're turning into one of them."

"I do work there every day."

"I know, but just because you work on a farm, doesn't mean you have to shag sheep. Anyway, I eventually get directions to Floyd's house from some bloke called Jason. Bit thick, but harmless enough. He was slurring his words and couldn't stop staring at my tits. So off I go to Floyd's; knock on the door. After waiting ages while he hides something I reckon cos I could hear him moving stuff around inside, he answers the door in his pants. I could smell the weed from the doorway. It stank so much he must have been doing hot-knives in there, and his eyes were as red as tomatoes. He's got a stupid grin on his face when he sees me, as if I've called round for his pleasure or something: home help or whatever. Anyway, he invites me in for a drink, but I refuse. Instead, I explain the situation, who I am, why I'm there etc and he just looks confused. Long story short, I ask if I can speak to you and he says 'of course you can but you'll have to shout as he lives about four miles away'. Eventually, he tells me where you are and about the shortcut and here I am. A right fuckin' palaver thank you very much!"

"Sorry."

"Why did you lie to us, Al?"

I consider my words carefully before answering. "I didn't want

Will's pity or charity... I don't know. I live in a shed, Mia, that's the bottom line."

"You don't have to be ashamed."

"I'm not ashamed, it's just... well... I'm happy here. Life's uncomplicated, simple..."

"Well you should have told him the truth..."

"I know." The silence returns. I drain my bottle, pop the cap off another and try my best not to look at her chest. Although our relationship seems to have become platonic, I can't help but appreciate her beauty.

"What have you got to tell me then?"

"What?" Mia asks absently.

"You said you had something to tell me..."

"I do, yes. Right..." This is obviously more serious than I thought, as she seems stressed. She furrows her forehead until it's as crinkled as a McCoy crisp. "I don't know where to begin. Well, I want to apologise, that goes without saying..."

"For what?"

"For using you. For... you know..."

"Please don't apologise, it was my fault as much as anyone's."

"No, Al, it *wasn't*. I used you to get at Will, but I know the whole episode fucked your family up..."

"Mia, stop! Please stop. If that night hadn't happened..."

"Don't say it."

"Ok, I won't... Why did you tell them, Mia?" Tears well in the corner of her eyes.

"It just got to me, that's all. I was feeling soooo guilty, you wouldn't believe..."

"Trust me, I would."

"Of course, sorry, I should have..."

"Don't worry."

"After our little fling, things gradually got better between Will and me but not without the help of some serious antidepressants. I was confused, emotional, upset, borderline hysterical. Fucked up. Seriously. Will changed during that time. I mean, we both did obviously, but especially Will. He stopped being such a wanker, he stopped hanging out with his dickhead mates, took care of Sophie, loved me like he'd never loved me before. He admitted he'd cheated on me but I held off telling him about us because of who you were, and then it was too late. We were getting on better, getting on very well, he was happy, I was happy, and then you did what you did and everything fell apart…"

"So it's my fault?"

"No, not at all. Although you did play your part, young man!" She smiles. "We were all in a state of shock on New Year's Day around your parents' house. Everyone was confused and it occurred to me: how could I go on living this lie when Will had been so honest? How can you start afresh when there are secrets festering that could come back to haunt you in the future? I realised that to make a clean start, a proper one, I'd have to muddy the water. I had to tell him. I had no choice."

"But you didn't have to tell my parents."

"I know, I know, the timing wasn't the best, but I was a mess and out it came. I'm sorry."

"Don't apologise," I repeat. "As I said, if that night hadn't happened, you'd still be talking to a virgin by here…"

"If that night hadn't happened…"

"But it did happen."

"I know." She falls silent again before the tears start flowing. I get up from my chair and kneel next to her, embracing her tightly.

"There's something else, Al," she admits without moving her chin from my shoulder.

"Tell me," I insist, confident that the worse is already behind us.

"You," she begins, "I mean, *we've* got a daughter."

And that's it, the end of my simple life. Over. Kaput. Finito. Slowly, I peel myself away from her, and that's where we pause – her crying uncontrollably and me in muted incredulity – for a long time. Is this good news, or the worst of my life? At last, Mia stops crying, while I manage to keep it all in. For now. I try to clear my mind. Why did she need to tell me at all? Ignorance is bliss, after all. Lauren has already got a father, and a sister and a Mam… and even an uncle, although she's never met him. And now she never will…

"How... Why..."

"You know how, Al, so I won't answer that..."

"But why?"

"Why what?"

"Why tell me? Why now? I thought things were sorted between you and Will."

"They are, Al, they are..."

"But they won't be if he finds out about this!" I bellow. Mia turns away in tears again.

"I thought you'd be happy, I felt you deserved to know."

"Happy! How can I be happy about something that'll break my brother's heart... again. We've done it once before, and I swore I'd never do it again."

"But she's *your* daughter, Al, she's *yours*, not his."

"I know, I know, but so what. I just wish you hadn't told me, that's all..."

"You selfish prick! Don't be so fuckin' ridiculous," she shouts. "This is your daughter we're talking about, not hearing the football scores before you watch Match of the Day!" I realise Mia's been carrying this burden for years with no one to confide in. I understand she isn't pressurising me to confess to Will, but just sharing the load with the only other person that *should* know the truth.

"Sorry, Mia. Please look at me." She turns towards me. "I'm sorry, it's a bit of a shock that's all." She smiles weakly.

"A bit of a shock?" We laugh.

"Yes, ok, quite a big one. Massive if you want the truth. What now though, what about Will?"

"Dunnow really, I suppose it's up to you. I've lived with this for so long it just feels good to share it with someone..."

"No one else knows?"

"Not a soul."

"So we keep it that way... for the time being at least. I've got to do some serious thinking about this one..."

She gets to her feet and grabs some kitchen roll from the windowsill. Wiping her eyes, she aims for the door, but turns to face me once again. I get up and go to her, and we hug again.

"I'm sorry to dump all this on you, but I had to," she whispers in my ear, which causes the hair on the back of my neck to stand to attention. "You had to know..."

"I know, I know, but please don't apologise, it's great news... sort of." But if I was lucky, those words would never need to have been spoken. If I was lucky, the fateful fumbling wouldn't have happened in the first place. If I was honest, I'd tell her that I was devastated. Once again she is threatening to wreck my fragile relationship with Will. Not to mention her marriage to him. She didn't need to tell me anything. I didn't want to know and now I find myself in another complicated situation. I'm sure that sounds selfish, but I live in a shed and work in a pub, cash in hand. I'm hardly what you'd call 'dad material'. Lauren's happy with Will as her father and what Mia's just told me has the potential to ruin her life as much as everyone else's. I don't want to lose my family all over again. She's shared the weight and now I have the power to ruin her life, Will's life, and the girls' all over again. What *should* I do? What *will* I do? Nothing for the time being, that's for sure. Think about things for a little while... or maybe even forever.

"We'll see you soon, ok Al. You should call over, Will would love that..."

"Not if I tell him the news."

"No, obviously, but you should come over... there's someone else you should meet."

"That's too weird to even think about, Mia."

"I know, sorry. But don't be a stranger, ok." And I nod weakly, refusing to commit to anything. Mia leaves and as I watch her disappear into the darkness I don't lust after her at all. Our relationship has developed way past those kinds of instincts in the last hour.

I lean on the door frame for a little while, staring into oblivion. Paddy's already sitting in my comfy chair, shaking his head slowly. He was there the night Lauren was conceived, and he's here on the night when the truth was revealed.

Chapter 14: GREEN LIGHT

The stairs of my home seem steeper than ever. I'm carrying a tray of food up to Paddy's room. As his condition deteriorates, sitting by his bedside feels more like a burden. Breathing is such an effort for him that he finds it difficult to even hold a conversation. Our chats are a little one sided. I hate hearing my own voice echoing in his room's icy atmosphere. But more than that, I hate seeing him having to depend on his oxygen mask even to whisper a sentence. I still want to soak up all his wisdom and hear about his experiences before his innings comes to an end. But I don't want to put him under any more strain. I hate to see him fade before my eyes when I've only just got to know him.

Will appears before me on the landing, his long black leather coat as dark as a bat's wing in a deep cavern. I join him, placing the tray precariously on the oak banister's square angle.

"Alright, Al?"

"Ok. You?"

"Aye. Just dropped in to see what condition his condition was in…"

I smile at my brother's *Big Lebowski* reference and ask, "How's he doing?"

"Not too good really," Will whispers. "He's more fucked up every time I see him... and he's starting to turn yellow, have you noticed?"

I nod. "I know. Something to do with his liver? It's so unfair..."

"You're right. Look, Al, I gotta go, I'm in a bit of a rush like..."

"Oh. Where you going?"

"Swimming. With Sophie."

"Swimming?"

"I know, I know... I've never done anything like it before, but I'm determined to change. It's about time."

"Brownie points, is it?"

"Something like that. Sharing the burden. The responsibility. Being a better dad. You know what I mean..."

"No. Actually I don't." He smiles wanly. "How's things with Mia by now?" I blush.

"Not bad, but not great either. One day at a time and all that, you know." I nod. "Anyway, I'm off. See you soon..."

"Alright. See you." I lift the tray with its proper winter fare – sausage casserole with mash – and Will disappears downstairs.

Paddy seems to be asleep, but when my chair groans as I sit down, his eyes – which are also yellowing – open, and he gives me a cheeky little welcoming smile.

Placing the tray carefully on my lap, I zip my cardigan until it tickles my Adam's apple. I notice the layer of sweat clinging to my grandfather's paisley-packaged skeleton. I eat my supper to the oompa band of Paddy's chest and uneven panting.

Having finished my meal, I reach for a pad of A4 paper and hand it, along with a biro, to Paddy. He looks at me, eyebrows raised.

"I want you to write down what you want for Christmas, ok? Books, CDs, anything. You name it and I'll get it for you. It's only a couple of weeks away now, and I've left it 'til the last minute as usual. I hate shopping so I keep putting it off, putting it off, anything to delay the inevitable."

This Christmas promises to be busier than usual, with Paddy in residence and Will and his family also coming for lunch. My festering guilt is trying to talk me into buying my brother something extravagant, while common sense tells me not to show myself up.

Paddy hands me the pad which he's been scribbling on. I read his infantile scrawl:

There's only one thing I want from you this Christmas...

"I know that, Paddy." Our eyes meet for the first time tonight. "I'd *really* like to help you... I mean, I hate seeing you like this. I know how you must feel and I..." He takes a long suck on his oxygen mask and asks, "You know how I feel do you, Al?" Of course I don't *know* how he feels. He takes another drag of oxygen, "Do you know how it feels to have your own son wipe the shite off your body while being unable to move from your bed?" Another hit. "Do you know how it feels to lie here, all day, all night, do you?" And another. "This is my life, Al! This is my existence! Do you really *know* how it feels?" As he sucks more air and begins to calm down, I try to hold back the tears.

"No, I don't. Sorry Paddy."

"I know you don't, Al. It's your help that I need, son, not your pity."

"I know, I know, but I don't think I can..." And the old man nods his head in understanding and disappointment. After another lengthy intake of oxygen, he starts to rant a little, "Six months ago I was working on my allotment without a care in the world. That little piece of land was my salvation after your gran died. It kept me active; body, mind and soul. At least that's what I thought until everything unravelled." He talks in a high-speed whisper. "Since being bedridden, I can't stop thinking about her. Your gran, that is. I miss her so much, Alan, she was a truly great woman." He fills his lungs, "I've got nothing left to live for and I'm expecting the results for this oesopha-thingy-me-bob of mine any day now. More bad news. Guaranteed. Anyway, I just want to go quietly, in my sleep or wide-awake I don't care, as long as I go. Now I'm not even sure if I believe in the afterlife and I'm pretty sure I'll never see her there even if such a place *does* exist,

I'm not *that* gullible." He sucks air again. "But you see, Al, I'd rather be *there* looking for her than *here* just thinking about her…" He's so spent he falls asleep. This is our relationship these days – unfinished conversations and silence where once there was a spark.

I sit and watch him, attempting to imagine how he feels. Failing, I turn to a collection of poetry by Jim Dodge which Paddy's been reading recently. I reach for the book from a pile on his bedside table, and it falls open on a page with its top left corner tucked in.

The acceptance of death
Clear down in our hearts
Is the faith we bring to life
That love may go on

Returning to the kitchen, I feed Dwdi although I know he's already had his supper. As I scrape the meat and gravy into his little silver bowl, I keep on considering Paddy's words. I know he's in serious pain and I know I could help him reach Paradise. But even though I can see he's suffering, something holds me back. It is my parents' opinion of the whole situation that's stopping me helping Paddy. That and what the Good Book has to say about it. Not to mention that I'm a bit of a coward…

I leave the kitchen in darkness and head for the attic to see if Paddy's unfortunate situation can inspire some poetry. After all, don't the best poems stem from the darkest corners?

I aim for the lounge to say good night to my parents, but pause at the entrance, which is slightly ajar, and listen to their loudly-whispered conversation rising above the crackle of the open fire.

"So you haven't said anything to him yet?"

"No, I haven't. That's your responsibility, don't you think, Brian?"

"Yes, well, maybe…"

"*Maybe*! He's your father, you know that?"

"Of course I do. But I just don't know where to start… I think the news could send him over the edge…"

"Don't say that!"

"But it's what we both believe could happen, and remember, the cancer they've found is already showing signs of spreading…"

My mother starts crying, but my father carries on as if he's just glad to be getting it off his chest.

"It's in his oesophagus now, and the doctor said it's already gone to his stomach…"

"At least the end will come sooner rather than later…" Mam manages to say between sobs.

"They can't even guarantee *that*, Gwen. Not in any way. These things can take months… years even…"

"Don't say that."

"But that's the truth, Gwen. That's the way it is. He's suffered so much already; it sickens me to think that the worse is still to come…"

"What are you trying to say, Brian?"

My father pauses. "You know exactly what I'm saying, Gwen."

"Yes. Yes, I do…" Paddy's suspicions were right: the cancer has arrived. But hearing my father claim that the worse is still ahead of him is somehow worse. Hasn't Paddy already suffered enough?

I climb the stairs. My parents' conversation has cleared any doubts I had about my decision.

By helping Paddy, I'll be helping everyone…

Chapter 15: DEBT, DOUBT & DESPERATION

The morning's unnaturally intense heat saps my energy before the day's even started. There are five letters lying on the worktop by the sink. After twelve hours, over a period of four days, the task is at an end. But all I feel is anxiety. I've sorted through and read over six hundred letters but only five remain of any relevance.

The first is the latest statement from HSBC which informs me that I have less than a tenner in my current account. Obviously, that's not the best news, but compared to the other four pieces of correspondence, it's like winning the lottery. The second letter tells me that I owe the Inland Revenue six thousand seven hundred and ninety-three pounds in back-taxes and invites me, in a friendly tone, to contact them to resolve the situation. I have no idea where the debt came from, but I heard enough stories on the inside of what can happen to take the threat seriously. The letter was sent to me almost three months ago, when I was still locked up. The third, on pink paper, accuses me of 'ignoring' the earlier letter! In it, the Inland Revenue insists that I contact them as soon as possible to discuss the debt. *If you do not contact us before the aforementioned date* (4 July – two weeks ago) *you will be summoned to appear in court to answer the charges brought against you.*

The fourth letter is a court order setting a date for my court appearance (8 August – less than three weeks away) and explaining that I still have time to clear the debt and postpone my trial for an indefinite period.

The fifth, from the Inland Revenue's 'Collection Department' (aka Bailiffs and Heavy Mob), states that failure to be present in court on the 8 August will lead to bailiffs coming for me... at Will's address. Failure to pay the debt will also lead to the 'repossession of goods worth up to and including the amount due by the Inland Revenue Collection Department or an outsourced collection company'.

Failure to pay with either money or belongings will lead me straight back to jail... without passing Go. If I don't pay the debt within twenty-one days, I'll be back with Knocker quicker than you can say 'life sentence no parole'. Considering that I intend never to return to jail, I'm left with only one option: paying. My next problem: finding the money, leading to another problem, and another, then another. Since finding out about my 'debt', my new status as Lauren's father has taken a bit of a back seat. I still think it'd be best for everyone if I kept quiet about it all, but one thing's for sure; my simple life is already a distant memory.

I don't know who to turn to for help, except maybe Floyd and Will, but first of all I'm going to phone the Inland Revenue to explain my situation and hopefully come to some kind of agreement. I close the blinds and lock the door behind me, leaving Paddy snoozing lazily. With the letters in my pocket, I pedal slowly towards the Arches, as if the weight of my worries are dragging on the road behind me.

The day, like any quiet day in a public house when your head's full of worry, moves slowly. As the clock ticks towards four, the bottom bar is completely empty for the first time today. Apart from Paddy who sits in his usual place smoking and drinking. I decide to take advantage of the situation and call the Inland Revenue. Although I'm hoping that this is all just a big mistake, my heart's pounding.

The public phone is situated at the end of the bar, next to the jukebox, so I don't even have to leave my post. I set the letters in front of me, with the latest one on top of the pile, and dial the Collection Department's number. A female voice answers, and things quickly go downhill from that very moment... I'd forgotten that a secretary's main function is to defend her particular department from the public and to be as vague and unhelpful as possible... especially at the Inland Revenue.

"Collections, how can I help?"

"My name's Alun Brady..."

"Yes."

"My name's Alun Brady..."

"Mr Brady, yes."

"I've got a letter in front of me here threatening me with court action, repossession and jail if I don't pay my debt to the Inland Revenue. I think there's been some mistake..."

"Is it from this department, Mr Brady?"

"One of them is, yes."

"And what does it say?"

"I just told you!" I exclaim, feeling my fingers tighten around my glass, setting the ice clinking.

"Can you repeat that please, Mr Brady?"

"Apparently," I breathe heavily, "I owe almost seven thousand pounds and have been threatened with court action, repossession and jail if I fail to settle the debt."

"That's right."

"What? That's it?"

"Yes, I have your details on my screen in front of me here now. Mr Alun Brady, you owe six thousand seven hundred and ninety-three pounds exactly. Back taxes between nineteen ninety-two and two thousand and one. It says here you didn't pay the correct amount during these years. You were probably entered into the wrong category where you worked..."

"So it's someone else's fault, not mine?"

"No. It's *your* debt, Mr Brady, no one else's. Tax is taken directly from your paycheques, and even though the initial mistake was made by someone else, probably the accounts manager at the firm you worked for, you still received your income without paying all your taxes…"

"But that can't be right, I didn't even know."

"I'm sorry, Mr Brady, there's nothing else I can say. That's the situation according to our records."

"But, but… is there someone else I can talk to? I need to explain…" I hope she can hear the desperation in my voice, but I have forgotten I'm talking to a seriously icy individual.

"No, there's no one here you can talk to…"

"No one?"

"That's right. It's standard procedure, Mr Brady. You owe us a lot of money, and considering that you've been ignoring our correspondence this is the only way left to deal with you…"

"I haven't been ignoring anything!"

"Mr Brady, you were contacted over two months ago…"

"But I only received the letter four days ago, I've been away…"

"Work or leisure?"

"Neither."

"What then?"

"Jail," I whisper.

"Oh!" she exclaims, showing a brief moment of emotion at last. "Unfortunately, Mr Brady, you'll be going back there shortly if you don't pay your debt!"

"Are you serious? That's not even close to being fair. How can I *ignore* something that I didn't even know existed?"

"I'm sorry, Mr Brady, I'm afraid there's nothing I can do to help. You might want to contact the CAB though…"

"The who?"

"The Citizens' Advice Bureau on Charles Street in town, although I'm pretty sure they'll tell you exactly what I've just said."

I slam the phone down and grab the glass with the intention of throwing it against the nearest wall. But, I feel light-headed so I put the glass back on the bar and lean against it, breathing heavily.

I leave the pub as soon as John appears from upstairs to relieve me of my duties, and aim my bike towards Roath Park Lake. Within a few minutes I'm leaning it against the veranda of Will's house. It looks more like a bungalow from the outside and has a wooden façade, with the veranda stretching around the front third of the building, offering a spectacular view over the lake.

Will's Merc is parked in front of the garage at the back, leaving enough space to park at least another two cars at the side of the house. There's a trampoline in the front garden and kids toys scattered everywhere. The house is painted sky blue, with white borders around the windows and doors. Somehow, it seems to be a happy home, although I have the power to change all that.

I ring the bell and step back, enjoying the coolness provided by the shade at the side. I can hear movement and feel a mixture of nervousness, awkwardness, fear and quiet confidence that Will will agree to help me restore my life to its simple state. The door is opened eventually by Will, wearing one of those comedy aprons with a fat woman's body in a bikini on it. He seems resentful, and instead of the warm welcome I was expecting, my brother just stands there in silence, staring at me.

"Alright Will?"

"What do you want?" He doesn't try to mask his indifference. I step back and look closely at his face.

"Just a quick word. A favour…"

"A favour!" he guffaws. "I'm busy."

"Please Will, it's really important." Sighing heavily, he invites me in. Georgeous cooking smells are coming from the kitchen. The house is a combination of expensive furniture (I recognise some from my parents' home) and colourful toys. In the hall I spot the 'The Shepherd' hanging by three photos of Will and me when we were kids – one of us on our BMXs, one of us dressed as cowboys and another of us in Legoland. This trilogy of memories was a present from me a few Christmases ago. I'm quite touched to see it at all, as I'd imagined Will would have burned it after Mia's confession.

"I'm cooking tea for the girls. Mia's picking them up from soft play or something, so sit down by there and say what you've got to say, ok?"

"Thanks," I say, but when I pull a chair from under the kitchen table, I find Dwdi asleep on it already. I smile and bend down to stroke him, amazed that he's managed to grow fatter since the last time I saw him. I didn't think that was physically possible. When Dwdi starts to purr, I'm glad that at least one member of my family's pleased to see me.

"What d'you want then Al?" Will asks crouching to the oven. My brother's attitude confuses me, but I decide to get straight to the point so I can get out of here as soon as possible. After all, it's quite obvious Will doesn't want me here.

"I'm in a bit of trouble..."

"Trouble?" He faces me with a ladel in one hand and a saucepan in the other. "What kind of trouble?"

"Well," I begin, as Will returns to his cooking, giving me the chance to look around the room. The kitchen is huge. It has a trendy, yet practical, slate floor, chocolate-coloured cabinets and chrome everywhere. It reflects Will's wealth and Mia's tastes. The cabinets and units dominate two whole walls; the oven, SMEG fridge (covered in childish paintings and magnetic letters) and washing machines line up against another wall, while the other is home to numerous coats and bags hanging untidily on unseen hooks. Above the coats there's a nice professional photo of our parents. I wonder if the picture was there before they died? The room's at the back corner of the house, the back garden directly in front, beyond some patio doors. The back garden is Japanese in style with low-growing Acers, wooden walkways across a network of ponds (which are undoubtedly home to numerous Koi Carp), various Eastern statues, buried spotlights and one of those double swing-chairs in the far corner under the weeping willow, "money troubles, to tell you the truth."

Will doesn't appear to hear what I've said. He doesn't even look at me. He carries on stirring the saucepan's contents. I just sit there, stroking Dwdi's fat belly. Eventually, Will reacts.

"Why are you telling me this?"

"Because I need your help or I'll get sent back to jail..."

"Help? You're 'avin' a fuckin' laugh!" His back is still turned.

"What are you on about, Will? You said that all I had to do was ask..."

"Yes, well, that was then, this is now."

"What? I don't understand... what's changed since then?" It dawns on me that maybe he knows the truth about Lauren...

"How much money do you owe?"

"Seven grand." Will sucks air through his teeth.

"To who?"

"Inland Revenue."

"Bastards." He faces me at last.

"Too right! Back taxes since '92, apparently..."

"Have you phoned them?"

"Yes."

"And?"

"And nothing. I've got three weeks to cough up or they're taking me to court, sending me to jail and sending the bailiffs..."

"Bailiffs?"

"Yep."

"What's the point of that – you haven't got anything..."

"I know that. That's why I'll be going back to jail."

After a short silence, Will comes to a stupefying conclusion.

"Hang on! Where will the bailiffs go?"

"No idea..." I lie, knowing exactly what's on his mind. He turns towards me once again, furrowing his forehead.

"Here, Al!" he spits. "Fuck! This is where your post gets delivered. *This* is where the bailiffs'll come." In fact, I'm not registered as living here – it's just this is where my post gets redirected. Still, I'm not going to tell Will that since he's more likely to help me if he thinks his own property might be under threat. "You stupid little prick, Al. How the fuck did you manage this?"

"It's not my fau..."

"No, of course it isn't. Sorry for doubting you. This is so fuckin typical. Jeezuz Al, what's the matter with you? You haven't got a clue have you? Not a fuckin clue!"

"I need your help, Will, not a lecture." He stares at me in disgust.

"No, *Al*, it's not help that you need, but a lesson. It's about time you learnt to stand on your own two feet. Long overdue if you ask me. You were always a mummy's boy. You're fuckin pathetic, look at you!" I can't believe what I'm hearing. He was so happy to see me a few weeks ago.

"But Will..."

"But nothing, Al. I can't believe this. You won't be happy until this family's ruined, will you? Again!"

"Why're you acting like this?"

"She came to see you, didn't she?"

"Who?"

"Who the fuck d'you think? Mia, of course."

Well, at least that kind of confirms that he knows nothing about the other 'thing'.

"So that's the reason you're..."

"Just answer the question, Casanova!"

"Yes, yes she did," I admit, after all, I've got nothing to hide. Well, almost nothing... "She bought my post over the other night..."

"Was there anything *extra* in her bag?"

"What does that mean?"

"You know exactly what I mean, you prick!"

"Mia came to drop my post off the other night. That's it. If you want to know the truth, we talked about you and the girls most of the time..."

"Yeah-yeah," he says, turning his back on me again.

"Look, Will, that's the truth. And anyway, what was all that stuff you said about forgiving and forgetting the other night?"

"I wasn't completely honest with you..."

"What?"

"I realise now that one can't exist without the other..."

"*What?*"

"Forgive *and* forget, Al. Both have to be in order for everything to be ok. You have to forgive *and* forget..."

"And?"

"I told you I'd forgiven you for what you did but I could never forget... I mean, the image is always there whenever I close my eyes... I can't just forgive *and* forget."

"But you said…"

"I know what I said. I *was* happy to see you, but now… well… I'm not so sure. Sorry Al, but that's the way it is." And just like that, Will changes back to the person he was years ago. I'm gutted, and even Dwdi leaves me as he waddles towards the back garden. He has shattered all my hopes.

"I thought out of the two of us, it was you that had changed the most," I pick my words carefully, "First of all, I've lost my faith. But listening to you refuse me just now on top of everything else I've suffered in the last four years just ices the cake! There is no God, because if there was, you wouldn't treat me like this. You see, *brother*, it's me that's changed. Not you. You haven't changed at all." This makes him turn around once more.

"If you've lost your faith, Al," he points at me with a wooden spoon. "And if you've changed so much, why the fuck are you wearing that cross around your neck – to welcome Jesus on his second coming?"

"Don't be so sick!"

"Why then?"

"It was a present…" My answer makes him smile slyly, like a hit-man acting friendly before fulfilling his contract.

"Oh yes, I remember now. It belonged to Paddy, didn't it? What did you do, Al, snatch it from his still-warm corpse?"

I shake my head sadly.

"You haven't changed at all!" I shout. "You're as nasty and selfish as you ever were! Once a wanker, always a wanker! And anyway, what right have you got to judge me? What right have you got to refuse to help me? I was the loyal one. Not you! I was true to Mam and Dad. Not you! I was…"

"Shut up, Al, you're being pathetic. You lost all your rights when you did what you did…" But what's he referring to here – Paddy, Mia or Lauren?

"What d'you mean?"

"Are you serious?" He shakes his head. "You fucked my wife, and now I'm fucking you. How does it feel, Al?"

"You're just like the old Will!" I struggle to my feet and stumble towards the back door. I need to get out of here. I get to the door and breathe deeply, turn back to Will. He shrugs and shakes his head again, and I'm about to tell him about Lauren's real father, just for revenge, but he says, "I'm a shit brother, Al, what can I say? Always have been, always will. Mam and Dad forgave you, but I don't think I can. I'm sorry... *brother*."

I turn away as the tears flow. I walk down the drive with one hand against the wall as my head spins. I lean on my bike and ride out the storm. Calming down, I straddle the saddle and aim towards Lake Road West. But, before I reach the pillars at the bottom of the drive, a car turns in and I break hard. Although my bike doesn't touch the car, my body glides forward, crashing my balls straight into the handlebars. The wind goes from my stomach as if I were a boxless-batsman taking a full-toss to his middle stump. Then I come face to face with Mia, Sophie and Lauren.

All three of them are staring straight at me as I writhe in agony in front of them. I'm aware of what a mess I must look – cupping my sack with tears streaming down my face.

Mia mouths "Are you ok?" through the windscreen, but I'm far from it. Sophie's sat in the passenger seat, but I'm not looking at her today. My eyes are glued on little Lauren in a carseat in the middle of the back. Peering at her through the reflections on the glass, I remember that my parents told me that I too insisted on sitting in the middle of the back seat when I was young, in order to get an unobscured view of the journey. Mia is still gesturing at me from behind the wheel, but I don't take any notice of her. Instead, I start shuffling along between the car and the hedge, nudging my way slowly towards the road.

When I reach the car's back window, I bend down to get a good look at Lauren. She turns to face me and our eyes lock for an instant. Staring into Lauren's eyes is like looking into a mirror, and I can clearly see myself and Mia within her, as well as some of my mother's features. I hear the car door open so I start pedalling away before Mia gets to ask any questions.

By the time I reach the Arches, my heart has regained its natural rhythm. I leave my bike in the usual place and ignore a few friendly 'alrights' from some of the locals who are sat outside, enjoying the early evening sunshine. I'm so wound up after my clash with Will that when I find Floyd propping up the bar, I can hardly speak. He looks at me through bloodshot eyes as I lean heavily beside him.

"You ok, Al?" he asks, and I nod. "You look fucked, mate. Where have you been, eating supper's not the same without you." He adds with a warm smile.

"Will's," I manage. "Can I have a word?"

"Of course. Me and Jase were about to do one in the car park..."

"In private," I say, which makes them both look a little awkward.

"Ok," Floyd says after a short pause. "I'll give you a shout in a minute, all right Jase?"

"Aye," says Jase, turning back to his pint sheepishly.

I head outside and wait for Floyd by Jack Brown's locked entrance. Floyd lights his spliff as he walks towards me, pulling hard to get the embers glowing. His skin's as burnt as a well done T-Bone after another day in the sun. He looks at me oddly.

"What's going on, Al? I've never seen you so wound up..."

"I'm in trouble, Floyd. Big time."

"Go on," he invites me to explain, while spitting a stray piece of tobacco on the floor.

"I'm in debt and I've got nowhere else to go," I pause. "I don't know how to do this..."

"Just ask, mate, just ask."

"OK... I need seven grand in two weeks time or it's back to jail for me."

Floyd looks at me and whistles.

"Jeezus," he says at last. "Who d'you owe it to?"

"The Inland Revenue."

"Bastards, fuckin' bastards... Is it definite?"

"It is," I confirm, and pass him the letters to scan.

"Can you help me?"

"Yes and no."

"What do you mean?"

"Well, I can't lend you that sort of money cos I ain't got that sort of money. It's all tied up in this an' that if you knows what I mean…"

"So what are you saying?"

"Well, I can't *give* it to you but I can offer you the opportunity to *earn* it…"

"In two weeks? That's impossible!"

"In one day, mate, in *one day*…"

"How?" I ask, although in truth I don't really want to know. You can only earn money like that by breaking the law, or being a professional footballer, and I don't think Floyd's about to offer me a contract with Cardiff City.

"Look, if you're interested – and I don't think you've got much choice here, have you? – I'm having a business meeting at my house the day after tomorrow. You should come up, listen to what's on offer and make up your mind. No pressure, like, but I think you'll like what you hear. It'll sort your financial troubles out, no worries."

"OK," I agree. "But if I come I'm not committed to anything, right?"

"Absofuckinlutely," he confirms, and with a big smile on his face he offers me the smoke.

"No thanks, Floyd, not now…" although the herb's sweet smell is tempting. "I've got far too much going on in my head…"

"More for me then," he says, sucking greedily.

"What about Jase?"

"Fuck Jase, he's just a fuckin' scav! He never buys his own…"

"Look Floyd, I have to go. I've got a lot to think about…"

"Well, don't think *too* hard now. But Al, there is one thing…"

"What?"

"You should call your parole officer too. He might be able to help."

"Good idea," I agree. "I will…"

After a horrendous night of tossing and turning, sweating and worrying, I phone my parole officer at precisely nine a.m. from the phone box opposite Cathays Library. The kiosk's outer shell is practically covered in puke, and although the diced kebab hasn't penetrated the inner sanctum, unfortunately for me the smell has, so I pull my T-shirt over my nose to keep it at bay.

"Can I speak to Bruce Robertson, please?" I ask, retching.

"I'm sorry, sir," the secretary answers politely. "Bruce is away on holiday at the moment. Can I ask who's calling, please?"

On his hols! His jollies! Not now, surely...

"My name's Alun Brady, he's my parole officer..."

"Mr Brady, yes, he's been trying to get in touch with you. He wanted to meet you before he went away. He left a message for you with a Mr Fortune..."

"Who?"

"Mr Fortune, Floyd Fortune."

"I didn't get the message, I'm afraid," I say, smiling at my friend's fantastic surname.

"Not to worry, Mr Brady, I'll make a note of your call and make sure Bruce contacts you as soon as he returns."

"When will that be?"

"Let me just check for you... a week yesterday, Mr Brady, he'll be back in the office next Tuesday and I'll make sure he comes to see you the following day, OK?"

"Thank you. Can you please tell him it's very urgent? It's very important that I see him as soon as possible..."

"Of course, Mr Brady, I'll make a note of that. Where can he find you? It says here the caretaker's shed at Cathays Cemetery. Is that correct?"

"Yes," I confirm. "That's right. If he can come as early as possible I'd be grateful. I won't be there from quarter-to-eleven onwards, though; can you tell him that?"

"I can, I'll make sure he comes just after nine. Will that be OK?"

"Yes, yes it will. Thank you..."

"No problem, Mr Brady, is there anything else?"

"No."

Any hope of receiving help from that particular source disappears along with my leftover change. Even if Bruce comes to see me next week, there won't be much time to do anything anyway. If he *can* do anything to help, that is. Like the Collections Department secretary said yesterday, it's my debt and no one else's...

Chapter 16: THE BEST CHRISTMAS PRESENT IN THE WORLD... EVER!

I open my eyes on another bleak mid-winter day. It takes me a few seconds to remember that today's a little different. The sensational smell coming from the beast of a turkey in the oven downstairs reminds me it's Christmas day. I check the digital clock on my bedside table, and am shocked at how late it is. Although the early morning rush of childhood excitement is gone, I usually attend our chapel's morning service to thank God for what He's given me.

Every year as a family we visit a little chapel in the heart of the Vale of Glamorgan on Christmas Eve for Midnight Mass. This is my personal highlight of the year: the candle-lit service and soft unaccompanied singing give me goosebumps.

However, last night was different somehow. Instead of joining in the singing and revelling in the wonderful Victoriana of the whole spectacle, I bowed my head and closed my eyes without whispering a word throughout the service. Instead of thanking Him, my thoughts were focused on only one thing – Patrick Brady's tragic existence. I prayed to the Almighty, I begged and pleaded with Him to take Paddy to Paradise and free my family from the burden of dealing with his slow death.

I roll out of my warm bed and remember that today promises to be a different kind of Christmas. Usually I accompany my father to chapel in the morning, before returning to help Mam in the kitchen. After a late, long lunch we retire to the lounge to open our presents in front of the open fire while sipping a special bottle of wine from Dad's cellar and roasting chestnuts on the flames. But with Paddy's presence casting a long shadow over proceedings, along with Will, Mia and Sophie's company, today promises to be 'interesting', to say the least.

After washing in my bedroom's sink, I grab the bulging Santa Sack I bought from *It's A Pound* the other day, and struggle to Paddy's room. I fish in the sack for Paddy's Christmas stocking and quietly nudge the door open. The old man is snoring nasally and his chest is trumpeting: God didn't hear my prayers. Like Santa Clause himself, I approach the bed on tip-toe and place the stocking carefully beside his spindly form. His eyes, which are closed, burrow further into his skull every day. Still, though, the red hat with white trim on his head makes me smile, and I leave the room in a better mood.

In the hallway, I drop off my other presents at the eight-foot Christmas tree. Dad insists on buying a huge tree every year, even though our celebrations are always pretty quiet. Maybe men do mature, but they never really grow up.

I give Mam a big hug in the kitchen. As I hold her tight, I can smell the sherry on her breath, and when she steps back I notice how red her eyes are.

"What's wrong, Mam, have you been crying?"

"No, no," she claims, and returns her attention to the food.

"Are you sure?"

"Yes. It's the onions, bach, the onions..."

"Not to mention the sherry," I say, half joking, which makes her titter.

"Maybe," she says, reaching for the bottle and turning to face me. "Do you want a drop?"

"No way! Tea and toast is my morning medicine." And without a word, she turns away again, refilling her glass to the very top.

This is completely at odds with how my mother usually behaves, but she's not the only one in the world who's drunk before noon on Christmas day. There are similar scenes being played out all across the land – eggnog on the cornflakes, whiskey in the tea, sherry chasers and snoring before three.

"Have you seen Paddy this morning?"

"Yes, we washed him first thing so we could spend the rest of the day with you, your brother and the girls."

She yawns as she says this, stifling the end of the sentence with the back of her hand.

"That explains the hat then!"

"He's still wearing it?"

"Yes. We should get a photo of him. Where's the camera?"

"In Dad's study. Top drawer of his desk."

Having gobbled two pieces of toast, I find the camera and return to Paddy's room. But unfortunately, when I arrive the old man's awake and the candid camera moment has gone forever. He's still wearing the Santa hat, but his face is scrunched up angrily and the only Christmas spirit near him is the bottle of whiskey which I bought him. His nose is red and he's covered in sweat although the room's icier than the outside of an igloo.

"Happy Christmas, Paddy," I say, all smiles and good cheer.

"You think so?" he says, and although his voice is a soft whisper, he is obviously angry... not to mention a little bit drunk.

"Should you be drinking that?"

"You bought it for me, so what do *you* think?" After taking a gulp of oxygen, he lifts the bottle to his lips and sucks greedily.

"That's not what I meant, Paddy. Just, you know, it's not even midday and you've already polished quarter of the bottle." Filling his lungs again, he slurs, "Why the feck not, boy?" He smiles cheekily, "It's Chrisshmush!"

I avert my eyes and look at my newspaper gift-wrapping which is strewn all over the bed. Paddy hasn't touched the rest of my gifts.

"Are you going to open your other presents?" I ask.

"No," he whispers. "I told you before, Alan, there's only one thing I want from you today and you can't wrap it up in paper."

"I know that, Paddy, I really do, and I wish I could help you out..."

"Every night before I shleep, I pray the Lord my shoul to take... but he never feckin' lishens, doesh he... probably getting pished up with Jeeshus or shomeshing," I lean in closer to concentrate on his words, "either that or he doeshn't exist, ey... ey." He pauses to suck air. "He'sh made a right fool of me, sho he hassss. I've believed in him all me life. All me life. Mash thish, communion that, confeshion over there. The fecker! I never did anything as bad as making shomeone shuffer like I am today, I'm telling you. I hope the bastard's in a confesssssssion boosh right now. Feckin' hail Mary!" Spittle cascades down his chin. "He can't even do me one thing in return for a lifetime of living in awe. In fear. The feckin' bashtard!" He takes a swig of whiskey this time, although I think he might have mistaken the bottle for his oxygen mask. "What have war, famine and fecked up old people got in common, Alan?"

"I don't know."

"They're all evidensh that He doeshn't exist... or at the very leasht that He doeshn't care..."

"Don't say that!"

"Why the feck not, it'sh Chrishtmush!" And with that, his eyes close and the bottle slips from his grasp, spilling the single malt over the bed-sheets. Replacing the cap and patting the puddle with tissue, I sit there replaying his words. I can certainly appreciate how things look from his perspective. I hear the front doorbell signalling Will and his girls' arrival, so I turn my back on one problem and go down to welcome another.

As soon as I open the door, my home's tranquility disappears. Outside, the city is grey and lifeless, like every Christmas I can remember. Cloudy and dry. Dull. It's the kind of day that God himself would turn his back on. Sophie comes in first wearing a fairy costume and pushing a posh pram crammed with dollies and other toys. Will is next, struggling under the weight of two huge sacks. He's wearing a colourful and stripey jumper which doesn't suit him at all.

Mia follows my brother. This is the first time I've seen her since 'you know what' and my heart starts pounding like an industrial drill. My blushing goes unnoticed in the chaos. Mia's makeup doesn't appear to be laid on so thick today. She isn't wearing a skirt (belt) either, but tight jeans and a loose fitting cardigan over a low-cut top which shows off her cleavage. Her face, her cheeks, appear to be more rounded somehow... and her eyes dart in all directions to avoid looking at me.

Mam breathes sherry-fuelled halitosis all over Sophie as she gives her a hug. I greet my brother with a manly handshake. There's no awkwardness in our greetings... until I have to welcome Mia.

We move towards each other. She can't bring herself to look at me, but I'm pretty sure she's recalling, like me, exactly what we were doing together here the last time we met. We embrace coldly, then Mia pushes me away.

Will says, "What have you got to tell Mam-gu, Soph?" Sophie doesn't answer but buries her face in my brother's jeans. Will bribes her with the promise of another pressie if she does as they've rehearsed. Slowly, Sophie detaches herself from the denim and looks at my mother, before stuttering through her lines.

"Nah-doll-ig-thlah-when-a-blue-thin-new-yv-dah," she whispers, which makes my mother beam. It even makes me well up a little too: hearing this tiny seed of Welshness seems like a light in dark days. Mam pulls Sophie towards her again and the tears start to flow. She eventually sets Sophie free, and the child turns her attention to her pram, as Mam embraces Will and Mia at once to celebrate this joyful development.

"*Diolch! Diolch!* Thank you so much..." Mam gushes.

"It's Mia's turn next, innit, Mi?" Will declares.

"We'll see," Mia says noncommitally, as the first smile of the day appears on her face.

"This is the best present you could have ever given me," Mam says.

"We'll see about that," Will retorts, winking at me provocatively.

After the group hug ends, Mam steps back and looks at Will's jumper.

"What a lovely jumper, Will, is it new?"

"You *are* joking, aren't you, Mam?"

"No, why, don't you like it?"

"Mam, it's disgusting," Mia slaps him and calls him an 'ungrateful sod', "but I had to put it on round Mad Marge's this morning..." This is what Will calls his mother-in-law. "I was all 'wwww, it's lovely' and 'of course I'll wear it' but the truth is it's going straight to the Salvos first thing in the morning."

"But it looks nice, Will, it *really* suits you."

"I told you so," Mia agrees, but Will just sighs and lifts his eyebrows.

"You're both full of it! I look like Giles Brandreth at best, and that's not good." The sound of tearing paper grabs our attention and we all turn to see Sophie crouched under the tree opening a present without permission.

"No way, young lady!" Mia shouts, stepping towards her daughter and pulling her to her feet without ceremony.

"Easy Mia!" Will yells. Sophie starts to cry, so Will lifts her up and whispers in her ear, "You remember what I told you, don't you Soph? You have to wait until Gramps gets here before you get any more pressies, ok?" The sobbing subsides and Sophie nods. Mia and Mam disappear into the kitchen, leaving the three of us in the hall.

"How's Paddy doing today?"

"Not good. He's angry, unhappy, a bit drunk..."

"In that order?"

"Emmm, maybe his drunkness is most obvious to begin with, but when he opens his mouth, the others sort of take over."

"Are you saying I shouldn't give him this bottle of Danzy Jones, then?"

"No way! He's already polished a quarter of a bottle of Glen Moray, and spilt another quarter over his bed. It stinks up there."

"This should be interesting then."

"What?"

"You wanna see Paddy, Soph?" Sophie shakes her head. "She was a bit freaked out when she saw him last, like…"

"I'm not surprised!"

"I know, but tuff-tiddies, Sophie, cos you have to wish him happy crimbo, so come on." Will carries her upstairs, to Sophie's protestation.

I decide to set the table for the feast, as I don't want to join Mia and Mam. But when I get to the dining room, I find it has already been done – including some seriously posh crackers from Harrods – so I return to the hall to dither, and take a closer look at Sophie's pram. It's full of brand new toys – dollies and teddies and kiddies' make-up, roller blades and a trendy poncho from Gap. I look from the pram to the tree and then to the ocean of gifts strewn over the floor, and wonder if such a young child can truly appreciate all this. It's not her fault, of course, but there was something so magical about receiving one big present on Christmas day – a bike, a footy kit or maybe a Scalextric set – and nothing much else. That's how it was when I was growing up – a sock filled with satsumas, nuts and chocolate coins at the end of the bed, followed by one memorable present later on. I can remember almost every gift I received for my childhood Christmases because of this. I wonder how many Sophie will remember in a few days time?

I get depressed as I realise the true meaning of Christmas is long forgotten. Consumerism is the modern Messiah, and we're all guilty of bowing down next to his manger.

"You're happy with your new pram then, Al?" Dad says, stepping towards me from the kitchen, lighting a monstrous Cohiba.

"It's just what I always wanted!" I say, as we greet each other with a warm embrace. "Happy Christmas, Pops. Sorry I didn't come with you this morning."

"Don't worry, I put in a word on your behalf…"

"Thanks. Was it full this morning?"

"As always. Everyone wants to show their faces on Christmas day, as you know."

"Fairweathers!"

"Something like that. Where's your brother and Sophie?"

"Up with Paddy…"

And right on cue, Sophie bounds down the stairs with a huge smile. It's a pleasure to see Gramps, compared to what she's just witnessed in Paddy's room. Then I remember what Will promised her earlier and realise that Dad's presence is the green light to further presents. She dives from the third step towards my father's arms, as he clenches his cigar between his teeth in order to catch her. He tickles her ribs, making her bare her baby teeth and close her eyes in ecstasy.

Sophie soon wriggles free, as Will saunters down the stairs to join us. After he and Dad embrace and swap boxes of Cuban cigars, Mia and Mam appear and it's time to open some presents.

Within five minutes of filling everyone's glasses with Bucks Fizz (apart from Mam's, who's already complaining of a headache.), Will and I have joined Dad in wearing some brand new slippers. The floor is covered in paper and ribbon and personal piles of presents. Sophie's in seventh heaven and is busily helping everyone else with their presents, having already ripped open her own. She seems to be drowning under the shiny waves of paper as she dips for yet more gifts in the murky depths beneath the tree.

The 'thank yous', the kisses and the cuddles are enough to make me spin, but I feel warm inside as I watch everyone's faces light up as they open their gifts. Mia's happy with her Samsara, although she still can't look at me when she whispers her appreciation. Everyone apart from Sophie seems unhappy with the African Djembe drum I bought my niece.

"Cheers for that, Al," Will says as Sophie bangs out some stuttering beats. "Just what we need."

Mam's on her knees by the tree, calling Dwdi to come and join us. He struts across the hall towards her, sniffing at a few things along the way. When he reaches Mam, she opens his present and dangles a few treats in front of him. Dwdi, like any self-respecting feline, ignores the presents, curls up on the paper she's just discarded and falls asleep.

Mam struggles to her feet and I pass an envelope to her.

"For you and Dad," I explain. "I couldn't afford one each for you this year."

"Don't worry, bach," Mam says without noticing my joke, and steps towards Dad to open it. What I've bought them is a relaxing weekend at Nant Ddu Lodge and Spa. Seeing its contents, Mam mumbles her thanks but I can see that the burden of looking after Paddy has made the prospect of a weekend or even a night away impossible. I wanted them to have a nice break away from all this, but I know I've just wasted over two hundred pounds.

I sip my drink and hope that Will likes his present. After all, this is the one I've sweated over most. In the end, I went for a small personal gift.

"Nice paper, Al. You couldn't afford any wrapping paper either could you?" This time, I take the bait.

"It's called recycling, Will." This year I decided to wrap all my presents in newspaper, and although it might not be to everyone's taste, the lake of shimmering paper on the floor justifies my decision.

Will crouches down and like a true surgeon, unwraps the paper carefully. I watch as his face transforms from initial confusion to joy. It's a picture frame from Habitat, containing three photos from our childhood before the onset of puberty and the bullying that followed. The first image is of the pair of us on our brand new BMXs one Christmas morning when I was about eight and Will was elevenish. The middle image is of both of us when we were very young – maybe three and six years old – again taken on Christmas Day, but this time we're dressed as cowboys, six-shooters and all. In the third picture, we're still pretty young, this time taking our 'driving tests' at Legoland.

I begin to worry that something's wrong when Will puts his head in his hand and just stares at my gift. Nat King Cole's voice is the only sound to be heard, as everyone waits. Mia steps towards him and puts her hand on his shoulder. Will gets to his feet and I'm shocked to see tears. I haven't seen him cry since childhood. When he steps towards me and holds me in a vice-like grip, the tears flow from my own eyes. Through the mist, with my chin resting on his shoulder and my tears soaking his new jumper, my eyes meet Mia's for the first time in two months… behind my brother's back.

As if I didn't feel confused enough already, Will thanks me and apologises in the same breath for the way he's treated me in the past. The photos were meant to ease my guilt and remind him of the good old days before he turned into a teenager. As we gaze at each other though, the guilt's still as strong. Will's the only person on this planet who's grown from the same stock as me. Despite our troubled past, my betrayal is much worse than Will's childish misdemeanours. We eventually step back and dry our faces with the back of our hands.

"Bloody hell!" Will exclaims. "Sorry about that, I don't know what came over me."

"That's all right, Macho Man," Mia says. "Your feminine side had to make an appearance sooner or later!" Everyone laughs as more Bucks Fizz is poured. The oven's alarm sounds, which means that the turkey's ready.

The table is loaded; glasses are filled and we watch Dad carve the turkey as carefully as a child playing Operation for fudge-money. Will insists on saying grace. Now I know that I have no right to judge anyone, and I know that it's nice to see him making such an effort to change, but hearing an atheist praying to God is as fake as a six pound note as well as being inappropriate and pointless. But I keep my mouth shut and play along.

As soon as the "Amens" are uttered, Dad turns to Will and asks for permission to 'pull his cracker' and before any meat, stuffing or veggies have passed anyone's lips, we're all wearing paper crowns and cracking terrible jokes.

Thankfully, silence follows as we all tuck in. Mam's food is so tasty that I don't want the meal to end. I have to rest after a little while, and sit back to clean my palate with some ice cold water, before taking a swig of my father's excellent wine. As I roll the Rioja around my mouth, I lean back in my chair to allow the food to settle, and look around the room. For the first time in ages, my parents actually look happy, as if they've forgotten all their worries. I watch Will, who's as patient and loving towards Mia and Sophie as I've ever seen him. I'm envious as I watch him cut Sophie's turkey and pour Mia some Sancerre. Apart from Paddy's chest which can be heard through the baby monitor, we appear to be a normal happy family. Although we all know different, it's nice to pretend. My mind fills with memories of past Christmas: gleaming bikes and Lego garages; Action Men, Bucking Broncos and extra pressies for Will and I if we eat all our sprouts. In fact, Will's using the exact same tactic with Sophie – I'm glad to say that McDonalds seems far from her mind today.

"No more for me Will!" Mia exclaims, breaking the silence and placing her hand over her wineglass. Will, much to everyone's surprise, says nothing and obeys her without making any kind of fuss.

"Go on, Mia, it'll do you the world of good." Dad insists through a mouthful of cheesey greens.

"I can't," Mia pleads, looking at Will for some support.

"Can't or won't?" Dad asks, holding the bottle within striking distance.

"Can't," Will answers emphatically.

"Will!" Mia snorts, as her cheeks blush the colour of rosè.

"Designated driver for the day, are you, bach?" Mam now, joining in.

"Something like tha…" Mia starts, but before finishing her sentence, Will buts in.

"For the next few months, more like…" which makes Mia stare him down, her eyes threatening.

The room falls silent and everyone looks at Mia. The question is obvious. Mia carries on chewing as she tries to ignore us, but Will just can't help himself.

"Ok, ok," he starts, holding his hands in front of him. "We weren't going to tell anyone for a while as it's still early days…"

"A-a-and?" Mam, hanging on my brother's every word.

"Well I'm sure you can guess already…"

"What?" Mam again, her eyes open and her hands flapping like the wings of an injured bird.

"Blinkin' 'eck, Mam, if you stop interrupting I'll tell you." Mam mouths a silent 'sorry' in Will's direction. "Mia's pregnant. We're gonna have another baby." Mam jumps to her feet and goes round the table hugging everyone.

"How early?" asks Dad.

"Two months gone," Will answers, and as I hear the words I look up and catch Mia staring in my direction. But when our eyes meet, she looks away and starts explaining the situation to Sophie.

"Mia's having the twelve week scan at the start of February."

Mam tempts fate by claiming 'nothing could spoil today now', and everyone's back in their seats. The main course is followed by an extremely alcoholic plum pudding, which proceeds cheese and biscuits and coffee and mints. Then it's all over for another year and we loosen our belts as the conversation returns to the new baby blah blah blah. Like a television set at five in the morning, I'm switched off. I slowly zone out and get sucked into the muzak and Paddy's trumpeting chest, which is keeping better time than some renowned horn sections. The seindorf stops as the old man regains consciousness.

"Acorns and oranges... it'sh that shimple..." The gibberish enters the room through the baby monitor, stopping everyone's conversation. Mam, like an inexperienced new mother, gets to her feet and is ready to go and deal with the situation, but Dad tells her to wait a moment before climbing the stairs, 'just in case he's sleep-talking'. He's nothing of the sort, in fact Paddy's clearer now than he's been in a long time.

"Can ya hear me down there?" he asks and sucks air. "I know ya can and I jusht wanted to shay," another deep breath, "Merry Chrishtmush to you all, even the tart." Though everyone else takes this to be nothing more than the confused rant of a drunk old man, Mia and I can guess who he's referring to. "Now I know I'm a burden and I alsho know that I didn't get any of you any preshentsh, so I'm now going to read you a few wordsh that I hope will ring true with shome, if not all, of yoush."

Mam looks at Dad, fear sketched upon her face. Dad does his best to ignore his wife and father by pouring and draining another glass of red. Will smiles at Mia first and then Sophie, twirling his index finger next to his forehead. I hang on to Paddy's every word, dreading what's about to come next.

"Right... 'Here', by RShhh Thomash..." He's reading from the poetry collection I gave him this morning. I'm glad he's making some use of my other gifts, and not just the whiskey. The whole room is silent, even Sophie, and remains that way throughout the recital until Mam starts to sob when Paddy reads: "Why are my handsh thish way that they will not do as I shay? Doesh no God hear when I pray?" She then leaves the room as Paddy reaches the last verse.

It ish too late to shtart
For deshtinationsh not of the heart.
I musht shtay here with my hurt.

As soon as Paddy finishes, Mam returns, drying her eyes on some kitchen roll.

"Merry Chrishtmush!" Paddy hollers once more, then starts snoring, filling the room with grunts.

"Will someone please switch him off," Will demands. I get up and press the off switch, banishing Paddy from our family gathering.

The mood darkens: no one knows quite what to say. My parents look helplessly at each other across the table. I'm still absorbing the significance of Paddy's words when Will says, "Right. There's only one thing left to do now, isn't there?" Everyone looks at him vacantly.

"What?" Sophie bellows in hope of more presents.

"Monopoly, of course!" Will smiles widely. This is one of our discontinued childhood traditions – a marathon game of Monopoly after Christmas dinner. Once the table's clear, we're ready for battle. Within ten minutes, Sophie's disappeared to play with her dollies. Within twenty, Mia's gone, blaming her pregnancy for the urgent need to lie down in front of the fire. Mam joins them a few minutes later, complaining of a bad head and heartburn. Which leaves us, the men... in the form of competitive schoolboys. We go to work, building our empires over the course of the next hour, building houses and hotels faster then Wimpey Homes. Dad concentrates on the lower rungs of the property market – your Old Kent Roads, Pentonvilles and various other fleapits; I go for the orange and red corners, as well as the railway stations – making it nigh on impossible for anyone to pass without coughing up. Will, surprise surprise, goes for the top end of the market.

Dad's the first to fall, as Will snares him twice in quick succession – once on Regent Street, followed by the stinger on Park Lane. I battle on for a little while longer but Will's competitive streak sees me off. You'd think that he'd just won Wimbledon or something the way he's punching the air and rubbing our noses in it. I've seen it all before of course, and as usual I keep schtumm.

As dusk paints the grey clouds black, Will, Mia and Sophie collect their presents and leave for Mia's sister's house in a frenzy of hugs, kisses and thank yous. They leave behind them a slight uneasy sensation. I try and force my parents to leave the dirty dishes to me, but they don't listen. Only after the dishwasher's full and the rest of the crockery's been returned to the cupboards do they finally leave me to wipe the tables and retire to the lounge to watch some telly.

I go and see how Paddy's doing. Not brilliantly as it happens; a pretty mean hangover seems to have kicked in. Apparently, his mouth's "as dry as an Arab's arsehole", but I don't press him for any further details. I fetch him a glass of water instead.

"How did they like my performance?" he whispers.

"Not too well, if I'm honest."

"Good!" He smiles.

"What do you mean?" After filling his lungs, he explains. "When I read that poem for the first time, it rang so true, Al, so true. I just wanted to remind everyone that I'm here and without some help I might still be here next Christmas. And no one wants that do they?"

"There's no chance of that, Paddy," I say, and as my words find their mark, Paddy's eyes sparkle.

"What do you mean?"

"You know what I mean, Paddy, so don't pretend otherwise."

"But I need to hear you say it…"

"I'm ready to help you, Paddy. There, happy now?" He sucks more air, smiling cheekily.

"Very. Thank you, Alan. It means a lot to me."

"I know, Paddy. I know."

"When?"

"Next chance we get."

"A toast!" he exclaims excitedly, reaching for the whiskey bottle.

"I think you've had enough already, Paddy..." I reply, not wanting to taste the malty liquid.

"Nonsense, boy! Tonight we celebrate." I reluctantly pour us both a small measure. "To death!" is Paddy's morbid toast, delivered with a huge grin on his face.

"To life!" is my reply.

Chapter 17: REBIRTH

I leave the shed at half past eight and struggle towards Thornhill in the searing heat for a 'business meeting' at Floyd's house. Now, if we lived in a perfect world, I wouldn't have to go near the place, but as the hole widens beneath my feet with every passing hour, I don't have a choice in the matter. I have to at least listen to my friend's offer. Beggars and choosers...

After leaving the Crystals and pumping my little legs up Heol Hir towards Llanishen High School, I stop and get off my bike just after passing the school's main entrance as the hill's too steep and my lungs too small. I have a bit of a rest on a nearby wall, in the shade of a big old magnolia tree. I regret not bringing a bottle of water with me, as well as a change of clothes: I'm already sweating profusely and have to go straight on to work after the meeting.

I decide to walk the rest of the way, since I've got plenty of time and little spare energy. Schoolchildren go past me, oblivious to my presence. I don't remember it ever being this hot and sunny when I was a kid. Inexplicably, I'm suddenly standing on the yard of my own high school over in Llandaf North, covered in zits and wearing a tie made of Welsh tapestry which tickles my underdeveloped Adam's apple. As always, I'm alone. The whole scene is greyish – from the concrete beneath my feet to the sky above and the faces of my fellow pupils as they head for who knows where.

It's lunchtime and I'm eating some egg and cress sandwiches as I walk in circles around the school, impatient to return to the relative safety of the classroom. All the other kids are in groups or gangs, but I'm not really bothered by that. I'm already used to my own company. That's where I feel most comfortable. I'm a private child, thanks mainly to my dear brother.

I cross the playground, I'm aware that my fellow pupils are pointing and staring at me. They whisper to each other, chuckling quietly as I pass. I check my clothes to make sure they're free of guano and chalk penises, before thinking what I always do when these incidents occur: what has Will done this time? The sniggers and stares continue as I walk casually past the annexe where the sixth formers play ping-pong and babyfoot during lunchtime. I find Will on the hockey field around the back, addressing an assembly of fellow pupils. I stand at the back to listen. My dear brother is reading extracts from my diary to the assembled crowd. Sharing my childish feelings and naïve secrets with my fellow pupils. The diary's full of confused childish wonderings, as well as endless questions directed at God. I'm christened with a new nickname – Al the Baptist.

I turn onto Heol y Cadno, just north of Sainsbury's, and find Floyd's home at the far end of the cul-de-sac. You wouldn't think Floyd would suit the suburbs, but really Thornhill's warren-like network of pathways, dead-ends, identikit houses and pockets of woodland is the perfect home for him. It would be quite easy to escape and disappear here.

Floyd's detached home is in need of external TLC. The red bricks have faded and the yucca by the front door needs watering. Cutting the grass would be a good idea too. By the side of his house, there's a pathway leading to some woods and a double drive where Floyd's Ute is parked next to an inconspicuous silver-grey VW Polo. His and hers, if ever I saw one.

I go up to the front door and knock quietly. The door opens slightly but there's no one on the other side. I enter and am overwhelmed by the funk of skunk and bacon butties. Floyd Fortune's favourite brekkie! I'm about to bellow his name, when the door slams shut behind me and my mouth's covered by a cold hand. I feel cold steel touch my temple and the unmistakable click of a gun cocking next to my ear. I'm on the point of fainting when I see Floyd walking past with a tray of tea and bacon sarnies.

"Put him down, Dee Dee, for fuck's sake. That's just Al, our driver."

I turn to face "Dee Dee", breathing heavily as the colour returns to my cheeks. He doesn't look anything like a criminal; more like a rock star. Ripped denim drainpipes, biker boots and Mr No Muscles T-shirt with the words 'Kill Everyone' on his chest; long dark, unkempt hair and scarred face: proof enough that this man has lived life to its fullest. His dark, deepset eyes are devoid of emotion.

"What did you do that for?"

"Sorry man. It's just a replica, like, not a real shooter or nuffin. And anyway, I thought you woz a cop."

"Do I *look* like a cop?" Looking me up and down, Dee Dee smiles.

"Nah, you look more like a barman come to think of it."

"Makes sense, seeing that's what I am!" I push past him to join Floyd in the front room.

The inside of Floyd's home is a palace; a proper bachelor pad: humungous flat screen TV hanging in one corner, a leather La-z-boy placed in prime position, a library of DVDs, videos and CDs, a tropical aquarium stretching the length of one wall and about half a tonne of ganja packed and stacked in nine ounce bricks on the floor by my feet. I'm looking at the contraband when Floyd comes over to me.

"I know, I know," he says, arms held wide like an Italian footballer claiming his innocence. "Tubbs just delivered that lot. I don't usually keep that much on show. I mean, that's why I built the bunker... Anyway, Al, welcome to my humble abode." Floyd's like a kid on Christmas morning introducing his motley crew. "Here are some friends of mine. You've already met Dee Dee." The rocker goes past us, taking the spliff from Floyd. "This by 'ere's Silent Gee." A giant of a man sits in silence at the table in the conservatory. "Silent on account of his muteness and Gee because his name's Gary.

Gee nods his approval and takes the joint from Dee Dee. I notice the big man's trousers; the waist pulled so high above his belly that it looks like an anaconda's eating him whole. The pale scar that runs the length of his face – from forehead to jaw – stands out spectacularly on his liquorice coloured skin. "Gee's Dee Dee's partner…"

"Objection!" Dee Dee bellows. "Don't say that Floyd for fuckssake; you make us sound like a right pair of hommes." All the men are doubled up laughing.

I relax a little and ask: "Old friends of Floyd's are you?"

"Friends? Sort of. We met him inside about three years ago…"

"Inside what?" I ask like a fool. The place erupts again and I smile.

"Top gag, Al! Where the fuck did you find him, Floyd? Jongleurs, was it?" Dee Dee asks as Floyd turns to the third dark knight of this round table – a tubby man with arms as wide as a row of terraced houses. His skin's like leather and tattoos climb all over his body. Despite appearing to be an unpleasant person, his thick black hair, chubby cheeks and crooked smile gives him a childlike grace. As Floyd introduces him, I notice him refusing the spliff that's offered.

"Last but not least, this is Tubbs. Alan, Tubbs, Tubbs, Alan. He's one of yours by 'ere, Tubbs…"

"What's that supposed to mean?" Tubbs asks, in a quiet but menacing voice.

"He's proper Welsh like, speaks the lingo an' all that."

Tubbs smiles at me.

"Do you really, Alan," he asks in Welsh.

"I do, and my name's Alun, not Alan." I continue our private conversation.

"That's a good name. What are you doing with this bunch of nut-jobs then, Al?"

But before I have a chance to respond, Dee Dee pipes up.

"What the fuck are you two sayin'? It sounds like fuckin' bollocks to me…"

"It would though, Dee Dee, wouldn't it," Tubbs retorts; totally calm, totally cool, "seeing you can't speak the language." He shakes his head and mutters, "*Ma-mwy-o-freins-'da-ni-yn-ein-twll-tin-na-sy-'da-hwn-yn-'i-ben!*" for my benefit.

"Wot was that, mate, wot the fuck d'you say?" Dee Dee asks.

"All I said was it's nice to meet a proper fellow Welshman for a change, instead of one of you phoney fuckers!" Tubbs answers with conviction.

Once again the whole room laughs together. Tubbs catches my eye and holds my gaze.

"Right, down to business gentlemen," Floyd announces. I'm pretty sure we're not here to discuss rigging the local raffle. "Tubbs, what have you got for us this time?"

"Good question, Floyd," he starts. "What I've got for you today is probably the easiest job ever... it also happens to be very high yielding, thanks to the incompetence and short-sightedness of our arch enemies, the bureaucrats." Floyd and Dee Dee *booooooooooo* loudly and laugh. "The job in hand centres on the Post Office in the tiny hamlet of Trellech, which is about ten miles south of Monmouth. Now Monmouthshire, as we all know, is rich cunt country, which is pretty much why we're targeting this area and not some fuckin' place like Porth or Ponty. Rich cunts equal *muchos mula* after all.

"Right, in Trellech there's what's known in the business as a Holding Office. To you and me, it looks like any other small country Post Office – you know the kind: flowers outside, old biddy behind the counter. But gentlemen, it's so much more, you wouldn't believe. The Holding Office, or holder as it'll be known from here on in, collects weekly takings from four other small Post Offices within an eight-mile radius and holds the money in a safe for collection on the last Wednesday of every month. That's next Wednesday, by the way. Now for those of you that are crap at maths, that's five weekly takings because we also count the holder's takings too – which average five grand a week, by the way – from five Post Offices, which equals 20 weekly instalments in one lovely safe in the holder. What we're looking at is a figure in the region of one hundred thousand pounds, gentlemen. It's so fuckin' easy I don't know why I don't just do it myself. The reason all this lovely cash is hoarded in this place as opposed to the main post office in Monmouth is plain old bureaucratic bullshit. They don't want weekly takings at the main offices, only monthly… which is beautiful for people like us…"

My jaw drops. The plan seems so simple; I wonder why everyone doesn't turn to a life of crime.

"Why don't we go up there tomorrow and just take what's there?"

"Good question, Dee Dee; the answer is because the safe's code changes every thirty seconds and the only people who know the codes are the Securicor dudes who visit once a week with the weekly takings from the other four post offices. And, as we're greedy fuckers, we want to wait 'til the last possible moment to claim all the booty…"

"And that's next Wednesday, right?"

"Exactly, Floyd; the Securicor blokes arrive at roughly eleven o'clock, when you'll be waiting to accompany them inside for a spot of safe cleaning…"

"What about the posters they got up in them post offices? You know the ones; they say somethin like 'no cash kept on premises'. You see 'em everywhere…" Dee Dee again.

"They're absolute bullshit, my friend. Nothing more than propaganda, nothing more than lies…"

"Where will you be, Tubbs?" I ask.

"Who knows, who knows? I certainly don't. I'm just the man with the plan by here. That's the way I like it. Ten per cent and a quiet life…"

"How do you know all this, then?"

"Fair question, Al, but I'm sure you've noticed that none of these boys asked before you and the reason for this is I don't disclose my sources and I never let people down. Would you agree, Floyd?"

"Too right Tubbs, you da man!"

"This is how I see it," Tubbs continues. "Floyd and Gee, you take care of the post master, first Securicor dude and safe. Dee Dee, you control the second Securicor dude, the driver that is. Pistol-whip him, shit him up. You know these fucks are cowards and won't do nothing to stop you. They're just doing their jobs and want to get home to wifey at the end of the shift. While Floyd and Gee are inside, you need to drag the driver out of the van and get him to open the back door because there'll be the final weekly takings from the four other post offices in there. Once he opens the van, knock him out and exchange his body for the bags inside. Al, you're driving..." What? Are you sure? Is this the time to confess to never passing my driving test? No. Probably not... I think I might be a little out of my depth here... I just nod and look serious, as if being the getaway driver in a Post Office robbery's as normal as pulling a pint to me. "...park the car about a hundred yards down the road from the holder; when you see the Securicor arrive, you three walk to the post office, all casual like, don't run. Al, stay put as the job goes down. It won't take more that sixty seconds. When Dee Dee opens the back of the van, drive the car up and pop the boot so he can put the bags in. By that time Floyd and Gee will be out with their loot. As soon as everyone's in, drive off. I take it this is your first time, a late replacement for Floorboard George, as I understand, so, a few tips. Actually, just one, keep to the speed limit. No, sorry, two. Don't run any lights; the last thing you want is to be pulled on your way home. And that's it, I think, gentlemen..." That's it! Seriously? That's it! Easy peasy lemon squeezy! "Any questions?" Tubbs shows us the village on a map, along with photos of the holder.

I say, "I don't want to be part of anything that involves guns," and am amazed when everyone starts laughing as if I've just cracked the ferret gag. Floyd shushes everyone, before explaining. Although he's talking to me as he usually does, there's a glint in his eye which suggests that maybe my friend Floyd is somehow a different beast in the company of these men.

"Al, we *have* to use guns, 'cos you can't really do an armed robbery with pea shooters, know what I mean? But don't worry, 'cos we only use replicas so no one gets hurt. OK?" And I nod my head as if everything's tickety-boo. "And anyway, Al, you're just the driver so if we get caught..."

"We won't get caught!" Dee Dee buts in.

"I know that, Dee. But, even if we did, the driver never gets a heavy sentence, right?"

And they all mumble their agreement. I'm well out of my depth. Unfortunately, I'm also out of options...

After Tubbs re-explains a few things, and promises to phone Floyd on Tuesday night to confirm that we Thunderbirds are go, he struggles to his feet and says his goodbyes. At the last minute, Dee Dee asks, "Ey, Tubbs, what's with the gangsta limp?" Tubbs lifts his right trouser leg to reveal the outline of his latest tattoo and the source of his pain – a fierce and intricate dragon scaling his entire leg. "How far up does that bad boy go?" Dee Dee lights another joint.

"All the way..." Tubbs answers with a cheeky smile, lets his trouser leg fall back down and takes from Floyd a chunky envelope as they both leave.

Then, silence. The most uncomfortable silence I've ever known. Here I am sitting in the company of two career crims. They both stare at me. No smiles. No apparent feelings at all, really. They're both completely neutral, as if they're assessing my ability to do the job. Or maybe they're just a bit too stoned... after all, the purple haze which hangs above us is making my mouth drier than Mr Bond's Martini... and I haven't even smoked anything. The spliff's passed to Gee, and after he fills his lungs, it's offered to me.

"No thanks, Gee," I say. "I've got to go to work..." and I look at my watch. "...right now, actually." Gee keeps the joint and sucks hard on the roach until smoke billows from his nostrils, his mouth and every other orifice. It dances above his head in the morning light and I notice a subtle change in attitude towards me. I can definitely sense something – as if my refusal of the smoke somehow insults his way of life.

As I get up, I offer my hand to my new accomplices. They both refuse to shake it. I just say, "See you next Wednesday."

I'm glad to get out of there. On my way out, I notice Tubbs leave in his little Polo: I imagined him on the back of a Harley. Floyd joins me on the front step.

"You leavin?"

"Yeah, I'm workin' in ten minutes..."

"Safe. So, what d'you reckon then?"

"About what?"

"The fuckin job, Al, the job!"

"Well I don't like it, but..."

"But what?"

"But I don't have much of a choice, do I?"

"I guess not..."

"There's something I have to tell you, though, Floyd."

"If it's the shooters you're worried about Al, don't be. They're for show only. A threat, nothing more. They're not even real..."

"No it's not the guns, although I'm not over the moon about them either..."

"What then?"

"I'm the driver right?"

"Right."

"Floyd... I've never passed my test..."

He makes a wide grin but it soon straightens.

"You're serious, aren't you?"

"Of course I'm serious!"

"You *can* drive though, right?"

"Well yes, although I'm a bit rusty..."

"That's not a problem, it's like riding a bike and you can practise in mine over the weekend..."

"But what about a licence?"

"Leave that to me, Al. I've got you covered." He places a hand on my shoulder. "I know you're worried about returning to clink and all that, but this is a piece of piss. Tubbs never lets us down; he's a real pro. It'll be over in a matter of hours. All you've got to do is drive and then, wham; we're back here counting the cash. At least fifteen grand a pop, probably closer to twenty. That'll cover your debt and get you a deposit on a nice flat or something. Sort you out proper like. What d'you say?"

Like a star-struck schoolgirl romanced by the rugby captain, I say, "That sounds good, Floyd..."

I spend the rest of the day in a strange daze. Customers talk to me but I'm not sure if I answer them, or even acknowledge their existence. Visions of Dee Dee, his gun and the blatant madness in his glazed eyes are haunting me. Gee's silence was worse. At least with Dee Dee you know what's what, but you could only guess at what Gee was thinking.

I'm in Catch-22. I don't want to break the law and return to jail. But even if I don't break the law, I'll still return to jail. What a choice. I have some recollection of agreeing to be a part of 'the plan' too. What a mess. There's only one way out of this gazpacho...

I could blame Will and his selfishness, but really I'm the only person responsible. I don't like what I've become, what I'm becoming, but have no idea how to dig my way out of this hole. In the past, I'd have turned to God for guidance, but I've even turned my back on Him by now.

I'm a weak, weak man. Lost. Damned.

At five o'clock, in walks Floyd, catching me as I prepare to leave for the day. He persuades me to stay for 'one', which inevitably turns into three and then six...

I tell him everything – the tongue loosens somewhat after a few Stellas – and Floyd listens, explains and slowly persuades me that everything's going to be ok. He even promises not to offer me any kind of 'work' after this one-off job, but it's getting harder to believe anything he says after what I've seen recently. I noticed something different in him this morning that reminded me of his fight with Fabio. A wild streak. A darker beast.

As the clock tick-tocks towards eleven, I leave the pub when Floyd accompanies another customer to his 'office'. Regardless of what I've heard tonight, I'm not happy. Leaving with a full belly of beer, I don't feel drunk in the slightest. It's as if my problems are suppressing the usual feelings of euphoria. I walk through the sweating bodies still drinking outside, and am overjoyed to see my old friend Paddy waiting for me by my bike. At least I have some kind of choice, which is more than Paddy has where he is. As I reach for my bike, Paddy places his hand on my shoulder, and I can feel him on a certain spiritual level. I smile at him and offer him a backie. As if sensing my loneliness, he jumps on and I start to pedal.

The roads are quiet at this time of night, so I swing out onto Fidlas Avenue, and then Heathwood Road which runs directly in front of the Arches. The weather's been so dry recently that the dust and chippings on the road make my front wheel slip when I attempt to straighten up and head for home. All three of us – Paddy, the bike and me – are tipped into the floor in the middle of the road. Blood stings my knees and a lorry thunders towards us with its headlights blinding me and its horn bellowing. I freeze, and the lorry's right on top of me in the click of a camera. I hit the ground and close my eyes.

The horn blasts again and time stands still. The lorry rips right through me and I find myself in a strange place; some brightly lit, restful netherworld. The light blinds me to begin with, but once my eyes grow accustomed to it, I see Paddy walking away from me towards two figures closeby. I rub my eyes. My parents are standing there, reaching out to Paddy, welcoming him to Paradise. I try to move my legs so I can follow, but I can't. So I watch Paddy as he joins my parents. They are all smiling. They all look younger than when they left their earthly bodies, and Paddy's shaved another decade off his age, while my parents look closer to forty than sixty. At last Paddy's arrived. I try to shout at them, begging them to wait for me, but can't for some reason. I start to cry out of sheer frustration, and through the tears I see the holy trinity turn to face me. Mam blows me a kiss, Dad gives me the old thumbs-up, while Paddy lights another Woodbine and takes a swig from a fresh pint of Dark. Heaven indeed! I wave them off as someone, something shakes me back to earth.

I open my eyes and lift my hand to my head. My bike's mangled by my side and the lorry's come to a stop about fifty yards down the road. There's a crowd surrounding me and the driver, judging by his Esso Oil baseball cap, is kneeling by my side. He stops shaking me and helps me to my feet. My knees are ripped to shreds and the palms of my hands too. But instead of wincing, I smile.

"Mate-are-you-ok-mate-jeezus-fuck-me-christ-you-came-from-nowhere-I-had-no-chance-of-stopping-like-no-chance-I-can't-believe-I-didn't-hit-you-must-have-gone-right-over-you..." His words are all a blur, and his hands are shaking uncontrollably.

"It's a miracle!" someone shouts.

"The bike's not been so lucky though," adds a difference voice.

"Talk to me, mate! Are you ok?"

"Yes," I confirm. I'm better than 'ok', in fact. It's difficult to explain how I feel, so close to what I've just experienced, but something's changed within me.

The driver helps me over to a nearby wall opposite the pub. Someone else carries my bike and hands me a pint of water. I'm not even shaking. But I drink the water anyway. Slowly but surely, the crowd disperses.

"I'll be back in a sec," the driver says, before jogging towards his lorry. I watch him go, and then lift my bike and place it on some black bags lying close-by.

"What happened, Al, are you OK?" Floyd appears next to me, wild eyed and out of breath. "Someone just said you'd been hit by a fuckin' lorry!"

"Not quite," I drain the last of the water.

The driver returns with his insurance details, but I refuse to take them. He thinks he's harmed me but he actually saved me.

"Only if you're sure, mate, I mean, I did wreck your bike…"

"Thanks anyway," I say. "But seriously, there's no need."

Floyd tries to change my mind, but I refuse again.

"Are you ok to get home now? Let me at least pay for your cab," the driver says.

"I'll give him a lift…" says Floyd.

"Not a chance, Floyd, you've had a skinful. And anyway, I'd rather walk. I need to clear my head and have a think. It's not far anyway…"

"Only if you're sure, mate."

"I am, thanks."

So Floyd returns to his drinking, while the driver returns to his truck. I watch him leave, smiling as I recall my sweet visions.

I walk home alone, properly alone that is. I can't stop smiling at what I saw. I feel brilliant. Full of energy. Powerful, as if I'd overdone it on the old guarana juice. There's some new strength within me. Some certainty, some force flowing through my veins – God in liquid form? Everything around me has some newfound gravity. I've felt the Truth. I've heard the Word. And now I can see His Glory all around me through clear eyes. All my uncertainty over the past few years has disappeared. I'm so happy to *know* that His belief in me never waned, although I turned my back on Him. That's the difference between God and man, I suppose...

I finger the silver cross that still hangs around my neck, and feel some strange thrill as I do so. I see my parents' faces every time I blink, and once again I'm embraced by some unexplained warmth. I feel amazing. Privileged. Chosen. Not many people get to see Heaven while they're still alive... That's when it actually hits me. I've *seen* Paradise. With my own eyes. And I'm not talking about some soft focus clouds; angels playing their harps or an old man with a long white beard either. It was more of a feeling, a sensation, some spiritual certainty in truth. Touched by the Hand of God. I know I saw the truth. I felt God. Although He wasn't present in person, you don't need to *see* God to know when He's appeared.

Is He protecting me, keeping me for some higher purpose? Who knows? But as I walk along the dark path towards my shed, I know that Paddy's left me for a better place. As I say goodbye to Paddy, I feel a new presence in my life. I now know, as I turn the key and open the door, that I'm walking in the shadow of the Creator.

I sit in my chair, feeling slightly strange without Paddy sitting next to me, but I'm glad he's gone. I grab a Breezer from the fridge and take off my trainers, relaxing and letting the energy flow through me. I think back to this morning's meeting. Even without God's influence, I knew it wasn't the right thing to do. After all, the Ten Commandments are nothing more than common sense which applies to everyone, regardless of faith. But now, as the insects chirp in the humid night, I know I can't be part of Floyd's plan. Even if I have to return to jail, I must obey God's commands and take my punishment like a man. Like a disciple.

The only problem is how to tell Floyd. I don't think he'll be quite so enthusiastic about my spiritual rebirth. Nor accept it as a good enough reason to back out.

I must be strong, and with Him by my side once again, I feel indestructible…

Chapter 18: HAPPY NEW FEAR

I open my eyes just in time to stop myself from wetting the bed.

My early morning dream is to blame. In the seconds proceeding my pant-wetting panic attack, my subconscious took me back twenty years to when I was about thirteen and Will was fifteen-ish. There we were, like a teenage Mole and Toad, in a rowing boat on Roath Park Lake. The sun was shining and the sky was blue. My parents were in a pedalo, heading for the islands at the opposite end of the lake. Will was rowing towards Captain Scott's lighthouse, the opposite way to my parents, with me imprisoned in the back of the boat. My brother, who by now is master of the dark art of tormenting me, sits facing me. His wide shoulders and toned biceps are on show under a tight, bright Ocean Pacific vest and his blond hair falls from his head in waves.

My parents disappear in the heat haze above the tiny waves. Waiting for Will are four girls from the lower sixth, hanging off the railings like a quartet of caged monkeys. Even though Will's a year below them in school, they appear to be huge fans of his. Within ten yards of them, Will does as any boy in his position would – he starts showing off. He takes off his vest, making the girls scream like the front row of a

Take That concert. I hang my head in shame.

One of the girls is taking photos of Will who is now standing up in the boat and posing like Mr Universe. The boat starts tilting. I am terrified since I'm a poor swimmer. Will notices my discomfort, and to the girls' continued encouragement, sits down and starts rocking the boat from side to side. I close my eyes and hold on tightly to the side of the boat. I open them a little: a crowd has gathered on the shore to see what all the fuss is about. They're all pointing and laughing at me. Will carries on rocking the boat, water splashing everywhere. Suddenly the rocking stops, I breathe deeply and open my eyes to the sight of Will back on his feet, pointing at my midriff with a demonic grin on his face.

"Al's fuckin' pissed himself!" he screams. The crowd laughs and howls. I hear a few cameras click. I now have no hope of ever holding my head up high in school again.

I want to dive into the water and swim towards the opposite shore, but instead I just sit there with my head in my hands and warm wetness trickling down my leg.

That's when I woke up just in time to stop it happening all over again. I rub my eyes to try and erase the memory. It's only then I realise that the dream captured just how I feel on this strange morning: Patrick Brady's last on earth, the final day of 1998.

I get out of bed, press PLAY on the stereo and wash in the sink accompanied by Miles Davis' trumpet on *Shades of Blue*. I've spent the past week since Christmas going through the motions, acting as if everything's a-ok in front of my parents, while counting the hours, minutes, seconds until Paddy's termination. I've spent every possible minute in Paddy's company, as I took a week's holiday from work. We've listened to a lot of music and watched many movies – all his choices – and even though the conversation's not what it once was, our friendship is stronger than ever, and I now know that what I've agreed to do is right. One hundred per cent. Mainly for Paddy's sake, but also for everyone connected to him. And even though I haven't thought too much about what lies ahead, we've discussed the matter and decided to keep things as simple as possible. I sometimes feel like my family's saviour, their liberator... and like Judas himself on other occasions.

I've been to the January sales a couple of times mainly to get some fresh air, but also to add to the facade of normality that Paddy and I were trying to create. As per usual, I have no plans to celebrate New Year's Eve, which made persuading my parents to accept an invitation to the Camilleri's annual party at number eleven quite an easy task. Mam didn't want to leave Paddy, but Dad and I managed to twist her arm and she agreed in the end. After getting dressed, I have a moment of inspiration and grab my notebook in order to add to the poem I've been working on all week. I'm writing an ode to Patrick Brady, some kind of farewell to an old friend.

I drag myself downstairs and pop my head round the door to Paddy's bedroom. The old man's fast asleep. Dwdi opens his eyes for a second and looks in my direction from his position at the foot of the bed. After a leisurely breakfast, I join my parents as they go for a walk around the lake. It is a mild day of mid-winter but my deception weighs heavily. I hate being so conniving, especially considering how close I am to them. I want to share everything with my parents, but know that now is not the right time to do so.

As we near Captain Scott's whitewashed memorial, this morning's dream comes back to me. My discomfort is worsened by my parents' suggestion that we call in on Will and the girls at their lakeside home. I thank God from the bottom of my heart when I see that Will's Merc's not parked in the drive and there's no answer when we knock on the door. We head for home through the woods by Cardiff High School, all the way up Llandennis Avenue's mansion-flanked incline, across Cyncoed Road and down Hollybush.

I make myself a ham and cheese sarnie and take it with me, along with a packet of Frazzles and an apple to rid my teeth of the starchy debris, to Paddy's room. The old man's awake, stroking Dwdi's thick fur, causing the cat to purrrrrrrr. I sit, smiling broadly.

"He likes it when you stroke him hard on the chin." As Paddy tries this, Dwdi's volume skyrockets and his long tail dances like a cobra. I eat my meal and watch. Every house should have a cat in my opinion, and Dwdi's presence – as well as the certainty in Paddy's mind that his end is nigh – has helped the old man hugely. Calm has descended on him, and although he's still in some pain, it's as if Paddy's accepted the discomfort because he knows it won't last long.

I finish my sandwich and open the crisps. The sound scares Dwdi back to the bottom of the bed where he curls into a tight ball and falls asleep.

"Sorry about that Paddy."

"Not a problem, Alan," the old man whispers with a hefty chug on his oxygen mask. He points a long yellow finger at Dwdi. "Isn't it ironic?" he whispers but his voice fades away.

"What is?" I ask, as he reaches again for his inhaler.

"So ironic... if I was a cat... like old Dwdi by here... they'd have put me down a long time ago... and they call humans humane," more air, "when they're only humane towards all animals except their own species. Pah!" Paddy closes his eyes and follows Dwdi to the land of nod.

I'm back at Paddy's bedside as night falls. I turn on the bedside lamp so I can read some of Joyce's masterpiece. When my parents appear, dressed up and ready to party, my heart skips a few beats. I gently shake Paddy's arm to wake him, and watch as my parents take turns to kiss him goodnight. As usual, Mam goes through the motions – "You know where we are if you need us" and "Don't hesitate to call if you need anything" – before Dad shakes my hand and wishes us both a Happy New Year. I catch Paddy's eye and see a sly little smile curling his emaciated lips. And then they're gone, wishing us a 'good night', whereas 'good bye' would have been more appropriate.

As soon as the front door closes, Paddy grabs hold of my hand and with that smile still firmly in place, asks, "Are you ready, Al?"

Nodding, I feel far from ready. Dry phlegm sticks to the walls of my mouth. I leave the room without saying a word and proceed to collect all the stuff I need for Paddy's final act.

I grab a bottle of eighteen-year-old Laphroaig whiskey from my room, which is meant to numb Paddy a little while giving me some much-needed Dutch courage. After slipping my notebook into my pocket, I return to Paddy's bedside. He's asleep again by now so I slip a Count Basie CD into the stereo, and press PLAY, before placing *Whiskey Galore* into the video and taking my seat at his side.

I sit there, listening to the Count's piano accompanying Paddy's horn section, and pray. I pray for guidance and confirmation that what I'm about to do is the right thing... and when Paddy coughs violently, bloody-green phlegm arcing from his mouth onto the print of his pyjamas, I take that as a sign from above.

"The film's ready to go, Paddy," I explain, as I wipe the gunk from his chest and chin.

"Forget the film," he whispers. "I'm ready to go now... I'm ready to start looking for her." My heart flutters and my mouth crimps up like a carcass in the desert. I nod and open the bottle of whiskey to pour us both a hefty measure.

We drink in silence – Paddy savouring every drop. I down mine in one which makes my lips curl back over my teeth. Paddy chuckles, puts his away discreetly and holds out his glass for a refill. I start sweating, although the window's wide open as usual. Paddy's also covered in his usual salty sheen. He reaches for his mask, sucks and whispers, "Don't you worry now, Alan, you're definitely doing the right thing..."

"I know that, Paddy, but it just feels, you know," he nods his head, "weird, that's all. I mean, I know how much pain you're in and I want to help you more than anything, but..."

"There's always a but."

"I know, and I'm not pulling out or anything, it's just, I suppose I don't want to hurt you..." He takes a long, long pull on the oxygen.

"Hurt me! Al, Al, Alan, you won't hurt me any more than I'm hurting already. You're setting me free. Liberating me from this world of pain. And for that, there's only forgiveness, there's only joy. Do you like seeing me like this?"

"No, I mean, yes, of course I like having you here..."

"That's not what I asked..."

"Then, no, I don't like seeing you lying here like this. In fact it breaks my heart..."

"And that's why this isn't wrong, Alan. Letting me live is what's wrong. They treat animals better than humans when it comes to death and suffering," he repeats, sucking more air. "Reach into that drawer for me, would you son?" I retrieve a sealed white envelope with my parents' names on the front in Paddy's childlike scrawl. Paddy explains that it's a letter explaining the situation and taking sole responsibility for what's about to happen. I thank him and start to cry.

"Stop that, right now!" he insists. "This is *not* wrong, Alan." He fills his lungs, unlocks the silver necklace hanging around his chicken neck and hands the cross and chain to me. "This is for you, and that book too. Look after them, they're both antiques." I give him a huge hug and can feel his bones through his yellow skin. Paddy's sweat already reeks of death. His chest struggles under the weight of my love.

I pull away when Paddy asks me to replay his favourite song – *Count's Place*. This is a party tune: Paddy lies back and smiles, sips some more whiskey and says, "Ok, Al, I'm ready. Do it now…" He finishes the whiskey and places the glass on the bedside table. I get up and slowly remove a pillow from beneath his head. Paddy lies back with his eyes closed. I remove the statue of Christ on the cross that hangs above his headboard and place it in the drawer. I whisper a short prayer, kiss both his cheeks and take one last look at him. His eyes are closed and his breath is so quiet it's as if he's in a coma. He's already at peace in the knowledge that the end, at last, has arrived.

As carefully as I can, I place the pillow over his face and press down. I wait for five minutes… five long minutes, five hideous minutes, until my back aches and my skull thunders. Dwdi gets up from the bottom of the bed, walks over to me and rubs his chin against my elbow. The cat leaves the room in disapproval of my lack of attention.

When the clock reaches 19:53, I take off the pillow and kneel by the side of the bed. I hold his skeletal hand and pray. Paddy's completely still. His chest has stopped trumpeting, which means that the pain has stopped and Paddy's on his way to Paradise. I place my finger beneath his nose to make sure that we've succeeded. Then I get up and sit once again in the chair by his bed, breathing deeply. I feel guilty to begin with, but Paddy's words come back to comfort me. *This is not wrong, Alan.* The stillness and silence return to the room, the house, my home. When I lift my eyes from Paddy's face, I see his ghost sitting on the opposite side of the bed, looking about twenty years younger.

The spectre smiles, sparks a match and lights a Woodbine.

I cannot speak nor move. I'm so sad that Paddy hasn't reached Paradise at all. We failed. I feel the notebook in my pocket and feel even worse. I forgot to read Paddy his poem, the poem I've been working on all week. The panic subsides though and I decide to read it to his ghost instead.

I open the book to the appropriate page, clear my throat and whisper the words in the hope of assisting his spirit to cross to the other side.

Your body's a wreck
But your mind's like a blade;
The time has come
To find peace and rest.

An inspiration to the very end
My hero, my teacher, my one true friend.

Listen and learn
That was my plan
And follow your example as time marches on.

Guilty as charged,
Neglected you so long.
My past behaviour
So very wrong.

But sunshine hit me over the past few months,
Your wisdom and humour has taught me so much.

And here we are on New Year's Eve
I thank the Lord for what you gave.

I know for sure that we'll meet again
In Heaven above, but who knows when.

I look up as I finish the poem and see Paddy's ghost blow a lungful of smoke towards the ceiling, unaware of what I've read. I can't smell the smoke, which suggests that we're not of the same dimension. I close the book and put it back in my pocket. I'll never write another word...

I look again at Paddy's corpse as his ghost disappears. I recall how close we became over the past few months. Then I reach for the Bat Phone and dial 999.

Chapter 19: NEW DAWN, DARK HORIZON

17:05. The last Tuesday of the month. Right on cue, Floyd struts in to the Arches' lower bar, which is full today for the first time in ages due to the change in weather. Although it's still humid and hot outside, the blue skies have been replaced by dark clouds. Floyd's eyes are like a pair of bloodshot marbles. His wide smile is gone. For the first time since I've known him, he looks serious; no doubt focusing on what awaits us in the morning. He makes his way towards me, ignoring those who greet him.

Floyd doesn't even order a drink tonight. Instead, he whispers *"it's-on-be-ready-at-nine-o'clock-we'll-pick-you-up-from-the-cemetery's-main-entrance-don't-be-late"*, moving his eyes from side to side as if he's an Action Man gone AWOL. He then leaves the pub with no further word. I watch him go taking with him any hope of a reprieve. I was hoping that my constant prayers over the past week would have paid dividends by now, with Tubbs calling to cancel the job. But it's *on*.

Since last Thursday's meeting, I've seen a subtle change in my friend. Darkness has been pushing itself to the surface: Floyd seems constantly on edge. Despite my spiritual reawakening, I've failed to share my true feelings with him. I'm afraid I'm almost out of time. I've even been practising my driving in Floyd's Ute around the cemetery's narrow paths. We've also been discussing the job and dreaming about what we plan to do with the money. I'm scared of what I can see simmering just below Floyd's surface. On some other perverse level, I don't want to let him down after everything he's done for me. Without him, who knows where I'd be?

After Floyd leaves, I grab my bag and head for home. I hear Hoff say "See you tomorrow, Al" so I turn back.

"I've got a day off, Hoff…"

"Serious? I didn't think you knew what a day off was!" I smile and wave. I didn't even take a day off after my accident. But that doesn't mean it didn't have a lasting impact on me. I don't know why God saved me, but hopefully that reason will become clear before dawn. Before it's too late. I head home on my new mountain bike which I bought off one of the locals for twenty pounds.

It is muggy outside, despite the strong wind. A storm is inevitable: the overhanging trees and flags on the garage forecourt opposite the pub are swaying. The bulging clouds above threaten to burst. Still, I take a different route home from usual. I decide to cycle past my brother's home, and as I approach I slow down and crawl past so I can sneak a peak through their front window, like I did when I came out of prison. I spy Mia carrying Lauren and Sophie skipping shakily. They all look so contented. I've decided not to tell Will about Lauren's paternity. I can deal with how my brother treated me, but I cannot ruin his life and his family's by revealing the truth. I'm going to be the best uncle possible to Lauren and Sophie… if Will allows me back into their lives. My desire for revenge left me soon after my last visit. They all seem so happy at the moment. And I know better than most the importance of family. I lost mine, and I don't want Will to experience something similar. What I want most of all is a return to the simple life I knew a few weeks ago. Although that is pretty unlikely if I go on with tomorrow's plan…

By the time I turn onto Wedal Road, the rain has started to fall. Thunder growls in the distance. As I push my bike along the path towards my shed, rainwater on foliage stirs my sense of smell and

217

reminds me again of His eternal presence. Still, I've got to think about tomorrow morning. I'm ashamed that I'm so weak. When I see a dark figure leaning on the shed I hope it's Floyd come to tell me the job is off.

I'm disappointed to see that it is Will. What does he want now? Has he come to rub salt on my wounds? I walk towards him. He smiles, but I don't react in any way. Why should I be pleasant after the way he treated me last week?

I lean my bike against the wall, open the door and walk right in, ignoring him completely. I aim for the fridge where I grab a chicken korma meal-for-one and place it in the microwave, setting the clock to three minutes. I reach for a towel and start drying myself. As I rub my hair, all my problems go through my head. I'm desperate for some guidance from somewhere... what can I do – run, disappear, end it all?

"Alright if I sit down?" Will asks. I shrug and watch him take a seat in the comfy chair... *my* comfy chair! He holds a brown envelope in his right hand, and in his eyes I can maybe see repentance. I turn my back to him and watch my dinner spin.

When the oven *pings* I grab a plate, some cutlery and sit down on Paddy's old seat without even acknowledging my brother. If he wants to break the ice, I hope he's bought a pickaxe. Amazingly, that's exactly what he does, and I almost choke on my korma when Will says, "Sorry. Look at me, Al. C'mon! Please," he pleads, "Fine, if you don't want to talk, fair enough, but you're gonna listen. Firstly, I'm sorry for the way I treated you last week and how I ignored your problem and bought everything back to me, as usual. Typical, I know, but it's hard to change after years of perfecting the art of being a twat." I start to thaw. "This'll probably sound like a lame excuse, but I've been having a pretty hideous time in work recently. I lost a patient during surgery about three weeks ago and her family's threatening a lawsuit. I'm stressed. Under pressure. Simple as that. Anyway, that's not an excuse, just an explanation. I understand now that no matter how hard my life seems, at least I've got my family's support. Their full backing. And after considering that, I came to realise that's exactly what you need right now... support, that is, not condemnation and a lecture from yours truly." He's got my full attention now. "I spoke to Mia about everything and in the end I decided, without too much convincing I'd like to add, that I'd come over and clear the air. I'm tired of fighting, Al. And I'm sorry. For everything I've put you through. Now I don't expect total forgiveness tonight, but I hope this helps to smooth things over a little until maybe you can manage it." He waves the envelope in my direction. I hesitate then snatch it from his grasp. Inside is a really cheesy birthday card. I take it out and look at the cover – a bad watercolour of an ancient-looking racing car, the kind you usually get from some aunt you've never met.

"Very nice," I say, although I'm secretly chuffed. "I didn't think you'd remember... especially after last week."

"Well, you know... it's just a little something, a gesture, and sorry about the card. I want to be your friend, Al. I want to bury the past, if that's at all possible. There's nothing more important than family, I know that now."

"You're right," I agree, opening the card. I nearly faint. I stare at the cheque within. I'm light headed. I'm speechless. I look at Will, then back at the cheque again, just to make sure. I try to speak but only manage a whisper. "Is this some kind of joke?"

Will smiles as he answers. "No. No joke. Just what belongs to you, that's all..."

"How... explain... please..."

"There's nothing to explain. That's your inheritance. Simple..."

"Simple!" I exclaim. "But... but... but there's over half a million pounds here!"

Will's smile expands. "Like I said: your inheritance."

I stare at the piece of paper in my hand for a long time. I'm saved. Liberated. Free. So this is what He had in mind. Everything suddenly makes sense. Sort of. My brother. My angel. My redeemer. How ironic. I can pull out of the job in the morning without having to worry about returning to jail. All my prayers have been answered. But even so, I still need an explanation for this huge sum of money...

"Thanks Will, but where did all of this come from?

"What d'you want, a breakdown of funds?"

"Something like that..."

"Ok, here we go. This won't be one hundred per cent right though, just a general breakdown to the nearest few hundred quid." I nod. "Right, it goes a little something like this. I sold Mam and Dad's house for six hundred gees. That figure was reduced to around four hundred after paying the inheritance tax. Mam and Dad's combined life insurance came to roughly three hundred grand. So, that's seven hundred thousand so far. Add to that their savings, Paddy's stash which was almost two hundred gees itself plus other assets which I also sold and we have a grand total of roughly nine hundred and fifty thousand smackaroonies..."

"So why is this cheque made out for almost six hundred thousand pounds, then?"

"Well, after a little consideration, I figured that you deserved the majority after all the shit I put them, and you, through over the years. I went for a sixty-forty split in the end. Do you want some more or something?"

His question makes us both crack up. "Not at all, there's enough here to sort this mess out with the Inland Revenue..."

"And enough to help you move out of this shed too, I hope!" Will adds, as he reaches into his pocket and retrieves a little wooden pipe and a bag of weed. "You don't mind, do you?" He asks rhetorically, already packing the bowl with a pinch of sweet smelling skunk.

"Not at all, as long as you offer it to me when you're done." I get up, grab a couple of Breezers from the fridge and pass one to Will.

"Nice," he says without sarcasm. I watch my brother put the bottle carefully between his legs and the tightly-packed pipe between his lips. He lights the pipe's contents and sucks down a lungful, holding his breath for as long as he can. Then he blows the smoke towards the open door. His eyes glaze instantly and he passes me the pipe. I copy his technique and am proud to report that I didn't choke, cough, cry, splutter or spit.

You took it like a pro would be Floyd's conclusion. Jase would say, *Sucked it like the cock of doom!*

"Beautiful," I say, smiling like my man Jack in the role of the Joker.

Unlike Floyd, Will doesn't smoke tobacco, so the rush I feel after smoking the pipe is much more pure than my friend's polluted spliffters. Will's already packing the pipe again, but this time we smoke its contents standing at the door watching the rain pour down and lightning dazzle the sky.

We laugh at who knows what and talk in depth about topics we forget immediately. At one point, Will asks me what I want to do with my money. I announce a plan to buy and run a pub. Only when I say that do I realise that this *is* my ambition, but even after thinking about it seriously, it appears to be an excellent idea. A chance to serve the community and return to the simple life…

Although the conversation flows, I decide not to tell Will about my spiritual reawakening. I've decided to keep my special relationship with the Almighty close to my chest. I know He's looking after me; Will's appearance tonight proves this. Maybe no one else will notice me worshipping him on the qt, but I know for a fact that He will…

The tropical rain turns to drizzle around ten o'clock, and Will turns to go.

"I hope that cheque means you don't have to sell your ass on Bute Street or do some other stupid thing to pay off your debts," he says.

After a huge hug, I watch my brother disappear into the darkness.

I lock the door, pull out my bed and lie down. I'm happy. I'm thankful. I'm relieved. I lie there in darkness, listening to the pitter patter of the rain on the shed's tin roof. Drifting off into the deepest of sleeps I know that everything's going to be ok now. Everything…

The next thing I hear is heavy knocking on the door. I open my eyes and look at the clock. 09:15. Uh oh! More knocking. Some kicking. Aggressive voices. Threatening whispers. I get up. What do I do?

I hear Dee Dee say, "He's done a fuckin' runner, the cunt's done a runner."

Floyd retorts, calmly, "Calm down Dee, I can hear him moving inside."

My heart bangs the beat of a million bongos and my mind's a

mess. I put on some trousers and go over to the door. What can I do to cool them down? Tell the truth? It's as good as place as any to start, I suppose…

I turn the key to unlock the door and am pushed off my feet as the trio barge through the door like the All Blacks' front row through Romania's defence. Dee Dee leads the charge, then Gee followed by Floyd. I'm pushed towards the back wall and come to a stop, slightly winded. I look at them though a tearful haze. They're all wearing black. Trousers. Boots. Tops. Black. Their voices are cloaked in darkness too. I think I might have pissed them off…

Dee Dee stops growling, and Floyd steps towards me. "What the fuck's going on, Al? Now's not the time to have a lie in."

"He's a fuckin' amateur, for fuck's sake!" Dee Dee barks. The Devil dances in his glassy eyes… moshing to the Ramones, most probably.

"Shut up, Dee." Floyd orders. He's more serious than I've ever seen him and his position as leader of the gang is respected by the demented rocker. "What's the story, Al, alarm didn't go off?"

The question's asked in a mock friendly tone, and I struggle to create enough saliva so that I can answer. I start shaking. I look at the floor.

"I can't do it, Floyd…" I whisper.

"Can't do what, mate?"

"Yeah! Can't do what, ya fuckin' cunt?"

"I can't be a part of," I point towards them, "a part of this…"

"Too fuckin' late, Al," Floyd says, shaking his head in disgust. Dee Dee pipes up again. "Too late, boy, you're in it up to your fuckin' neck!"

Floyd comes so close to me I can smell the nicotine on his breath. I can't look at him. My eyes dart around the room but they can't escape. I'm surrounded. Scared. Silent Gee stands by the door, his six foot six frame reaching towards the roof. He closes it without taking his eyes off me. The sweat cascades from my forehead. Then, without warning, Floyd hits me across my face with the back of his hand. A "bitch slap", I believe. I cower into the corner, but they all follow. Floyd lifts his hand to strike me again. I cover my face with my hands like a boxer on the ropes, and close my eyes. When Floyd doesn't hit me again, I slowly open my eyes and come face to face with two guns pointing at my head. Dee Dee holds one, Gee the other. They stand either side of Floyd, and even though I know they're only replicas, this doesn't stop me from almost passing out.

"You can't pull a sicky on this job, Al," Floyd explains, nice and calm, but bereft of kindness. At last I realise what Floyd actually is. He is a bad man with a friendly nature. I begin to doubt everything he's told me. How could I have trusted him? I needed a friend, not another oppressor. "Now, please tell me why you want to pull out; I mean, if you've got a good reason we might reconsider..."

"There's no time, Floyd, let me fuckin' do 'im and let's go." Dee Dee again.

"Hang on! Let's hear what he's got to say. Al?"

I realise there's no way I can reveal my new found wealth to these three. They'd just take the lot and leave me for dead, surely. Worse still, I can't find the strength to admit my pact with God. I break down and cry. This enrages them further, and Floyd strikes me again, harder this time, making me fall to my knees.

"C'mon Floyd, let me finish the fuckka! We don't need 'im anyway..."

"No. Nothing changes. Not now. No way. The plan stays the same. Get him on his feet, we'll deal with him when we get back."

Silent Gee pulls me up by the scruff of my neck and shoves a pair of trainers to my chest. I put them on under the watchful gaze of the two guns, breathing deeply to calm the shakes. There's no way out now, no escape – from the job, jail nor whatever else awaits me when we return from Trellech.

I stand up. I'm ready. It's time to find the inner strength that's needed to fight these bullies... I must dig deep. Very deep.

As we're about to leave the shed there comes a quiet knock on the door which makes everyone freeze. Floyd looks at Dee Dee, who shrugs, and then at me. He mouths "you expecting someone?" and even though I shake my head, I know exactly who's outside. Unfortunately, I don't think parole officers carry firearms.

"Mr Brady! Anyone home?" Bruce Robertson bellows, pushing the door ajar. Time stands still. Bruce's mind does some calculations. He's faced with four men. Three wearing black. Ninjas. SAS. Terrorists. Fathers For Justice. The Johnny Cash Appreciation Society. Take your pick. Two of the men point guns at the fourth man's head, the only one not dressed in black. This man is also crying and trembling. His mind does the math and comes up with the answer. Run.

What happens next takes place in super slo-mo, as Bruce scarpers away from the shed. Gee follows, taking the gun away from my temple. He steps to the door, aims, fires. The shot deafens me as it echoes off the walls, and it is clear that Floyd was lying about the replica guns. I scream but no sound comes from my mouth. I hear Bruce wince outside, and within seconds Gee's dragging him in by his feet and tying him to Paddy's chair.

My ears are numb. Blood gushes from Bruce's right leg, staining the carpet a dark crimson. Almost black. After securing him to the chair, Gee goes to work stemming the flow. The parole officer is silent, but the pain is painted across his face. Gee starts tying Bruce's ankles together while Floyd flips through his wallet.

"So, Bruce, you're a parole officer are you?" Bruce nods, wild eyed and scared as hell. "Well, you're not exactly doing a great job of stopping us lot re-offend, are you, mate!?" Floyd adds, drawing laughter from his accomplices.

"Let me kill him, Floyd, he's seen too much." Dee Dee again, itching for blood.

"Not now," is Floyd's icy retort. "We've got to go or we'll miss our window. Gag him Gee, we'll deal with him, and Al, when we return…"

I'm pushed out of the shed and towards a Ford Mondeo by the main entrance. I can feel Dee Dee's gun in the small of my back. Although the weather's cool today, I'm sweating. The clouds above are dark. The cemetery's plants are green, free of dust and shining after last night's downpour. I'm bundled into the car and take my seat behind the wheel. Dee Dee sits behind me, holding the gun to the back of my neck. The steel is ice cold. Gee joins him in the back; Floyd sits beside me.

"Right, let's go," Floyd orders, but I can't move. After a short pause, Floyd and Gee lift their guns in my direction, jolting me back to life. I start the engine and put my trembling hands on the steering wheel – at ten and two o'clock. Textbook stuff under such pressure.

"That's more like it," says Floyd, putting his gun away and inviting Gee to do the same. Without rushing, I press the clutch to the floor, put the car in gear, check the rear-view, indicate and pull out, moving slowly along the soaked asphalt towards the lake. Regardless of the severe stress I'm under, I do a good job of the driving – keeping to the speed limit at all times, just like Tubbs said, and being ultra careful. Pretty soon we're heading for Monmouth down the M48, then the M4. We travel in silence.

Will's words come back to haunt me. Then I'm back with Paddy and my parents last week and wish they could have taken me with them. I feel shame for betraying the Lord, even after he showed Himself to me, but I can still feel His presence.

I can feel His power giving me new strength and I realise I must stop all this... But how? I hate what I'm taking part in. Hate what I've become. I must change my ways so I can taste true freedom again. I imagine what they'll do to Bruce and me when we return to Cardiff. It's not pleasant. The only way is not to return... and there it is, the seed's been planted. I pray for guidance, but find none. I leave the M4 and join the B4923.

Dee Dee presses his gun into my neck and when I look in the rear view I see his eyes staring right back. They're lifeless, and his forehead's wrinkled like an old accordion. His hatred is aimed right at me. Who knows what this nut job's capable of? I'm so scared. For me. For Bruce... And then something very strange happens. I'm still looking in the rear view when Lauren appears in the back seat, perched in a baby seat between Dee and Gee. I try to keep my eyes on the road but my only child is hard to ignore under such circumstances. Our eyes meet. Lauren smiles a toothless grin. Is this a sign? If so, what kind of sign? Slowly, she lifts her hand, making the shape of a gun, and points it towards me. She shouts 'BANG!' and blows smoke from the barrel like some baby-faced assassin. Then she is gone, leaving me back in the company of these modern day desperadoes.

We crawl through Llanishen, as the village is packed. There are cars parked on both sides of the street, so I'm extra careful as I push on through. As we leave the village, Dee Dee winds down his window and shouts, "Haven't you heard of taking it up the arse?" at a teenaged girl who walks on by, pushing her young twins along the pavement. The girl gives him the bird, which makes Dee Dee even madder, but Floyd and Gee laugh at him. Talk about keeping a low profile.

We drive through rolling fields for the few miles between Llanishen and Trellech. Last night's rain has given the world a fresh sheen. As we pass the Welcome sign, Floyd says, "Easy now, Al, we're almost there."

Trellech is another one street village with a pub and a post office. Very traditional. Very quiet. The place seems lifeless. Floyd tells me to pull over about a hundred yards from the post office, on the opposite side of the street. The car's clock tells me we're just in time. 10:52. I kill the engine as the Securicor van drives past us within inches, coming to a stop outside the post office. I can feel some strange energy in the car. The adrenaline's pumping my heart along with it, even though I don't have to do anything except sit here.

One of the Securicor men leaves the van and goes into the Post Office. The atmosphere reaches boiling point.

"Rope?" Floyd.

"Check." Dee Dee.

"Duct tape?" Floyd.

"Check." Dee Dee.

"Lock…" Floyd.

Click Click. Click Click. Click Click.

"…and load." Dee Dee.

"Let's do it," says Floyd, and they all get out of the car as one well-oiled machine. Before closing his door behind him, Floyd bends down and looks me straight in the eyes.

"No fuckin' funny business now, Al. Don't even think about fucking this up or doing a runner or whatever. You're in trouble as it is, my friend, but if you fuck this up, you're a dead man… and so's your brother and the rest of your family. Those that are still alive, that is…"

I nod. I understand. I watch them walk slowly down the street. I hear Floyd tell Dee Dee not to hesitate to shoot me if he sees me try and get away. Dee Dee must be smiling, hoping that I'll do something stupid.

Although their guns are hidden, the men still look extremely dodgy as they head for the post office. Getting closer, they all pull balaclavas down over their faces. There isn't a soul in sight. When they get within ten yards, all I can think about is escaping. But I don't move an inch. I'm not going to put Will and the girls' lives in danger. All I can hope for now is that the job goes smoothly and no one gets hurt...

Floyd and Gee step into the post office. I watch Dee Dee go to work. He walks up to the Securicor van and sneaks towards the driver's window, keeping close to the side of the vehicle. When he reaches the driver's door, he opens it and points the gun at the man inside. I imagine Dee Dee demanding the keys to the back door. The driver must have refused: a huge explosion echoes around the village. A scarlet shower of blood and brains erupts out of the passenger window; smoke rises from Dee Dee's gun. Time stands still for the second time today as I open the car door and retch violently. I lift my head and watch as he reaches into the van, retrieves the keys from the unseen corpse and walks to the back of the van wiping blood from his eyes with a gloved hand.

I'm one hundred per cent bricking it, and know that I must take extreme measures in order to save my life. Bruce and I are in serious trouble if we ever make it back to the shed. Dee Dee has obviously lost the plot, and I need to find a way out of this mess. Quick. I turn to God for the answer but it dawns on me that the only way to save myself is to make sure no one gets back to Cardiff. The seed starts to sprout... I can't leave without them, but since I am in the driving seat, I'm the one who's in control of my own destiny.

After opening the van's back door, Dee Dee grabs some bulging bags and waves for me to drive over. He's shouting and waving, but I can't hear him. I'm numb. Floyd and Gee join him carrying two further bags of swag. Floyd leads the charge towards me. I pop the boot and after filling it, they join me in the car.

"What did you do that for?" I shout at Dee Dee, turning in my seat, wanting to hurt him.

"What?" he shrugs.

"You said no shooting, Floyd! No shooting!" I bellow, turning to face Floyd and feeling the warmth of Dee Dee's gun on my nape.

"There'll be some more shootin' in a second if you don't put your fuckin' foot down..." Dee Dee screams in my ear. I look at Floyd, my friend, but his eyes are cold.

"Let's get outta 'ere Al, right the fuck now!" He lifts his own gun and points it at my face. I start the engine. Passing the Securicor van, there is blood and skull spread all over the cockpit. I manage to suppress more retching, press the accelerator and get out of Dodge.

The clouds burst as we leave Trellech, pouring His wrath on the world around us. It's so localised and powerful that it feels like it's directed towards us alone. The road is soaked within a few minutes, which acts in favour of my slow-burning plan. After leaving the B-road and joining the A40 towards Newport somewhere near Monmouth, I work out how I can save Bruce and myself from almost certain death. I now know how to stop my companions from ever breaking the law again. I know how to please Him by doing His work and making the world a safer place for Lauren and Sophie to grow up in...

As was the case on the way to Trellech, I am the only one in the car wearing a seat belt. So, with that in mind, I hit the gas and hear the engine change its pitch as the car begins to accelerate. 39. The herds of horses powering the Mondeo neigh and snort as the trot becomes a canter. 45. The world outside and the reaction within to the sudden change in speed is chaotic. With blood thundering between my ears, I don't hear a word. I'm completely calm. Like a footballer preparing to take a penalty, the world around me is a complete irrelevance, my focus is absolute. 51. Lauren makes another appearance in the rear view, and I watch her change from a baby, to a girl to a woman. She seems happy, which lifts my spirits. 62. Will now with Lauren on his lap... and Mia too. All smiles. 69...

"What the fuck is this?" Dee Dee screams from the back seat, making my family disappear as we fly past one of those Smart Cars in the inside lane.

74. I see a grey bridge on the horizon, through the rain and spray and the metronomic motion of the windscreen wipers. Perfect. The final piece of my plan. 78. I spot a sign on the side of the dual carriageway warning motorists to slow down. No chance.

"What the fuck are you doing, Al?" Floyd asks, lifting the gun to my face once again.

The car falls silent as everyone stares through the windscreen. 85. I fight the urge to say "driving" in response to Floyd's question. I'm glad they're getting agitated. I say nothing. The car keeps on accelerating. My silence taunts Floyd, daring him to pull the trigger. He knows where that'll lead...

90. I feel my seat belt around my shoulder, as if His hands are holding me tightly. I feel safe, which is more than I can say for Floyd and the boys in the back seat. 96. "Slow down!" Floyd pleads as the steering wheel vibrates violently in my hands. The power Floyd's had over me since I met him evaporates. *The wheels on the bus go round and round, round and round...* Lauren, my angel, back in the rear view. 101. Dee and Gee take her place in the mirror. The threat is gone from their eyes. Fear is the new tenant. Alun Brady is his name. 106. As the grey bridge draws nearer, like a portal to another world, the calm belongs to me alone.

"I never told you why I went to prison, did I Floyd?" I shout over the scream of the engine.

"Is now the time?" he asks.

"Did I, Floyd?"

"No Al, you didn't."

110.

"I killed a man, Floyd. I'm a killer." I look at him as I say this, smiling like Hannibal Lecter. There is dread in his glazed eyes. "And now I'm gonna kill three more..." I turn the wheel and aim straight for the bridge. I know that God is by my side, protecting me from harm. I'm his Nikita. His Jules. His Vincent. His Jackal. By working with each other, we can make the world a better place. I check the speedometer just before the car hits the concrete wall – 112. I welcome the stillness, the darkness, the end.

I open my eyes very slowly and focus on the shambolic scene that surrounds me. Although I can't feel my body, my bones, my legs, I *can* feel the pain. Massive pain. Terminal pain. The driver's airbag failed to release. I'm one with the steering wheel. Eating the dashboard with bloody gums. I'm wearing Dee Dee's lifeless body like a cadaverous rucksack. I lick my lips, tasting the rust. To my left I see Silent Gee. His body's a crushed can of Coke; his neck's rammed down between his shoulder blades. Blood gushes from his ears. His eyes are open, staring straight at me. I look away.

Through the shattered windscreen, beyond the mangled engine, on the floor between the car and the bridge I see Floyd. Floyd's body, that is. Sweet memories flash before my eyes. Friendship. Laughter. Betrayal. Why? He moves. Just a little. But he definitely moves. He raises his head a fraction and stares right at me. The broken horn sounds a high-pitched *BEEEEEEEEEEEEEEEEEEEEEP*. Floyd – my friend, my enemy – attempts to speak. His head drops for the very last time.

As the sirens approach, I lose consciousness once again; turn my back on the carnage and bid farewell to my foes...

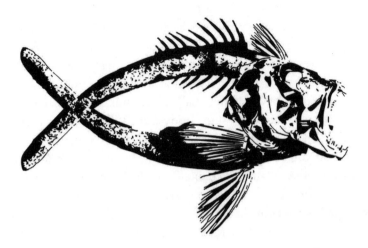

Epilogue: A TRUE LIFE SENTENCE

Darkness. Focus. Focusing. Through the visual mist to the other side. The light. His light? Heaven? Lift my head. Fail. Again. Fail. Blinding light. Stinging eyes. Slowly... very slowly... Dirty curtains and strange machines. Television? Surround sound? No sound, just sounds. Nothing definite. A monotonous hmmmmmmmmmmmmmm mmmmmmmmmmmm. Itchy nose. Can't move. Why? Darkness. And start again. Slowly. Lift my head. Can't. Lift my arm. Can't. Lift a leg. Can't. Why? Faces. Visions. Floyd. Dee Dee. Gee. Bruce. Knocker. Prison. Freedom. Prison. Same same but different somehow. A voice. From where?

"Are... sure you want... do this, Mr Brady?" Mr Brady! Mr Brady! Paddy? Dad? Heaven! Deaf again. Strange. Very strange. "Absolutely." Will. My brother. Mr Brady. "I know it's... tough, on all... us I mean, but this... what... all about..." "Family?" "Exactly." "Now, as Alan... out for... two months... his accident, he's severely damaged... Broken neck. Paralysed... neck down. He's mute. Possibly brain dead... brain damaged. Because... severity of... condition, we're not... sure if he... hear us. Hear anything..." Yes I can! Listen. Hear.

231

Can't reply. "It breaks... heart to... him like this. He was, is, such a good person. I've no... what he was doing... crashed the car, no idea why... mixed up in... things. What I do know is... he's received a true life sentence. Life imprisonment in his own body. It doesn't... any worse... that." Accident? What accident? "Sounds like... know what you're doing, Mr Brady. Shall we put him... the chair?" Chair? Chair? Electric chair? Eyes spin. Body still. Will. Standing above me. All smiles. Pity. A silver necklace in his hand. A silver cross. "They took this off you before theatre..." Theatre? What show? Will's hands around my neck. Hanging chain. Can't feel the cold. Partial recall. Knocker again. "There we are! You're ready now. I'm... look after... now. That's what families... for, after all." Too right, Will. Will! Will? Can you hear me? *WIIIIIIIILLLLLL!!!!!!* Sitting now. Moving. No. Hang on. No. Not of my own accord anyway. A male nurse on one side. Will on the other. Sitting. Seeing the world around me. The room. Where am I?

"Thanks... I'll take it... here." Will's voice. Smooth we move. Who? Where? Floating.

Leaving. Moving like a trolley round Tescos. Patients. Chatter. Cadaver. Left turn Clyde!

Automatic doors. Grey corridor. Right turn. Reception. People. Everywhere. Dressing gowns. Slippers. *Woman's Weekly. Bella. Best.* Another door. *Aaaaaghhhhhhhh! Noooooo!* Sunshine hits me. Sunshine blinds me. Stop. Please. No more. Another life. Change direction. A different result. Not my decision. Darkness. Black dots. Dark blood. Cracked skull. Floyd. Friend. Red sea. See red. Dark red. Black red. Paddy. Sorry. You there? No. Totally alone now. People stare. Stare back. What else *can* I do? Nothing. Move! Move you bastard! Can't. Float towards the parked cars. Warmth on my face, melting my skin. Voices merge with long forgotten sounds. Further confusion. What happened to me? What's happening to me? Breathe. Heart beating between my ears. *Bw-bwm, bw-bwm, bw-bwm...* Voice? No. A low hmmmmmmmmmmmmmmmmmm. Constant. Eternal. Hang on! A voice. A girl's voice. A young girl's voice. "Dad... where... taking... Al?" Good question. Where? Who? Dad? "For... walk... fresh air... indoors... long enough..." Two voices. Two plus two?

Father and daughter. Will and Sophie? Hope. Happiness. Bzzzzz
zzzzzzzzzzzzzzzzzzzzzzzzzzzzzzzzzz. Lifting now. Lift. Back of car.
New car. Vehicle. Another flash. Darkness. Metal on metal. Sparks.
Flashing blue lights. Far away voices. Near. Far. Far. Near. Will's
house. Mia. Sophie. Lauren's house. My Lauren! Smile. I think.
Cry. I think. Confused. No doubt. Out of the boot. Back to earth.
Away we go. Cross the road. Trees. Leaves. Branches. Polystyrene.
Rubbish. Water. Glistening. Clouds. Floating. Boating. Air. Fresh
air. Peculiar. Alien. Pedalo. Feel strange. Feel. Nothing. Weeping
willow. Geese. Bread. Warburtons. Braces. Best of Both. Feed the
ducks. Darkness. Uncertainty. White light. Bright light. Blinding.
Blind. Panic. A wishing well and promenade. Dog. Dog mess. Plastic
bag. Tescos. Square bins. Rubbish on the ground. To the left, water.
Swan. Swans. Lighthouse. Scott. Captain Scott. Great Scott. Cold.
Sensationless. Deep freeze. Arctic. Barren. Numb. Lifeless. Legs.
Arms. Body. Warmth. Above. Sun. Black dots in my field of vision.
Float on. Hand! C'mon! Move! Can't. Nothing. No pain. No gain.
No life. Voices. Man. Woman. Two young girls. Will. Mia. Sophie.
Lauren. Blood. Floyd. Glass. Death. Prison. Freedom. Gust of wind.
Palm trees. Flowers. People stare. At me. Pity. Look up. Where are
You when I need You most? Blue sky. No clouds. No clues. Look
left. Railings. Bars. Prison. Home. Rowing boat. Fisherman. Vest.
Red arms. Factor Nothing. Bait. Birds. Swans. Will's face next to
mine. Lips move. No sound. What? What? Nothing. Fate. Silence.
Darkness. Float on. Mechanical. Al, *NOOOOOOOOOO!!!!* Metal
meets metal. Mangle. The world spins. Or does it? Darkness. Calm.
Sirens. Pipes. *BEEEEEEEEEEEEEEEEEEEEP!* Pain. Will? I say.
No sound. To my right. Sophie. Big smile. "Uncle Al." That's right.
That's me. Uncle Al. Silence. Lipread. Look at me. Don't turn away!
She turns away. Silence. Loneliness. Will! Hey Will! No response.
Confusion. Confused. Alone. Will! Wiiiiil!!! To my left. Mia. Lips
moving. No sound. Mute. Deaf. Dream. Nightmare. Will! Come
on brother, I need you now. Nothing. Gun. Guns. Threats. Prayers.
Reaction. Take action. The answer. To my right. Lauren. She looks
just like Mia. Lucky for Will. Lucky for me. Button nose. Freckled
cheeks. Ice cream everywhere. Will! Can't feel. Future? Paddy. The

beginning of the end? Float on. In and out of the here and now. What's going on? What's happened to me? Why? The good suffer most. That's the truth. Bike. Mackintosh Place. Pint o'Daaaaaark please, Alan. Another bike. Rust red. Thin wheels. Razor saddle. Car. Asphalt. God? God? Sun through trees. Through the darkness. Paddy. Sorry. No. Correction. Thanks, Pad. Thanks my friend. Forgive me. Faces. Bodies. Cell. Cemetery. Mia. Thanks Mia. Thank God for Mia. "What's... with... Al?" Lauren speaks. "He's... an accident." Swings. Slides. Kids. Screams. Laughter. Tears. Frisbee. Red dog. Setter. Tubbs. Warning. Angel? Hell's Angel. Angel? Who knows? "Why... he speak?" Sophie. "He can't..." Will. Safety belt. Smashed glass. Bodies. Blood. Ice cream van. Mr Whippy. Mmmmmmm. 99 please! A queue of people. Fab or Zoom? Melting. Is this the end? Another beginning? "Is... going... to hospital?" Sophie again. Inquisitive. "No... live... us." Mia. "Why?" Lauren. "Because... what... families do. Look... each other." Will. I can hear almost everything now. But can't say a word. One big burden. Heavy chains on my brother's wrists. Ironic? Heartbreaking? Certainly. "Is he... pain?" Sophie. "We... know." Will. How can I be in pain when I can't feel a thing? Listening. Desperate to leave this world. Will's chance to be a normal family: wrecked. His dear brother. God's soldier. I don't want this. I thought we had a deal. Take me now. Now! It's time to go. I did what You asked of me. I've fullfilled my calling. My purpose. Faced my destiny. Lauren reaches out. Touch me, my daughter. Make me feel again. Or else put an end to this. I beg You. Skin on skin but no sensation. Without feeling. Without movement. Without purpose. I am nothing. Nothing. No good. God? No God.

Praise for *Ffydd, Gobaith, Cariad*

Llwyd Owen is a superlative plot-master; he is a messenger from the underworld whose narrative leads us through the mist.

Fflur Dafydd

Peppered with contemporary references, the intricately-woven narrative is alive with the pitch perfect voices of a host of characters... an affecting and haunting tale.

Wales Literature Exchange, www.walesliterature.org

Not unlike the Mike Leigh of Secrets and Lies, *who points out the black holes of family life. An outright talent and natural storyteller.*

Martin Davis, *Taliesin*

Another striking novel from Wales' most exciting author.

Dewi Prysor

"A wise and tender portrait of ordinary
lives slipping slowly out of kilter with
the brave new world around them."
John Williams
Author of *Cardiff Dead* and *Michael X*

Bumping
Tony Bianchi

"Reveals an amazing eye for detail. His portrayals of old Tom and of
teenagers Barry and Nicky… are classics." **Morning Star**

Always the love
of someone

Huw Lawrence

"Crisp, clear and illuminating." Emyr Humphreys

"Stopped me in my tracks… masterful throughout… I will be filing
this collection on my bookshelf next to Raymond Carver."
5-star review **http://americymru.ning.com**

TWENTY THOUSAND SAINTS

Fflur Dafydd

WINNER OF THE PROSE MEDAL –
NATIONAL EISTEDDFOD 2006

Oxfam
Emerging Writer of the Year 09

MxLexia
Woman to Watch 09

"Compelling, humane, a novel of remarkable delicacy and power."
Michael Symons Roberts

THE
DEER
WEDDING

PENNY SIMPSON

Published October 2010

PE 7/10

ALCEMI ✡

www.alcemi.eu

TALYBONT CEREDIGION CYMRU SY24 5HE
e-mail gwen@ylolfa.com
phone (01970) 832 304
fax 832 782